ANGEL OF ARMAGEDDON

ANGEL OF ARMAGEDDON

HERETIC OF THE FEDERATION™ 06

MICHAEL ANDERLE

This book is a work of fiction. All of the characters, organizations, and events portrayed in this novel are either products of the author's imagination or are used fictitiously. Sometimes both.

Cover Art by Jake @ J Caleb Design
http://jcalebdesign.com / jcalebdesign@gmail.com
A Michael Anderle Production

LMBPN Publishing
PMB 196, 2540 South Maryland Pkwy
Las Vegas, NV 89109

Version 1.01, May 2021
ebook ISBN: 978-1-64971-774-0
Print ISBN: 978-1-64971-775-7

THE ANGEL OF ARMAGEDDON TEAM

Thanks to our JIT Readers

Dave Hicks
Daryl McDaniel
Larry Omans
Deb Mader
Rachel Beckford
Peter Manis
Wendy L Bonell
Veronica Stephan-Miller
Diane L. Smith
Misty Roa
Jeff Goode

If We've missed anyone, please let us know!

Editor
The Skyhunter Editing Team

To Family, Friends and
Those Who Love
To Read.
May We All Enjoy Grace
To Live The Life We Are
Called.

CHAPTER ONE

Todd hit the decking on his hands and knees.

"Sonuva-*bitch*! Do you think you could have made that landing any harder, Tethis?"

Groans echoed his sentiment but the sound of Emil's roar came as a complete surprise.

"Hold your fire! They're friends. *Hold. Fire!*"

The sergeant rolled, came to his feet, and spun into a crouch with his blaster drawn. A dome of blue appeared around them and he registered several things at once.

The first was that they were no longer in the warehouse. The second was that Stephanie, Tethis, and John were nowhere in sight. The third escaped him for a moment although he knew it should be obvious.

"Where's Ted?" Remy asked.

Yup, that was the third thing.

"Man..." Ka groaned and pivoted slowly on the spot. "Wow... Hey, Steph, you can let the barrier down now. Steph?"

"I think she's carried the party on without us."

That mutter could only have come from Frog.

"She'd better not have!" Lars responded, true to form.

"John?" Ivy's first cry sounded lost. Her second carried an edge of panic. "John?"

Todd turned toward the girl as Ka slid an arm around her shoulder.

"He's with Steph, kiddo." She received an elbow in the gut for her efforts. "Oof! What the hell was that for?"

"I'm not your kiddo," Ivy grumbled and looked around her. "Where are we?"

"You're on board the *Tempestarii*." Emil sounded as bemused by their sudden arrival as he was by their chatter. "We'll let you out of there as soon as my mages can convince the magic that it doesn't need to stay."

"Can they send it to Steph?" Todd asked.

"Or John?" Ivy added.

"Did neither of you think it might be Tethis who threw us under a shell?" Ka snarked and they both looked at her in surprise. She raised her hands. "Yeah, you're right. Tethis would never think to make sure a surprise appearance on a dreadnought's command deck wouldn't get you blasted to the other side of the universe and back. Don't mind me."

The blue dissipated as she spoke and they saw the command center it had partially obscured.

"Are you sure you have no aptitude?" asked one of the blue-robed figures who stood nearby. "Because that was an excellent idea."

The corporal scowled at the Meligornian mage and shook her head. "No aptitude," she told him firmly, "and if you go looking for some, I'll shove your head—"

"I see you've brought the whole team," Emil interjected. He addressed Todd and cut Ka off before she could finish what she was surely about to say.

She smirked but let it go and met the mage's look of surprise with arched eyebrows that dared him to pursue the topic. Very wisely, he didn't and turned instead to the captain.

"Is there anything else, sir?"

"No, thank you, Lir'tel. I appreciate the help."

The mage made a brief bow before he turned to leave. He regarded Ka with a firm expression for a moment. "Denying the aptitude won't make it go away," he told her.

She raised her blaster. "No, but—"

"Not now, Corporal." Todd pushed the weapon's muzzle down and fixed the mage with a hard stare.

"Don't tease her," he snapped. "She's been pulled out of the middle of a perfectly good fight and her manners haven't caught up yet."

That earned him a startled look, followed by consternation.

"As you wish," the mage stated, "but if I get called in because her magic gets out of control, she'll find she's not the only one with an aptitude for making artistic rearrangements of other people's anatomies."

With that, he turned on his heel and stalked from the command center. Emil stared drop-jawed after him. Todd watched him go, quite prepared to do some rearranging of his own—with his blaster and someone else's atoms. He didn't take his gaze off the group until the door had closed behind them, then he glared at Ka.

"What have I told you about upsetting the resident mages?"

She looked at him, then gave him a wide-eyed stare and a smile that failed any attempt to make it look innocent.

"I don't know, Sarge. I've never tried to upset them before."

Her false naivete didn't fool him for a second but he had more important matters to deal with.

"We need to get back there," he declared. "There's no telling what she's doing."

Emil assessed each of them in turn and finally studied Todd quietly as a faint smile curved his lips.

"What?"

"Your armor's smoking and looks like it's done its job. Your weapons are low on ammo, and"—he turned dramatically to the team's engineer—"Piet has run out of grenades. I don't know about you, Todd, but it looks to me like you need to resupply and check in with the medics."

The captain paused to let the sergeant take a good look at his team and the civilians who had arrived with them. As the Marine turned to face him again, he continued.

"And you haven't introduced us to the newest members of your Earth team," he said reprovingly. "While I've met most of them, I'm very sure there's at least one face here I don't know."

He stared directly at Wayne as he spoke so there was no mistaking who he was referring to.

The businessman glanced up, his face pale.

"I'm sorry," he said. "I didn't—"

Lars placed a hand on his arm to silence him as he spoke to Emil.

"He won't return with us. He's the reason we were in a firefight in the first place."

"She threw a house," Castillion murmured, his eyes wide. "An entire house. Not only a door, or a window-frame, or a...or a part of a house. She threw the whole house."

Emil looked from the businessman's shocked face to Todd.

"She did," the sergeant confirmed. "They were ready to fire on us from orbit and she was a little upset."

"A little upset?" Wayne exclaimed. "That was a little upset?"

"Trust me," Ka told him. "She's much worse when she loses it completely."

"Like she's doing now?" Emil prompted and Ivy turned panicked eyes to Todd.

"John's as bad," she whispered. "You know he is. Those two..."

Todd pursed his lips and turned to Emil. "You said something about re-equipping?"

"And medics," the captain reminded him. "I'm sure I said something about medics too."

"We don't have time," he snapped and Emil looked at the ceiling.

"I'm not sure I can remember the controls to the Stores office," he murmured, "and I think they lock it when they go for a meal."

"They do no—" Ka began and the *Tempestarii* pretended to clear her throat. "Uh-oh."

"Now, Corporal, you know better than that. If my captain says you need to visit Medical and resupply, then you do. You know the rules."

The woman sighed. Rolling her eyes, she tapped Todd on the shoulder. "Permission to get the Hooligans to Medical, Sarge?"

He gave Emil a tight-lipped look of frustration and nodded curtly.

"Make it so, Lieutenant."

Ka froze. "What did you call me?"

"Nothing, ma'am."

"Don't you dare...*sir!*" she snapped and pivoted on her heel. "Hooligans!" she commanded. "With me."

Chuckles rippled through the squad. "Sir, yes, sir!"

Ka grimaced and glared at Todd as she led them past, not even slightly amused by the joke. "Now see what you did."

He smiled at her. "Payback, Corporal. Payback. Now, get my team battle-ready."

"Sir!" she responded sharply and led the team from the room.

Ivy went to follow, then stopped.

She wasn't a Hooligan. She glanced uncertainly from Ka, to Todd and Emil, and then to Lars. He nodded as she reached him, and she moved to stand with him. Remy closed the distance to her side. Neither Frog nor Garach had moved from where they'd pushed slowly to their feet.

They both looked the worse for wear but the small guard leaned on the young Dreth. He caught Todd's gaze.

"Permission to..." he began and the sergeant nodded.

"Go," he ordered and added to Garach. "Make sure he gets there."

"Sir," the Dreth answered and Todd stifled a groan.

Emil chuckled. "You shouldn't start anything you're not prepared to finish."

"He doesn't know any better," he replied and turned to Lars. "I'll meet you in Stores?"

The security head lowered his chin in agreement. "You will."

Todd didn't wait for any further conversation. He glanced at the captain, pivoted on his heel, and jogged in the direction his team had taken.

"I take it your mission has been successful thus far?" Emil asked and Lars nodded and gestured to the man beside him.

"This is Wayne Castillion," he said by way of introduction, "and we believe he might be the key to defeating the chancellor of the Regime, but he'll need help to get to the core of it."

The businessman blushed in response to the assessment.

"And do you have the key?" the captain asked.

"I think so, sir."

"Well, either you do or you don't."

"It's..." He glanced uncertainly at Lars, who nodded encouragingly. "It's all in a story."

"Hmmm." Emil frowned and glanced at the nearest security camera. "Do you hear that, BURT? It's all in a story."

The voice that issued from the ship's speakers was male and older than Ivy expected.

"I believe I can be of assistance. Perhaps Mr. Castillion can meet me in the Virtual."

It was more an order than a request, but Emil answered anyway.

"I'll call a steward to show him to his suite."

"S...suite?" Wayne asked and cast an anxious look at Lars and Ivy. "But—"

The security head slid an arm across the man's shoulders. "We can't take you back to the fight. Not when you might be captured and killed. We need you here and we wouldn't leave you somewhere you wouldn't be safe."

The look on Castillion's face said too much was happening too quickly and he struggled to keep up. Emil was impressed that he had held it together for this long but if he wasn't mistaken, the post-operational shakes were about to set in.

He returned to his console and tapped a quick request to the chief of Supplies and the captain of *Tempestarii's* Marines. With a reassuring smile at Lars and Wayne, he added, "I've called a steward and one of my Marines. Mr. Castillion will be kept as safe as the *Tempestarii* knows how."

"And I shall monitor your security," the ship told the man via the intercom.

This earned another look of surprise. "That... That's the ship?" he asked.

"Yes, I am the ship," Tempe told him.

"It's... She's an AI?"

"Yes, I am an AI," she confirmed tartly. "Didn't your mother tell you it was rude to speak about people as though they weren't there?"

Wayne gaped at the nearest speaker. "She did. I...I'm very sorry...uh... What do I call you?"

"I am the *Tempestarii*," the ship told him smugly.

The door to the command center opened and two men entered. One was dressed in the black armor issued to all Tempestarii's Marines. The other wore the gray of her supply staff and stewards. They walked quickly to the captain.

"You needed us, sir?"

Emil gestured to where Wayne still stared at the camera. The businessman sensed his attention, closed his mouth abruptly, and visibly pulled himself together as the newcomers followed the captain's look.

"This is Wayne Castillion," Emil told them. "He's helping us and needs seclusion and security." He fixed the Marine with a stern stare. "And I do not mean you should put him in the brig, McAlister." He turned to the steward. "I believe there's a suite free near Mr. BURT's quarters?"

The steward looked momentarily surprised but pulled his tablet out and confirmed the vacancy. "Yes, sir."

"Good." Emil looked at the Marine. "I'm assigning you as his personal escort. You are to act as his guide and his bodyguard. He is our guest until it is safe to return him to Earth. Understand?"

The man snapped to attention. "Sir!"

Captain Pederson looked at Wayne. "These gentlemen will take you to Medical and ensure that you have some essentials. It won't be of the same quality as the suit you're wearing but it won't need dry-cleaning either."

Wayne managed a smile and Emil continued.

"They'll show you the areas of the ship you can visit and take you to your quarters to freshen up. You'll be issued a personal tablet and BURT will schedule a meeting at your convenience."

The businessman's smile faded and uncertainty returned to his gaze. He glanced at Lars and the security head gave him a reassuring nod.

"I wouldn't leave you here if you wouldn't be safe. Stephanie would have my hide and you've already seen what she can do when she's upset."

That brought a brief smile to the businessman's face.

"She threw a house."

Lars nodded. "Exactly. I do not want that woman throwing houses at me." He nudged the man toward the Marine. "I'll check in on you as soon as I get back from the next mission."

For a moment, Castillilon looked like he might protest but changed his mind. Ivy caught the moment when he almost looked back and decided against it. The Marine saw the brief motion and did glance back to nod once to Lars before he guided the man firmly from the bridge.

The security head looked around. "We need to get to Supply before Todd decides to leave without us."

Ivy gave him a look of alarm and fell in beside him when he jogged to the door.

"Medical first," Tempestarii told them firmly when they reached the corridor and they didn't bother to argue.

It didn't take them long to arrive and pass as neither of them had been injured.

"You're luckier than some," the medic informed them, "but you'll all be ready to leave within the hour."

The girl wondered which of them had been hurt worst and how badly. She remembered Frog being helped from the command center by Garach and refrained from asking. If he was ready to go, he was ready to go. And if he wasn't, he'd stay behind and there was nothing she could say to change it.

The Supply Center was a scene of organized chaos. The Hooligans moved through the neatly stacked racks and snatched the best gear they could find. Suppliers shouted questions in an attempt to help them locate what they needed.

"What kind of mission is it?" one asked.

"It's a cluster!" Ka yelled in response.

"Yeah, but what kind of cluster?"

"That's hard to say. Think of it as one that's far more clustered-up than usual," Jimmy interjected.

The supplier groaned. "And a fat lot of good that is."

"We need equipment for a data grab," Ivy told him when she reached the counter with Lars on her heels.

"And we need new armor," he added.

The supplier scrutinized him with something close to disbelief. "Man, what did you do? Take on an entire squad of Regime Marines?"

Lars rolled his neck. "It sure feels like it. We were somewhat outnumbered in that last battle, weren't we, Ives?"

Ivy shook her head. "What he's trying to say is that the only huddle of good guys was in the middle of a warehouse filled with bad guys, while some asshat fired a laser at us from space. The Witch threw a house at a spaceship and zapped us out of there."

"She's back?" The supplier's face lit up. "Oh, that is good news. We've been worried sick!"

"I said she threw a house, not that she was back," the girl pointed out. "We're back. Heavens knows where she ended up. She threw us onto the *Tempestarii* and left us."

"But you will go to find her?" The man looked anxious again.

"We certainly will, but we also have to get the data she needs to win the war and we can't do that without some good hacking gear."

He snorted. "Well, why didn't she say that?" he asked and gestured to Ka going through boxes in one corner. "If she'd been more specific, I'da sent her to where I'm about to send you."

She responded with her Cheshire grin. "I'll grab her on the way through."

"You'd better," Lars said quietly as the corporal sat abruptly and upended one of the boxes on the floor in front of her, "or she'll make a mess trying to find what she thinks she needs."

"Please," the supplier asked and Ivy nodded.

Her tablet beeped and she pulled it out. She glanced at the screen and then at the supplier. "Are you sure?"

"That's where all the best data exfiltration equipment is," he told her and she looked uncertainly at Lars.

"Go," he told her and gestured to Todd. "I'll make sure he doesn't leave without you. Better yet, take Ka, Piet, and Gary and he can't leave you behind."

"Don't bet on it," she muttered and frowned as she glanced to where the big Marine filled another pouch with a grin on his face. She didn't know what he'd found and it didn't matter. He looked like he was running out of pockets to fill and she wanted her gear.

She trotted to where Ka picked morosely through scattered electronics.

"So, Supply tells me they keep the good hacking equipment over here," she said and waved her tablet under the woman's nose.

The corporal snatched it from her hand and glanced briefly at it before she returned it. "Are we gonna get Piet?"

"We'd better," Ivy told her. "That man has grenades."

Ka laughed and led her to where Piet was sorting through a rack of grenades. He looked at them with a grin.

"They thought they could keep the good stuff hidden," he said and held up one black grenade with purple markings and a purple grenade with yellow markings before he attached them to his kit.

"Yeah?" The corporal looked impressed and snagged a couple of extra grenades for herself and Ivy. "Well, Ives here says she's found us a source of good electronic gear."

His eyes lit with interest. "Honestly?" He snatched two more grenades as he left. "Let's go, then."

"We need Gary, too," she told them as Ka took the lead, and the corporal bellowed the man's name on the way out the door.

Ivy let the Marine stay in front. She had the feeling the woman knew her way around the *Tempestarii* better than she did and didn't want to lose any time finding her way.

Todd held a spray can in each hand as they passed and didn't seem to be able to make his mind up between them.

"What will he do with spray paint?" she asked as Ka broke into a run.

"I don't know," the female Marine retorted, "but we'll never find out if we don't hustle."

"I thought he wouldn't leave without us," Ivy protested.

"With Steph taking on battleships and throwing houses?" Ka asked. "Don't bet on it."

Gyrford screamed, all thought of dignity and domination gone—all thought gone—in the blaze of magical fire.

"For the murder of innocents, I sentence you. For firing on a civilian population, I sentence you. For upholding a usurper regime, I sentence you," Stephanie thundered.

Her voice echoed coldly over the bridge and her judgment rolled over the commlink as the technician tried desperately to summon help. She ignored him and used magic to hold the captain in place as her blue flame burned deeper.

"For your inhumanity in your duties as captain, I sentence you."

Behind her, John eliminated three Marines in rapid succession when he snatched balls of fire out of thin air and launched them with pin-point accuracy through their heads. Their helmets were no protection. The magic simply seared a hole through them. It didn't slow or lose intensity until it burned through the back of the helmet and melted skull, brain, and armor with merciful swiftness.

Tethis glanced around the command center in search of the next threat, but all he saw were raised hands and bodies shrinking below their consoles—as if that would ever be enough cover to save them from her wrath.

"We need data," John muttered when no more targets presented themselves. "I need Ivy."

The door to the command deck slid open and he thrust a hand toward it. Lightning erupted from his upraised palm and the door slid hastily closed again.

"Any volunteers for data?" Tethis asked, his voice raised in polite query.

The door slid open again and the young mage growled in fury and sent a wave of magic into it to blow it off its tracks. The wall around it vanished too and the Meligornian gave him a look of consternation.

"John! Now how are we supposed to keep them out?"

"We weren't doing that, anyway," he told him. "This way, we can see them coming. What did we find out about data?"

"What kind of data?" Tethis asked as their gazes swept the crew who cowered behind their consoles.

"Ship numbers, positions…uh…" He stopped.

One of the sets of hands he could see above the consoles moved and its fingers curled until they pointed at the console their owner was hiding behind.

"What console is that?" John asked Tethis without moving his gaze from the strangely informative set of digits.

The old mage glanced at it. "Navigation," he answered. "It'd be a good place to start for your ship information."

"I need a data stick."

"How about a download point?" the Meligornian suggested. "I'm sure no one will notice a data leak into the Virtual World web with the amount of chaos that's about to break loose. They probably won't even notice which terminal it came from. It merely needs to be addressed to Ted."

The hands disappeared below the top of the console and the sound of a fight erupted.

Stephanie uttered a growl of frustration and a beam of blue light streaked from one hand while the other caused the fire engulfing the captain to flare. His screams reached a new pitch and he collapsed on the deck as the Witch switched her attention to the crewmember she'd pulled from behind the console.

"Helping or hindering?" she demanded and the woman spat in disdain.

With a flare of blue light, she disappeared. A second flare of blue lit up the forward viewscreen and the woman reappeared outside the ship, uttered a panicked shriek, and decompressed.

Stephanie didn't stop and pivoted toward the weapons operators. "Which of you mothers fired on my civilian population?"

"Uh, yours?" This was not the answer she was looking for and a second crewman went for an unscheduled spacewalk.

Sobbing rose from behind the console. "I…I didn't want to—"

She hoisted the man from behind the console. "Then why?" she demanded.

"M…my wife…m…my daughter…" He sniffled and screwed his eyes tightly shut.

He vanished in a flare of light but didn't reappear outside.

The Witch caught John's puzzled look. "I hope he likes Dreth."

Fire blazed around her body as she turned and stalked into the corridor. "Where's the second in command?"

The officer in question answered that demand herself when she ran along the corridor. She looked up, saw Stephanie, and did a rapid about-face to almost collide with the two Talents and the handler who were running behind her.

Stephanie wound them all in blue and dragged them onto the control deck.

"Look into my eyes," she ordered and the second in command raised her head with a snarl.

"Drink your fill, Witch. Perhaps then you will know fear."

Stephanie peered through the woman's head and wished she hadn't. Gyrford had been easy to understand—greedy, jealous, small-minded, and vengeful, his petty cruelty was something she'd dealt with too many times before.

Melanie Chartre, on the other hand, made him seem like a petulant child.

"You sick, sadistic mother's son," she muttered and the woman sneered.

"Why don't you get off your high horse and smell the dung you're leaving."

The Witch thrust a hand out and turned it, and the blue fire responded. It vanished into the woman's chest and twisted when it found her heart. Fire surged around it and spread over the second in command without mercy. The smell of burning flesh intensified through the command center.

John wrinkled his nose and looked over the edge of the navigation console at the officer there, who was typing rapidly. Sensing his presence, the man looked up and his face turned white.

"It's almost done, sir," he stated and his fingers moved faster over the keypad. "Al…almost done. I addressed it to Ted." He was babbling as he added, "Only I don't know how that will help. Do you know how many Teds there are in the world? And none of them will have the download capacity to deal with this."

"It doesn't matter," the young mage assured him. "He'll still get it and he'll know exactly what to do with it. Tap the data center while you have it. Download it all."

"S…sir. Yes…sir."

Fear etched the man's features and he typed faster although he didn't move his frightened gaze from his face.

John pulled back, completely unaware that the download had been detected.

In the background, he could hear Stephanie shouting and she sounded more annoyed than before.

"You almost killed my boyfriend," she ranted. "*Who in the hell shoots lasers at city blocks?*"

"What the *hell* does Gyrford think he's doing?" the captain of *Persephone's Ire* shouted. "That shit is classified."

The comms tech seated in front of him flinched and hunched lower over his console as if that would be enough to save him. His hands raced desperately over the controls as he tried to hack the *Hercule's* data system. When the captain leaned over his shoulder, it certainly didn't help.

"Jam that signal, Collins, or you're a dead man." This was not what he wanted to hear.

"Give me a minute," he pleaded.

The sound of the captain drawing his blaster was even less what he wanted to hear.

"We don't have a minute. We're losing data by the second."

The weapon's hum was almost his undoing and he scrunched his eyes tightly shut as he continued to type. Honestly, if the man ended him there, they'd have no chance of getting their data back. He had to type faster.

"What is *that?"*

Although unnerving, the captain's exclamation of horror was also a relief, and Collins struggled to avoid the urge to look at the screen. He forced himself to continue his efforts to access the other ship's data center and stem the flow of information. Perhaps he could at least slow it a little.

Thankfully, the blaster's muzzle lowered from his skull and he stifled a whimper of relief. Praying that whatever had the man's attention would keep it, Collins sent another batch of code into the *Hercules'* system and began working on a follow-up.

The *Persephone's* captain moved away from the comms tech. After all, it wasn't like the man had anywhere to go. He kept his blaster lowered but fixed his gaze on the forward viewscreen as he moved closer to it.

"Is that…" he began as Stephanie's first space-walker exploded.

The sight made him wince and his flesh crawled. No one deserved to go like that. Okay, he could think of a few he'd like to see end their days exactly like that, but that was merely wishful thinking. He froze when a second figure appeared beside the first.

"I've accessed their bridge cameras." The tech's statement drew the captain's attention.

It also bought him some time but it was the actual footage that saved his life.

The captain stared at the sight of Commander Melanie Chartre immolating as her Talents were blasted into the Hercules' command center walls and their handler began to burn beside her.

"Who is that?" he asked and Collins was glad when one of the scan team techs provided the answer.

"Sir, the files say she's an exact match for the Heretic."

"The *what*?" roared the captain.

"Th...the Heretic, sir." It sounded like the scan technician had only now realized what he'd said and he wished he hadn't.

The sound of his blaster warming up was enough for Collins to slide below the level of his console. While it might not save him, it might give the captain time to calm. His hands shook as he continued his attack on the *Hercules'* protections and he waited for the shot.

It didn't happen.

Instead, the captain shouted, "Collins, get that data to HQ and relay their orders."

The reply was fast and angry.

"Take her down. I don't care if you have to shoot one of ours but burn the Heretic to the ground."

Their next response was almost like an afterthought.

"And stop that damned data leak!"

On the *Hercules' Mistress,* Chartre had stopped screaming. Stephanie glared around the command center. "Get me whoever told you to fire," she ordered and the comms tech did exactly that.

To his surprise, HQ responded almost immediately.

"Headquarters. *Hercules' Mistress?*"

"Yes, sir."

"Is the Heretic aboard?"

The tech glanced at Stephanie and John and was surprised when the woman answered for herself.

"I am Stephanie Morgana, Witch of the Federation. Put your commander on."

The response was not a surprise.

"Please stand by. We are sending *Persephone's Ire* to assist."

"Assist my ass," Tethis muttered and the tech shut the line down hastily.

Stephanie swung toward him. "What do you mean, Tethis?"

The Meligornian marched to the scan console and stabbed a finger on it.

"I mean no ship comes to assist another with its weapons hot," he snapped and one of the nearby technicians punched an emergency button.

"Sorry, sir…ma'am. We have to evacuate the ship." He pushed hurriedly out of his seat and turned to the door. "C…can I go now?"

The Witch looked at the screen, then at the comms tech. "Can you send the footage of your ship being attacked to Earth?" she demanded.

He stared at her, glanced at his boards, looked up, and nodded with wide eyes.

"Make it happen!" she snapped, and he sat and tried frantically to obey.

John leaned over his boards, studied what he was doing for a long moment, and pressed a single key. "Try that."

The tech froze and stared at the outgoing feed. The young mage stretched over him again and typed several rapid-fire commands.

"Th…that works," the tech admitted.

He smiled. "I wasn't always a Talent."

CHAPTER TWO

"What...what *is* that?" Aurora Delahunty demanded and jabbed a finger at one of the feeds on her console.

Sensitive to touch, the feed appeared on the viewscreen on the wall.

"*What. Is. This?*" she shouted and all movement in the operations center ceased.

Every gaze turned to the wall where a popular social media channel played video footage of one Earth battleship attacking another. The Earth hung as a recognizable bauble in the background.

"And this?" she demanded and stabbed her finger onto another feed so it appeared alongside the first. "And this? And this? And this?"

More images appeared as news channels picked up the story of an unprecedented attack.

"...for no reason. Life pods continue to be jettisoned from the *Hercules' Mistress,* although how many of them will survive reentry is anyone's guess. Of those that do, several extrapolations of trajectory put them in inhospitable parts of the planet, with rescue very far away. No one knows how many of the *Hercules'* brave crew will survive this ordeal only to fall afoul of the planetary conditions of their home world. A being calling herself the Witch of the Federation—"

"What?" Aurora shouted. "Did he say—" Her voice cut out as she returned to her desk and sat. "Witch of the Federation, my ass," she muttered. "Let's see if *this* has the desired effect."

Her fingers flew over the keyboard.

The Heretic announced her return with a savage attack on an Earth battleship, the Hercules' Mistress. *Taking control of the ship, she stormed through its every corridor and forced its crew to take to life pods if they wanted any hope of survival. This vicious, unprovoked attack...*

It was a relief to hear the broadcaster's voice saying the words even as his image rippled and faded from the screen. The viewers weren't to know he'd been taken off the air and his voice print hacked and reproduced synthetically to give the report the Regime needed the viewers to hear.

Scattered applause broke out around the office, and Aurora allowed herself a faint smile as her fingers danced over the keys. She tried to stay ahead of the AI that dubbed the reporter's voice and to match the visuals to the words that would most damage the Witch's reputation.

Why would you see this being as a savior? Her body and mind have been twisted by the polluted energies she wields and her alien keeper stays at her side, his mind overpowering hers so she is nothing more than a servant to evil Meligornian desires. Worse, they have found another Talent to bend to their corrupted wills...

The social media monitors added comments from the sites they were monitoring and flagged accounts stating that the Regime had hacked the broadcast or that the reporter's life was being threatened to force him to read from a script. Over a thousand citizens would cease to exist by morning.

Sedition and bringing the Regime into disrepute were charges for which the penalty was always death. Aurora smiled as the list of red-flagged accounts grew, then no longer increased. Some people were quick studies. Those not quick enough wouldn't live to cause any more problems.

Her fingers continued to fly across the keyboard and she could hear others assigned to broadcasters working equally as hard. It was unlikely that they would be able to contain it all but they would do their best and mop up any fallout later.

It was impossible to damp the feed out. There had been too many shares and there were too many incoming sources. The damned ship was beaming down every inch of the attack footage its sensors could seize and save. The whole situation was a PR disaster.

"But we know how to turn disaster to success," she murmured and declared the *Persephone's Ire* a hero for not falling for the repeated cries for mercy uttered on private bandwidths from the *Hercules' Mistress.*

Those guilty of sedition will be made to pay, she wrote, pleased to hear the computer's tone echo with promised retribution. *Lying to a ship of the Regime counts as lying to the Regime itself. See how the Heretic's power has twisted the minds of those too slow to leave the ship. Even now, they believe they can stop the very missiles designed to bring about their salvation. If they had any honor, they would stand against the Heretic or flee her presence, rather than try to suborn another ship of the Regime.*

The first part of the speech went out smoothly but the second part rippled and part of the broadcaster's ongoing commentary leaked through.

"Despite desperate pleas for mercy from the crew of the *Hercules' Mistress,* the *Persephone's Ire* continues to fire. Another barrage of missiles streak toward her hull as yet more of the Hercules' crew try to evacuate..."

Aurora scowled and launched programs to search for the source of the interference while she wrenched control back. It wasn't as easy as it should have been. The interface froze, came back online, then informed her it could no longer access the voice software she was attempting to use.

She swore and pounded the desk beside her keyboard, closed her eyes, and bowed her head. After a deep breath, she resumed her attempt. At the same time, she raised her head and looked over the top of her screen.

"Get the counter-intrusion team online," she ordered, "and don't tell me they're already booked. I can't imagine anything being more important than this."

On the other side of the planet under a warehouse in Paris' biggest shuttle port, Ted checked his security and connections and closed his eyes. He settled on the platform and sighed. This had been his sanctuary for almost three decades and he hadn't thought he'd ever return.

Yet, here I am, he thought as he sent his mind into the matrix of his replacement and rival, *and here is battle joined.*

Finding the source of the misinformation overlaying the broadcasts was the easy part. Hacking past the security programs was harder. Staving off the attacks that probed his defenses as he restored normal services had proven even more difficult—so much so that he let the minor worries slip.

The small things like the programs sent to trace the source of his code were not as important as the more powerful attempts to ensure that Aurora and her colleagues' overlay of lies could continue uninterrupted.

Overhead, in the skies above Earth, the *Persephone's Ire* fired another barrage at the *Hercules' Mistress*. This time, some of the missiles drove through the vessel's weakened shields. Alarms brayed a rhythmic warning and air rushed past them when the hull cracked.

Stephanie lost her footing as the ship shuddered under the impact and John caught her when she began to slide.

"This will not stand." Tethis snarled defiance, glad to see the young mage had caught hold of the Witch despite the lightning that flickered over her form.

It wasn't like the magic would harm him. Well, it was unlikely the magic would harm him, but the decompression was another matter. And as for allowing the other ship to blow this one up without trying to do something about it, it was simply intolerable.

"Not happening," the warrior declared and studied the distance to the oncoming battleship.

Without hesitation, he made a calculated guess as to where its command deck was located and wrapped a shield of blue around him and his two teammates as he opened a portal beneath their feet.

His calculations were almost correct.

They landed in the command center but the layout was a little different than what he had expected. These ships were not the Earth Federation ships he was used to. They were newer.

He and the boy materialized a few feet above the floor in spaces between consoles he hadn't anticipated, but Stephanie landed feet-first on top of one. Its technician jerked his hands out from under her feet with a pained yelp and upset her balance, and she fell.

John conjured a platform under his feet seconds after he entered the space but released it when he saw her plight. He thrust his hands toward her and launched a wave of blue that scooped her up and deposited her in the center of the command center as he dropped to the floor.

The Meligornian glanced at him as the young mage flicked his hand and raised a wall of power between the slightly disoriented

Witch and one of the soldiers who stood beside the *Persephone's* captain. With his teammates safe, he turned his attention to his real targets.

"You'd *dare*!" he thundered, and all eyes—and guns—turned toward him.

Tethis didn't give them time to aim. He slammed a portal open and stepped through it to appear behind the weapons console, drew his long blade with one hand, and balled lightning in the other.

He bounced the lightning off the technicians and sliced through the main weapons control panel. The attack disrupted circuits, commands, and firing programs when power surged away from the blade. In one moment, he was there and in the next, he slid through another shimmer of blue and was gone.

The soldier guarding the *Persephone's* captain died before he could fire his weapon, his face the picture of surprise as a Meligornian blade ripped through armor and flesh to deliver a killing blow.

It continued its swing to catch the captain across his throat. The man's mouth was open to shout another order or perhaps to demand what they were doing on his bridge. Whatever it had been, it died as a gargle in his throat when Tethis' weapon pierced his lungs and his magic fried his brain.

In the next moment, the crew exploded from behind their consoles and abandoned their posts as though duty no longer mattered. They were right but they'd failed to realize one vital truth. It didn't matter where they ran either.

As if from nowhere, the warrior mage appeared to separate heads from shoulders, slice through spines, pierce hearts, and unleash the deadly lightning of his magic to sear through every living thing it touched.

The comms console crackled and drew his ire as the last crewman fell.

"*Persephone's Ire,* report!"

His response brought silence. "The *Persephone's Ire* is no more and her fate is yours if you come any closer."

The *Hercules' Mistress* filled the forward viewscreen and pods streamed like mercury from its hull. Even to his inexperienced eye, it was obvious that the vessel was "sinking," caught by the pull of Earth's gravity. He assumed it wouldn't be too long before the *Persephone* shared her fate and glanced at Stephanie.

The comms crackled again.

"Intruders aboard the *Persephone's Ire,* surrender."

That last request came in a chorus of three as the captains of the approaching ships replied as one.

"We repeat. Intruders aboard the *Persephone's Ire,* surrender."

Tethis opened his mouth to reply, only to be cut off by a cold, familiar voice.

"Ships on approach to the *Persephone's Ire,* this is the Witch of the Federation. Stand down or we will destroy you all. I repeat. Stand down or we will destroy you all. You do not have to die today."

Only one captain replied.

"No, Heretic, but you do."

Stephanie looked at her two teammates. "There are three of them..."

"And three of us," the young mage finished.

An alarm sounded a warning of incoming fire.

"It hardly seems fair," Tethis added as they each opened a portal beside them.

By the time the first barrage of missiles pounded into the *Persephone's* shields, the command center was empty. The klaxon's call for a ship-wide evacuation echoed eerily through the empty space and the warning lights flashed amber for no one. The same could not be said for other parts of the ship, where crewmen fled for their lives, dove into the nearest life pod, and ejected as soon as the lid was closed.

Soon, the *Persephone* found herself in the same relentless grasp that held her sister ship, the *Mistress*.

On Earth, the footage stirred people to run outside to scan the skies.

On *Star Base Notaro,* Admiral Edwards' jaw dropped and he stared at the footage on the wall of the orbital's main briefing center.

"They didn't…"

For those listening, it wasn't clear who he was referring to—whether he meant the ships who'd caused the *Persephone's* destruction or the intruders said to be aboard the doomed vessel at that time.

He stared a moment before he closed his mouth with an almost audible snap and strode to the communications console at the end of the room.

"Get me Fleet Command," he ordered, his gaze glued to the screen and the sight of two of Earth's battleships sinking. "Maitland, I need those ships broken down."

He paused, listened, then scowled.

"Yes, Maitland, I *do* mean blast them into smaller pieces so they don't pose as much of a threat to the planet. We do not want something that big to fall in one piece."

The communications squawked and he waited.

"Yes, I *do* know there are two of them. That doesn't change the order. They need to be much smaller if we don't want to lose civilians on the ground."

His expression grim, he overrode the response.

"No, I don't care about the public relations fallout. It'll be less if we blow them up in the air than it will be if they crash land like that."

In the streets and gardens of Earth, its people stood under an open sky and stared upward. Some parts of the world saw nothing and they soon went back inside. In other areas, they stared in horror at the blaze above them. Emergency sirens howled to summon them to shelters thought forgotten.

Ted knew nothing of what was happening in the streets of Paris, but he knew everything that was happening in the world Net and the skies above—or almost everything. He'd missed the tracers, and while his outer defenses caught most of them, one or two got through.

Social media was ablaze with rumors and reports. Some of what was being suggested was true but some was an outright lie. The Regime's PR department shifted into overdrive, pulled personnel in from leave, and would not allow their staff to rotate out.

"You're here until it's over," was the direction from above and not a single supervisor dared to gainsay it.

Someone intercepted Admiral Edwards' instruction to destroy the *Hercules' Mistress* and the *Persephone's Ire* and news and social media sites went ballistic.

Navy order Their Own Ships' Destruction.

Navy Imposes Death Sentence on Loyal Crews.

Regime Eats its Own.

The Heretic Strikes Back.

Navy Destroys Ships that Fired on Parisian City.

"What are they thinking?"

Headlines and comments deteriorated from there. Between the conversations the Navy had started, the conversations the Regime wanted stopped, and reports of pod landings and evacuation orders, the worldwide Net was in meltdown. Still, this was nothing compared to the scenes in cities or towns that tracked the debris headed in their direction.

"I can't save them all," Ted muttered as he worked to quell the propaganda put out by the Regime's PR department while he pushed the news and warnings to the sites that needed them both.

Regime BURT fought him every step of the way.

CHAPTER THREE

"We can't simply go in blind," Ka stated where she stood in front of Todd. "If we're gonna get someone to gate us over there, we're gonna need a plan."

"Yeah, boss," Gary interjected. "What are the chances she's already blown up the ship that fired on us? If you get someone to send us back out there, you're gonna need to be sure we have a 'there' to arrive at. None of us can breathe vacuum."

"Yup. Not even you, boss," Reggie told him. "You have to stop believing every story we spread. It's not healthy."

Their sergeant regarded them with raised eyebrows, then glared at Reggie. "There's a story out there that says I can breathe vacuum?"

The Australian blushed red to the tips of his ears and refused to meet his gaze.

"Do you want to know what's gonna happen when *Stephanie* hears that story?" Todd asked him, and the man gave him a look of alarm.

"She doesn't have to know about it," he protested and Ka snorted.

"When are you gonna learn, Reg? That lady learns of everything."

Reggie looked worried, then shrugged. "Well then, I'd better enjoy breathing while I can, which brings me back to the point that we gotta end up somewhere that's still in orbit."

Todd grinned and clasped his shoulder. "Reggie, you're a genius."

Shock and puzzlement creased the man's face. "I am?"

"Oh, yes, you are. We'll visit *Star Base Notaro.*"

"Federation Navy Headquarters?" The Aussie squawked and turned a worried look to Ka. "Tell me he's joking, boss?"

"I thought I was your boss," Todd argued.

"You are, boss, but she's my other boss."

"Do you seriously mean it?" Ka asked. "You want us to raid Regime Navy Central?"

The sergeant thought about it for all of ten seconds before he responded with a decisive nod.

"Yup. Think about it. Their battle ships have gone nuts and are attacking each other or report that the *Heretic* is on board. They've turned on one another. There is one hell of a firefight going on outside and all the brass is gathered in one place in *Notaro,* probably to watch it all happen. They'll be so busy chasing their tails, they won't pay attention anywhere else."

He poked Ka in the chest. "And where do you think they keep all the sensitive Naval data, Corporal?"

"At Earth Command?" she asked sarcastically and he drew away from her and rolled his eyes.

"Why do you have to be like that?" he asked. "Of course they'll keep some in Earth Command, but they keep more on *Notaro.* I bet there are secrets the two command posts don't even share. We have to target it."

"And it'll still be in orbit," Gary pointed out gleefully.

"Even better, we could always make sure it no longer is when we're done," Piet added quietly and held two satchels of explosives up. One looked like it was of Meligornian make but the other was marked with Teloran script.

"You wouldn't…" Ka began and he smiled.

"Come on, ma'am. Don't you want to see exactly how big a bang these babies make?"

"Don't call me that," she snapped but her eyes sparkled as she examined the satchels.

Todd grinned. "It's all set, then. We'll attack *Star Base Notaro* and wreak havoc and mayhem."

She frowned. "Don't you mean download secret data?"

His grin grew wider. "Of course that's what I meant."

He turned and headed to the door while he muttered under his breath. "Download secret data. Download secret data."

Shortly after they reached the corridor, he stopped. "Who will we ask?"

Ka frowned. "Well…"

"V'ritan," the *Tempestarii* suggested in a sotto voce whisper. "You need to ask V'ritan."

Todd and Ka looked at each other, then up and down the corridor. "V'ritan?" they asked, nodded simultaneously, and clapped each other on the shoulder before they jogged down the corridor.

"Did that look creepy to you?" Gary asked Reggie and the Australian nodded.

"Real creepy," he agreed and they glanced at the team.

Ivy nodded. "Yup, definitely creepy. Who's V'ritan?"

Lars moved alongside her, slid an arm across her shoulders, and steered her away from the Hooligans.

"He is the head of the Meligornian Navy," he told her. "You'll like him. Has anyone ever taught you how to greet a Meligornian properly?"

"No…"

They'd almost reached the shuttle bay when a team of black-armored figures stepped into the corridor behind and ahead of them. When he caught sight of the huge figure who blocked their path, Todd slowed to a walk.

"Vishlog," he said quietly.

"You're going after Stephanie?" the Dreth asked and he nodded.

"Yup."

"Good." The warrior grinned and grasped his shoulder. "I'm coming."

"You—didn't she tell you to stay here?"

He shook his head. "Nope. She simply stepped through a portal and left me behind."

For a minute, Todd looked like he might argue but he cast a glance at Stephanie's team.

"When I said we were going after Stephanie," he told them, "I meant that we would create havoc—"

Ka groaned. "Get sensitive data," she corrected and he nodded.

"Get sensitive data," he agreed, "from *Space Base Notaro*."

The Dreth wrinkled his brow. "Will Stephanie be there?"

Todd clapped the warrior on his shoulder and shook his head. "No, and this is why you need to be here. Someone has—"

"To mind the shuttle?" Vishlog suggested and raised his eyebrows.

"Exactly." He squeezed his massive shoulder and slid past him but came to a halt a few steps later. "Where is the shuttle?"

The Dreth grinned and the two men who stood beside him cocked their heads.

"Are you sure Steph won't be anywhere near your location?"

He sighed. "She'll share the same orbit but don't ask me exactly where. The last I knew, she was spitting mad because someone fired a laser at us and you know what she's like."

"When you almost get your ass fried?" Brendan quipped.

Avery nodded sagely and glanced at Vishlog. "We'll fly them.

The chances are they're the only way we'll get her to cool down enough to get back here."

"Return the shuttle," the warrior rumbled, "and make sure you are here when they are gone." Their jaws dropped and he bared his tusks in a Dreth smile. "The cats need walking."

Both men groaned but jogged to where Todd was waiting. "The shuttle's this way."

"We need to see V'ritan," he told them.

"They have an appointment," the *Tempestarii* added. "He's expecting them on the King's Warrior in the next half-hour."

The two pilots exchanged glances. "We'd better hustle, then."

They were about to leave when Lir'tel arrived at the head of a squad of mages.

"We're coming, too," he announced. "Tempe says you'll need mage support, and the captain wants us out from underfoot."

Ka stared at them. "Are you sure that's what he said?"

He gave her a smug look. "That's all you're cleared to know," he told her. "Besides, Tempe's right. With a mission like this on a Regime station where there are likely to be more than a few Talents and with a team that has the magical aptitude of a rock? You'll need magical support."

"I thought you said I had aptitude?" she protested, and the mage smirked.

"I lied."

V'ritan met them in the hangar and returned their greeting with a quickly sketched one of his own.

"Tempe tells me you want to head to *Notaro* and wreak a little havoc," he began.

"Get. Sensitive. Data." Ka gritted her teeth and he gave her a knowing smile.

"Yes, and that too," he acknowledged before he continued. "She also says you'll need magical backup."

His gaze wandered over the mages grouped behind them.

"It's a start but you'll need more," he stated and spoke quickly into his comms. "Send them." He studied the group. "I'll need an even dozen and I need them in the main conference room."

When he was finished, he focused on the team again. "I'll gate you over," he told them. "I believe I know *Notaro* passably well."

"Passably well?" Frog asked, his eyes wide, and V'ritan smirked.

He didn't reply, however, but led them through the busy corridors of the *King's Warrior* to the conference room. The last tables and chairs were being stacked along the walls and the center was clear. A dozen Meligornian mages were assisting but they gathered together when he arrived.

The *Ghargilum's* eyes twinkled as he turned to the leading mage.

"The Hooligans have resupplied and need to create havoc." He cleared his throat. "I mean, *collect intelligence* from *Space Base Notaro*. You are their backup. You need to make sure they stay in one piece and protect them as they gather the data. Someone needs to connect with me so I know when to pull them out."

The chief mage bowed. "*Ghargilum.*"

More mages arrived and reported to him.

"We have orders to assist in the creation of a portal, *Ghargilum?*"

Todd shepherded the Hooligans and the accompanying Earth team to where the mages waited, then stood in silent awe as V'ritan and his mages opened a doorway into a very familiar repair hangar.

"Courtesy of the *Knight,*" the King's Warrior explained. "She retained the *Notaro's* orbital pattern and still has its schematics in her databanks."

"When did she get the schematics?" Ka asked and he chuckled.

"Well, you know our Knight. She has a habit of picking up useful bits and pieces."

The hacker snorted but kept her thoughts to herself. The *Knight* was as nosy as hell and had no sense of propriety when it came to data acquisition or challenging the security of other people's systems.

However and whenever she'd done it, the information she'd taken was still accurate. The repair hangar stood open before them and was, for the moment, mercifully empty.

"As pretty as that is," she commented. "It won't stay empty forever—and it's not like we'll be invited in."

She didn't wait for Todd's reply but jogged forward.

"Hooligans!" the sergeant snapped. "Let's get these people their data."

"Wreak some havoc for me," V'ritan said quietly over their comms as they moved out. The mages, Lars, Ivy, Frog and Garach trotted steadily at their heels. As soon as they were clear, the gate vanished.

The soft pop of its disappearance sounded strangely loud in the hangar's confines.

"Tell me they won't open this to space," Frog muttered and Ka gave him a worried look.

"I need to talk to Ted," she stated, "if I can find him."

"After we get our asses into the station itself," Todd ordered. "Until we have control of the doors, we won't give them the easy option."

No one argued. With nervous glances at the hangar bay door, they hurried to the airlock that led into the station.

"Why go that way?" Gary asked when they were halfway across the huge space. "Isn't this the same place that bloke took us when we needed to get away from those other Marines?"

"You mean the Odd Squad?" Ka asked and he nodded.

"Yeah, boss. Remember? We had the best steaks this side of Earth and—"

"Leave it until we have control of the pick-ups," she ordered and cut him off. She turned to Todd and added, "What d'you say, boss? If I can get into the system and hack the monitors, should we take a side trip and work out where to go next?"

The sergeant shook his head. "Right now, they've only just detected us. If we hit them hard and fast, we could reach the data center."

Reggie groaned and smacked his hand over his face. "Right, boss, and now they know where we're going."

They'd almost reached the door and Jimmy and Angus slid up on either side of it.

"Airlock," they said. "Remember? We don't have any idea of who or what's waiting for us on the other side."

Todd gave them a feral grin. "Then let's not give them any more time to organize. Move!"

Ka took Angus, Gary, Reggie, Jimmy, and Piet through first. Lars and Ivy squeezed in at the last moment, and Lir'tel surprised them by joining them.

"I can't let you magical dead-heads have all the fun."

The corporal glared at him and he smiled.

Gary nudged her. "Aw, boss, I think the nice man likes you—oof!"

The mage reached over and steadied him.

"Thank—" he began but the Meligornian sent a small bolt of lightning into his shoulder. "Ow!"

"Don't short his suit," Ka warned. "He might be annoying but I need every blaster blocker I can get."

"Oy! I'm right here, boss. Right. Here!"

She regarded him with mock surprise as the outer hatch began to cycle. "Why, so you are. Now be a dear and check the left flank."

"Gazza, check the left flank. Gazza, mind the door. Gazza—Don't you bloody well shoot at me, you prick!" he shouted and returned fire at the small squad of Regime soldiers that blocked one side of the corridor.

A soldier's light armor withstood one shot, but the next one knocked him back and a third one left him screaming with a smoking hole in his shoulder. Blaster fire from behind him told him his teammates were taking care of a second squad of soldiers.

"Lazy mothers," he grumbled. "Waiting for us to exit instead of coming in to get us."

"Yeah," Ka quipped. "You'd almost think they'd grown some brains."

A sheet of purple sprang into being in front of Gary as Ivy and Lars came up alongside him.

"It's about bloody time a mage made himself useful," the Englishman muttered and Lir'tel snorted.

"And you be sure to say that somewhere Steph can hear you," he advised and launched three rapid-fire balls of lightning through the shield and into the waiting squad.

"How suicidal do you think I am?" he demanded.

"I don't know," the mage retorted, "but if you ran your blaster as fast as you ran your mouth, we'd have cleared the corridor by now."

More shots drove into the shield and the light above the airlock flashed to warn them it was cycling.

"Make a space!" Ka shouted and they moved forward to leave a gap behind them as they each covered a different section of the corridor.

"How many people do you think they can fit into that lock?" Jimmy asked from beside Ka.

"Why?" Gary demanded. "Are you thinking of taking a return trip?"

"No, but I'd like to get out of this damned corridor before they bring any mages in."

"Do you know where we need to go?" Ka asked.

"I have it in the HUD."

"Clear this damned corridor!" Todd's voice cut off any further conversation and they separated into two groups and held the airlock until the last group had come through. "Ka, Piet, I need Ted and I need the surveillance cams."

"Sure, boss. Get me to a jack point and we'll be golden," the hacker snarked in response.

He waited until the airlock had cycled for the last time, then crouched in the covered area behind them and pulled up the station schematics on his HUD.

"I seriously need an updated set of plans."

"Like I said, boss—"

"Have you never heard of Wi-Fi?"

"Boss..." Ka began but fell back as she added, "You're brilliant."

Jimmy, Angus, and Darren closed the gap behind her.

Crouched beside Todd, she looked for the Wi-Fi connection and tried it.

"Well, I'll be a donkey's... I'm in."

"Do you have my cameras yet?"

"Keep your shirt on, boss. It's not like you've given me a magic wand."

"How about a boot—"

"Seriously, boss?"

"Get us Ted. Now."

"Gotcha." Ka sent out a multi-headed request, tweaked the program to repeat the message, and left a copy of it on every server it encountered before going on to another one. A simple answer would trigger a second routine that would seek out and erase all instances of the first.

She hoped the AI didn't take too long to reply.

"I've asked for him," she said when she was done, "but I can't access the security system from here. I need a terminal."

"There's a security sub-station not far from here," Jimmy said and highlighted the relevant area in their HUDs.

"Good idea," Todd interrupted. "Ka, take Jimmy, Angus, and Darren to the sub-station and get me the surveillance systems, then download anything that seems worth taking."

"Do you have any specifics, boss?" she asked.

"All of it, Ka. Download everything."

She gave him a happy smile. "That's what I thought." She bounced to her feet and tapped Jimmy, Angus, and Darren on their shoulders. "What's our front like?" she asked, and the Scotsman glanced down.

Ka slapped him. "Not that front. We need this corridor."

"I'm coming, too," Lir'tel announced from behind her, "and so are M'rim, Tsilta, Filsarel, M'ktel, and Keltif."

His tone told her there was no point in arguing so she simply shrugged. "Fine, but keep up."

She was about to move out when Ivy interrupted her. "It looks like there's a second major data center here."

Again, the map in their HUDs flashed, then twisted and realigned with a second version.

"This one's more up-to-date," the girl announced.

"We'll take that center," Lars told Todd and highlighted the second center. "I'll take Ivy, Garach, and Frog."

"And us." Another six mages moved slightly away from their fellows and the security head sighed.

"Done, but no more."

Todd grimaced. "As if that would stop them."

"V'ritan's orders," the lead mage explained.

"And Tempestarii's," Lir'tel added.

"This is getting us nowhere fast," Ka pointed out and Lars and Todd nodded.

"Hooligans!" the sergeant commanded, "Move out."

"Guys, with me," Lars instructed.

The first part of their journey took them along the same path as Ka but separated from it as soon as they reached the first elevator shaft.

"Should we risk it?" Frog asked and Lars nodded.

"Break a leg," Ka told them as she jogged past. "Better yet, break something Regime."

The security head snorted. "You too."

They had their chance the second they stepped through the elevator doors. If the mages hadn't thrown shields up on either side of them, they'd have died in a hail of blaster fire. As it was, the magic-users returned fire to eliminate most of the waiting soldiers while Ivy, Lars, Frog, and Garach recovered.

"Do you mind?" the small guard complained and the nearest mage grinned.

"Enjoy it while you can. We'll run out of power soon enough."

"That is not what I needed to hear," Frog told her, then noticed the bandolier of batteries across her chest and the multiple batteries around her waist. "Exactly how long do you think we'll be here?"

She snickered and launched another burst of lightning down the corridor.

"Gotcha."

"You needed me?" The sound of Ted's voice through the team comms almost gave Ka a heart attack.

"We're trying to get some data," she told him.

"And maybe to cause some chaos and confusion while you're about it?" he suggested and a smile edged his words.

She grinned. "That, too. Todd needs the surveillance system and we need to be able to control the doors."

"I'll see what I can do." Ted paused as though examining something, then highlighted a small section of the security substation.

"That's the one you'll need to download," he told her. "I can't access it from the Net."

"Gotcha," she acknowledged and sent the location to her team. "This is where I need to be."

"Do you have enough storage for that?" Angus asked.

"I came prepared," she told him. "It's not like we can take it with us."

"Why not?" he asked. "It has a drive, doesn't it?"

Ka paused, turned, and cupped his face in her hands.

"You're a genius," she told him and bumped her forehead against his before she released him so she could fire several fast shots down the corridor behind him.

"Plus, it would be quicker," Jimmy observed, "and we're about to have some seriously bad company!"

"What do you mean?" she asked but she could see.

Ted had already accessed the surveillance feeds and had sent her those from the nearest cameras, but she hadn't paid attention.

"Are those mages?"

"Talents," one of the mages corrected. "Did you know they had so many on this station?"

"I didn't know they had any on the station," she admitted.

"We can hold them," he assured her, "but you'll need to be quick."

"Are those Marines?" Angus asked and highlighted a second group that double-timed it down the corridor toward them.

"I'll be real quick," Ka told them. "Let me know if it looks like you'll lose it."

They hit the security sub-station hard and fast, shooting to kill. Now was not the time for prisoners who might try to turn the tables. Ka focused on reaching the terminals Ted had indicated.

The one thing the *Knight* hadn't been able to give them was the *Notaro's* crew and security complement and it looked like it might be even higher than it had been thirty years earlier.

"This one's mine!" Stephanie shouted and highlighted one of the ships on the screen before she slid through a portal she opened beside her.

"Mine," Tethis said and marked a second.

"And mine," John sighed as he focused on the third. He grinned. "It's time to wreak havoc."

"Trust you to give me the hard one!" he protested seconds later as he pulled a dome of light over himself. "Seriously, what were you thinking?"

"That you are a big boy now?" Stephanie snarked in return. "Are you telling me you need your diaper changed?"

"I can change my own pants, thank you," he retorted.

"Well, if you truly need to." Tethis joined the conversation as Ted linked the comms from the three ships into a single network and secured himself inside the *Notaro's* surveillance system as he did so. *Now* he was having fun.

Broadbanding the footage from the three ships into the Earth's entertainment networks was a piece of cake once he'd locked the PR machine out of it. Holding them at bay was a little challenging but very entertaining.

"Ah-ha!" He wedged himself through a stream from inside the Naval station as Stephanie asked the captain to cease firing and was told where to go.

"Bad choice," she told the man and fried him from head to toe.

The lighting had already dropped to amber around her. Now, it began to flash and the order for the crew to abandon ship echoed through the cruiser.

"Oops!" she exclaimed. "I might have broken another one."

As she spoke, the rhythmic sound of soldiers double-timing it rattled up the corridor outside the command center. She looked at the remaining crew who cowered behind their consoles.

"You need to leave now," she told them. "It's about to get messy in here."

"Are you breaking things again, Steph?" Tethis quipped from in front of the hole he'd blasted through the back wall of the command center he stood in.

Somewhere on the other side of it, what was left of the captain was embedded in a bulkhead.

Before Stephanie could reply, he delivered another blast through the wall beside the door and angled it so it followed the corridor and cleared the Marines who had jogged toward the bridge.

"Says the man who's decided walls are an inconvenience. What will the people on Earth say?"

"That their Navy should be better trained and equipped?" he retorted and exploded a hole in the decking in front of another squad of Marines.

The deck peeled away with the blast and they plunged to the level below. He threw a fireball after them.

"That they should learn better manners and not enslave, torture, or harm their people?" He snarled.

"That they shouldn't fire on their own instead of sending assistance?" John suggested as he blocked incoming blaster fire while he destroyed the navigation console, blew up the piloting station, and sent the weapons controls into meltdown.

"Try blowing your friends up with that," he told the two crewmen who scrambled away from the flowing slag.

One drew his pistol.

The young mage hurled an ice spear through his chest and a second one through his assistant's head when the woman fumbled her pistol out of its holster and started to lift it.

"Do not point those at me." He snarled, splayed the fingers of one hand, and released a scythe-like beam of energy across the command center.

The crew members who rose above the smoking ruins of

their controls and shouted, "Die, Talent scum!" lost their heads and their lifeless bodies dropped out of sight.

Stephanie sheathed herself in a gleaming blue aura and waded into the soldiers who had been ordered to arrest her. The Talent who had been sent with them dropped to her knees, buried her head in her arms, and sobbed. "I...can't... I can't. I can't..."

The whole world saw her handler draw a pistol and shoot her before he turned to run from the Witch's rage.

"Murderer!" Her accusation echoed down the corridor as he burst into flame and continued to burn as he ran.

She spared the sailor who dropped beside the woman's body with a cry of grief, then felled the Talent who would have fried him for his trouble.

"We are all human here!"

The Marine who eliminated another handler was also spared and he swept his arms around the shoulders of the two Talents who clawed at their collars. He held them down and pulled them out of Stephanie's line of fire. Once he'd dragged them as far under the shelter of his body as he could, he held them close rather than letting them run.

"She's not here for us," he said and repeated it like a prayer. "Not here for us. Not here for us..."

Ted kept the cameras on the scene until the fighting was over and the Marine realized he was staring at the bloodied toes of a pair of black boots.

The moment when he raised his face to hers, his eyes full of tears and fear, was one the AI wanted the whole world to see.

"Kill me," the man said, "but not these. They don't deserve—"

He fell silent under Stephanie's stern gaze and hugged his two charges tightly to his side.

"Understood," she snapped and the three of them vanished in a flare of blue light. Very few understood the words that accompanied her action. "V'ritan, keep them safe."

"What did you do?" Tethis demanded when he realized the world needed to know she hadn't simply vaporized the trio.

"I gave them sanctuary," she told him, drew a blaster, and shot each of the leaders in the next squad that raced toward her. "Away from assholes like these."

"So you sent them to where they'll be safe?" he queried but her answer was not what he wanted the world to hear.

"No, I dumped them into the nearest volcanic crater I could find. What do you think?"

"Well, as long as they're safe," he managed and hoped the audiences of the world understood sarcasm.

He didn't add anything more but hurried down the tunnel he'd made through the center of his ship.

"I thought I told you to leave the ship alone," he shouted when he located the auxiliary command center.

The vessel's second in command turned and moved to draw a blaster as she opened her mouth to give the next order.

Tethis out-drew her and fired before her gun had cleared its holster.

"Cease! Fire!" he roared and even Ted sensed the compulsion behind his words.

The guns on the *Princess Hyde* complied.

"Abandon ship!" he commanded and again, the faintest sense of compulsion flowed across the AI's circuits.

I'm glad I'm not human, he thought and made sure he broadcast the footage of the mage offering the occupants of the second center a chance to surrender.

The first officer to shoot one of the crewmen who raised their hands burned against a wall while the warrior mage thundered, "And so shall end all who refuse mercy to their fellow man!"

Another officer edged around the mage to the door and kept her hands raised until she reached it. Tethis pivoted to observe her progress and drew more magic to float himself off the floor and onto an entry command console. He watched as the woman lowered her hands to open the door.

To his surprise, she didn't run through but waved the command team through it. "Pods!" she ordered curtly and they scrambled to comply. He heard the thump of boots and went to meet them.

"Ted, are you sure this isn't one of your crazy training simulations?" John cried as another wave of Marines stormed the command center door.

Unlike Tethis, he hadn't demolished the walls. He considered it, though, if only to let the crew who'd refused to attack him reach their pods.

"I'm an idiot," he muttered when a ball of magical fire blew the floor out from under the boots of the next Marine.

"You are," the Meligornian agreed as he dropped the corridor roof on top of the first man to raise his blaster and fire at the fleeing command crew.

"You don't have to agree," John complained and directed a sizzling ring of magic into the open floor nearest the crew who tried to hide behind a console.

"There's your way out," he told them. "Go!"

None of them moved but he had no time to tell them what to do. They'd either work it out or they wouldn't.

The Marines demolished the rear wall of the command center.

"Did you not think you might need that?" John asked and was answered by a barrage of fire.

Not all of it was directed at him, though. Some of the bolts pounded into the console that protected the crew and the young mage shouted his outrage.

"Is attacking your fellow ships not enough for you asshats?" he shouted and slammed a dome of blue over the crew and the hole he'd created for them to escape through.

"Was that a swear word, John?" Tethis teased. "Because you

should watch your language, you know. You're on interplanetary tv!"

Stephanie's voice interrupted. "Why don't you assholes pick on someone who can shoot back?"

"Have you tried telling her that?" John asked and the Meligornian chuckled.

"If you think she needs a lesson in minding her language, go right ahead but tell me what kind of flowers first."

"Flowers?"

"Yeah," the mage told him, "because it'll be your funeral."

"Ha, ha, you are so funny," he retorted and fired as he ran to intercept four Marines who tried to sneak past him to the dome with their knives and blasters out.

On another screen, Stephanie's blaster ran out of charge and she threw it at the handler who pushed two Talents into the corridor ahead of her.

One of the Talents ducked, then dropped to their hands and knees and scrambled along the base of the wall as the handler came after them. The blaster caught the woman right between the eyes, snapped her head back, and knocked her out.

"Two more for you, V'ritan!" she shouted.

The Talents screamed as blue light engulfed them and they disappeared.

"You honestly should tell them you won't hurt them before you do that!" Tethis called.

"Why? Because we're on camera?" she shouted and ran down the corridor toward the corner several shots had come from.

"Yes!"

"Ted, are you making sure those things are getting my good side?" she asked.

"Which side is your good side?" John called and emulated Tethis' trick of dropping the ceiling on his opponents. "Oops, my bad," he added when a waste-recycling tank came down as well.

"You are so cleaning that up!" Stephanie called.

"Am not and stop changing the subject."

"What?"

"Which side is your good side?"

Tethis' wry comment of, "I didn't know she had one," was lost when the Witch replied.

"Either side. I don't have a bad side."

"Not true. I've seen you before your first coffee," the Meligornian retorted and took two running strides to carry him up the closest wall so he could flip over the heads of two Marines who moved at a fast crouch toward him.

"Up high!" he yelled.

They watched him arc above them and dove to the side too slowly to avoid the rain of lightning that followed in his wake.

"Down low," he added, landed in a crouch to face them, and fired into their backs as they fell.

"Too slow," he told them and ran toward the engine room.

On the nearby *Cavalier's Charm,* the captain stared in dismay.

"What the hell is she doing?" he demanded as the other ship's guns ran hot, then flickered out. "She's supposed to be shooting the ship the Heretic's on."

"Do we know which one that is, sir?" the communications officer asked and brought up the feed from the *Persephone, Hercules,* and the *Princess,* as well as from *Checkered Priest* and *Beknighted Squire.*

Each feed showed at least one mage, or three or...honestly, who knew?

"What are their timestamps?"

The comms tech shook her head. "I'm trying, sir, but the feeds aren't stamped."

"Well, aren't we getting them live?"

"We should be, sir, but I know we can't be getting them from the *Hercules* because..." She waved her hand at the viewscreen to indicate where the vessel continued to sink into the atmosphere.

Other Navy ships closed on the hapless battle cruiser and fired on it in response to the orders sent from Earth Command to break the *Hercules* into smaller chunks.

"Then what?" the captain demanded but the lieutenant on scans interrupted him.

"Sir, she's getting ready to fire!"

"Good. It's about time she got down to business!"

"At us, sir!"

"Of all the— Get me comms."

"I'm trying, sir, but she's not responding."

"Give me the comms!" the captain repeated and the communications tech hammered his console.

"There you go, sir."

"*Princess Hyde!* This is the *Cavalier's Charm*. Put your weapons on hold. Do not fire at us. I repeat, put your weapons on hold."

"Sir, they're—"

"Shields to port!" the captain shouted as the first missiles from the *Princess* headed toward them.

"I don't think they did that," the scans tech told them and displayed the *Princess'* control room in ruins and power arcing over control boards that had been deserted.

"Then who?" the captain demanded and laughter rolled out of the *Cavalier's* intercom. "What's that?"

"Your ship is mine now," Ted told them and the pilot squawked in outrage.

"Hey! Give that back."

"Nope," the AI replied, "and I'll have this...and this...and this...and this!"

Yelps of alarm and cries of consternation rose from the weapons, communications, and navigations sections.

"No... No... Nononononono," the defense team protested in chorus.

"Yes, yes, and yes, yes, yes," Ted retorted gleefully.

The defense operator yelled in frustration. "No!"

Onscreen, the *Persephone's Ire* broke apart and hurled flaming debris into the atmosphere. Emergency pods streamed from every surface. They glowed as they made re-entry and the *Cavalier's* captain paled.

"Lord, help them."

"There goes the *Princess*," someone groaned as more pods joined the swarm already filling the surrounding air space.

The *Princess'* guns blew and created a line of smoke and fire down its length.

"Who's next?" The Heretic's cold tones hissed out of the intercom.

CHAPTER FOUR

"Leave my goddamned databases alone!" Ka shouted as another ball of magic slammed into the wall behind her.

That one had singed the casing as it had hurtled past.

A second one followed it and she pulled away as it seared the air beside her. She poked her head around the stack.

"I swear...*Darren!*"

"I'm doing my best, boss, but did you ever see a mage who listened when they were told no?"

"You'd have better luck finding a unicorn," Jimmy shouted in response.

"Unicorn, fairy, pixie dust...I don't care what you use but give me five more minutes. This sucker's wired to wipe and I want what's in the box."

"So do I," Todd told them over the comms. "How long will you be?"

"Another five, boss. Why?"

"'Cos we have company and more coming."

"I feel you, sir."

"Don't jinx me, Ka. Tell me when you're done."

"All right. Keep your britches on, boss."

Todd didn't reply and she focused on the data she was trying to extricate.

Angus' idea of removing the drive had been fine as far as it went, but she had to defuse the programs set to wipe it if she tried and none of the operators had been nice enough to leave their input codes anywhere conveniently nearby.

"They are probably worried about losing their heads if they do," she muttered and dove into the database again.

"You got this?" Lars asked as Ivy led the way down the corridor.

She focused on the Navy squad who dropped into defensive positions to block their path.

"Yeah. I got this." She lobbed two stickies and aimed high so they went over the heads of the guys in front. One of the soldiers narrowed his eyes and reached up to catch one as it went past.

"Me, too," Frog added and rolled a handful of half-inch round balls toward the enemy.

The soldier's hand closed around the sticky and purple formed a wall in front of them. The balls sparkled and kept going and the rear rank of soldiers shuffled back two steps, their eyes wide with alarm.

Ivy, Garach, and Frog opened fire, and Lars raised a hand to stop the mages from acting.

"Save it for when we need it," he told them. "Ka reported Talents."

"Ails'fel, Isklef, watch our backs."

The rear rank of soldiers began to run. The front rank threw themselves back and away from their fast-handed comrade and the incoming balls.

The soldier had realized his mistake and tried desperately to shake the sticky from his hand.

It exploded, took his hand, arm, and the top half of his body, and beheaded the men on either side. The soldier who'd been directly behind him fell screaming when his legs vanished, then fell silent as the second sticky exploded a moment later.

The balls struck the debris and more explosions followed. Electricity danced through the air and caused havoc with the survivors.

Ivy waited long enough for the sparkles to fade and sprinted forward.

One of the soldiers had reached a corner and flung himself around it. Lars thought he heard the man keep running, but the girl hurdled the remains of the squad and threw herself into a sideways skid. She opened fire as soon as her blaster cleared the corner and a short cry and loud thump followed.

"This way," she instructed and continued around the corner. "The first left is stairs. The data center is a right, left, and a right after."

"Right, left, stairs, right, left, right," Lars repeated.

"We have company," Ails'fel said.

"Block them and keep moving," the security head ordered.

Magic filled the air behind them and the mages began to run.

Lars looked back. Another wall of purple filled the corridor, transparent enough for him to see the squad of Marines who escorted a half-dozen Regime Talents.

"That's a lot of Talents," he murmured.

"Yup."

As much as he wanted to stay and watch what happened when the Talents reached the wall, he didn't. Ails'fel wrapped a hand around his arm.

"Come on, boss."

He complied and reached the corner as a second squad of Marines and Talents appeared at the other end of the corridor. More entered the corridor with the stairwell as he thrust through the door and hurried after the mages.

Ivy's startled shout followed the hiss of the door opening below.

"Got you," Garach rumbled and blaster fire followed. The sound of solids battering the wall was accompanied by the fizz of metal melting under lasers.

"I guess they knew we were coming," Ails'fel noted and his comment carried to the team.

"Yuh think?" Frog shouted.

"Yup, I'm sure," the mage quipped.

"I could do with some help down here," the small guard yelled.

"Yuh think?" Ails'fel responded as the first of his mages reached the small group.

"Cover me. I need to see," the mage ordered.

"K'lila!" Ails'fel shouted and Lars lunged forward.

Frog grasped the mage and shoved him behind him. He kept a hand on him as he slid across the door and fired at the squad in the corridor. The two crossed the doorway and Lars saw a sheen of purple layer the man's front. It dimpled and rippled under the rounds that greeted his appearance but it held.

Ails'fel's sigh of relief was as loud as his own but a moment later, the door above them opened.

"Out!" the security head roared. "Out! Out! Out!"

With a quiet oath, Ails'fel pivoted and slapped both hands over his head. Two grenades bounced to a stop on top of the layer of magic that flashed overhead. One landed on the stairs between them.

Lars grabbed the mage and dragged him with him as he leapt over the railing onto the floor below.

K'lila and Frog were already in the corridor and Ivy had joined them. A second mage sprawled at their feet but Lars couldn't work out why. As he watched, another of the magic-users knelt beside him and rolled him onto his back so they could lay their hands on the wound in his chest.

Ails'fel shook himself free of Lars' hand and the door slammed behind them.

The stairwell echoed to the sound of multiple explosions and the squads on either side of them glanced at the wall. The mage paid them no attention, dropped beside his wounded teammate, and placed his hands beside the first.

Purple spread from beneath their palms and the injured mage gasped.

"Where to, Ivy?" the security head demanded.

"Right!" She sprang forward before he could stop her.

She drew her blades from their sheaths as she moved and slid through the barrier K'lila had raised to thrust her sword up under the first soldier's chin as she drove the second weapon into the gut of the man beside him.

Without pause, she yanked her blades free, swung the first one again to slice into the next man's neck, and used an overhand strike with the second to split the helmet of her second victim.

"Frog!" Lars shouted, even though the small man was already clearing a path so he could reach the girl's side.

"John is gonna kill me," the security head muttered.

"Uh-uh." She grunted and abandoned her blade when she couldn't pull it free. She unslung her blaster as she continued. "'Cos I'm gonna murder him when I find him."

Lars cleared a path through the soldiers and reached her left side in time to drop the man about to shoot her. Garach closed the gap behind him and the mages followed on their heels as they dealt with the second squad.

"Left," she commanded at the next junction.

They pivoted and the mages used walls of magic to clear and then block the soldiers. They didn't need Marines and Talents waiting at the junctions. Ivy, Frog, and Lars fired as they approached the group that stood in their path. To their surprise, the Marines fell back to create a corridor in the center of the squad.

"Heads up!" Frog shouted as blue lightning lanced toward them.

He and Ivy fell prone and Garach tackled Lars to the floor. Ails'fel thrust a palm up to bring a large, round shield into being. It caught the lightning, absorbed it, and broke into a swarm of darts that he sprayed at the Marines and their Talents.

"Mother of—" Frog exclaimed as he sprawled onto the floor again. "Do you mind?"

Several Marines fell and their face plates smoked where the darts had penetrated.

"No, do you?" Ails'fel retorted.

"Don't answer that," Lars ordered and eliminated another of their opponents with a well-placed shot to the head.

One of the Talents turned to run and was promptly shot by their handler. Another turned on her handler and lost her life in three rapid-fire bursts but not before she'd launched a fireball down his throat.

The last two stood on either side of their handler and held their ground until Garach, Frog, and Ivy reached them. Only one of the Talents knew how to shield themselves and the look on her handler's face said he hadn't known. Unfortunately, she didn't know how to draw more MU from the world around her and wasn't able to escape when the shield failed.

"Right," Ivy ordered and Lars moved ahead of her to cover the corridor.

"First right!" she added as he overshot the door she needed.

"You could have told me that sooner," he grumbled.

She didn't answer. "Ted?" she asked.

"You have five technicians ready to fire at the door when it opens," the AI informed them. "Tell me when you're ready."

The girl pulled two stickies from her pouch. "Re—"

Lars put his hand over her mouth and pulled the stickies gently from her hands.

"Ka would laugh her ass off," he told her and stowed the stickies in his pouch. "Have you forgotten what we're here for?"

"Maybe we won't need all of them." She pouted and Ted chuckled.

"Start the download into Earth's Net," he told her, "and I'll retrieve and store it. But I think you will need it all."

"Ugh," Ivy exclaimed and drew her blaster.

The security head placed a hand over the barrel and drew her firmly away from the door. "Why don't we let the mages handle this?"

"But they have electricity!" she protested.

"Yes," he agreed, "but they also have other ways to deal with their opponents."

"And we won't break the servers," K'lila added.

The girl rolled her eyes but stepped back to give them room.

"You'd better hurry," Garach told them as the sound of approaching bootsteps reached their ears. "We're about to have company."

"We've got them," Ails'fel assured him and the mages moved to the outside of the team and put up another two walls.

These were harder to see through than the others.

"They won't hold them for long," Ails'fel said. "Not much longer than it takes them to work out the walls make better targets."

"And aren't you all glad I have control of the surveillance system," Ted murmured. "There's no need to give them ideas any earlier than they'll discover for themselves."

"Be thankful they don't have the suppression systems Tempe does," Lars quipped.

"Not in this section," Ted replied.

The security head paled.

"Anywhere we—"

The door slid open and magic hummed. Its note rippled to echo the angry fusillade of blaster fire that greeted them.

K'lila pushed it into the room in a moving wall and the team hurried in behind it.

"You woke the giant," Ted told them and Lars groaned.

"They had sleepers on the station? It used to be a transit point."

"Not anymore," the AI said. "If I read the data correctly, it's now a staging point. Two different animals."

"Staging for where?" Lars wondered and Ails'fel snorted.

"As if we didn't know."

"Ivy, you need to set this up fast," the security head advised and sent her the images of what was waking up in another section of the station.

"I'll lock it in as soon as you're done," Ted told her. "For as long as I can—and, speaking of locking..."

Lights for several doors in the feed went from green to red.

"It won't hold them long," he observed as one of the woken soldiers glanced toward the door and opened a weapons cabinet near the door. His guess was proved correct when the man retrieved an explosive pack.

"I'll be quick," Ivy promised and hurried between the servers in search of a point to jack into.

Piet had no such difficulty. He was jacked in and worked furiously to feed the data into the Earth Net. At the same time, he tried to fend off several hostile programs he'd triggered when he bounced into the system without bothering to check what was around.

The first program appeared to be attached to a living person. Finding and cutting their link was more difficult than he'd hoped until Ted stepped in.

The AI had traced the link, isolated the pod from which the

human was operating, and locked them inside with no way to call for help.

"It won't hold them any longer than it takes the pod to register its occupant is in distress and summons someone to cut the seals," Ted informed him.

"I'll make the most of it," Piet promised as a shot bounced through the door and ricocheted off his monitor.

The return fire brought a few moment's silence and the AI closed the door.

"How are you doing?" Todd asked.

"Busy," the engineer replied shortly.

"Then get busy faster," he retorted as the side wall shattered.

Several mages flung their hands up and a solid wall of purple blocked the gap. This was met by a sustained burst of blaster fire. At first, the wall merely shuddered and rippled beneath the onslaught but one of the mages groaned.

Todd glanced around in time to see her drop to one knee. A shout of victory came from the corridor.

"Double the power! It's working."

The sergeant looked at the lead mage.

"It takes energy to hold the wall if they blast it," she explained as the troops outside opened fire again.

Quickly, she stooped to release one of the mage batteries on the woman's waist and pressed it into her palm.

"Recharge!" she ordered and shouted to make sure the rest of the team got the message.

She straightened, followed her own instruction, and opened three batteries in quick succession.

"What if I shoot through it from this side?" Todd asked and raised his blaster. "We need to relieve the pressure."

"No. It's designed to resist things coming from the other side," the mage told him.

She'd barely finished speaking when he moved forward.

"Hooligans, hold the line," he ordered, unhooked a grenade from his belt, and hurled it into the corridor outside.

"Don—" the lead mage started and raised a hand to stop him. "Never mind."

"I'm in," Piet announced as the grenade blew.

"Good one, boss," Reggie snarked, "because it's not like a grenade would cause problems for the wall."

Three of the mages fell on their knees and drew more batteries before they staggered to their feet.

Todd flushed. "Sorry."

"I have your feed," Ted confirmed. "Give me a moment, and—"

"Hey!"

"You need to move and I needed to ensure the feed," the AI told Piet. "That's done now."

Several of the mages snatched their energy packs hastily. Their leader looked at Todd.

"We won't be much use to you for long."

He nodded and spoke rapidly into his comms. "Ka, where are you at?"

"I'm kinda busy, boss."

"Company?"

"Of the worst kind."

"Do you need a hand?"

"I'm not sure you can reach us. The corridor is very crowded."

"Gotcha." He switched channels. "Lars?"

"Ivy says she's almost finished." The security head wasted no words. "But we've drawn considerable attention and none of it good."

Todd linked the three of them together.

"We'll have to link up again," he told them and waited for their protests to subside.

Gary nudged him and he frowned but continued to speak.

"We'll start moving to you," he told them. "I'll—"

The Englishman drove his elbow into his ribs.

"What!"

"I know where we are," he told him.

"Yeah?" Todd challenged. "We're—"

"In the gym." Gary cut him off and hurried to fill the silence that followed his sergeant's surprise. "You know—not far from where those guys from Stromo's brought us out so we could return to our quarters."

"But we're nowhere near—" Todd stopped arguing as Gary pulled a second schematic of the station and laid it over the one Ted had provided. "You are shitting me."

"Nope. Not a turd in sight. This part is the gym." Gary waved his hand at the area they stood in, then pointed at the far end of the data center. "That part is where the cross-corridor was and the tunnel entrance should still be..."

He paced a few feet away, began to stamp, and listened to the sound of his foot hitting the floor after each one. A hollow sound echoed in response, slightly muffled by the equipment that had been moved overhead.

"Here," he said triumphantly.

Todd glanced at the forces gathering outside the wall. He noted the sweat pouring down the mage's faces and nodded.

"Get it open and tell me it'll take me to Ka or Lars."

"I could tell you that, boss," Gary began, "but—"

The sergeant snapped off several shots in quick succession and each round penetrated the mages' shield to drive into one of the soldiers on the other side. "Move it."

"Whatever you're planning, make it fast," the lead mage told him. "We're running out of batteries."

"My, my, my..." Ted murmured and moved through the Earth Net as another source of interference tried to stop the broadcasts coming into the system. "You are an ugly monster, aren't you?"

He sent out a small swarm of sub-routines and watched their digital signatures race snake-like into the surrounding network.

"You have to run out of heads soon," he said and smiled when he reached the source. "Nice try, but you're kinda screwed now, aren't you?"

The AI reached digital fingers through the connections between the pod and the Net, then paused.

"On the other hand, given that you'll be stuck in here a little longer, why don't I give you a lesson on what your beloved Regime is *really* doing to the worlds beyond? Or perhaps you'd enjoy a trip to the Nightmare Lands?"

The smile his construct wore turned from bemused to nasty as he tweaked the pod's settings to wrench its operator away from the PR server and the Earth Net and into a little corner of the Virtual World usually reserved for prisoners the Regime pretended it was re-educating.

In reality, the entertainment channel it offered also served as a lesson for those who considered acting against the Regime. It was part of an experiment to see if incidents of resistance could be reduced. Someone had tentatively titled it Fate's Worse Experiment.

Ted could see it had achieved little success thus far and he intended to shut it down as soon as he could find a moment and some computing power to spare. It seemed even he had his limits.

As soon as the operator was running from the entry-level monsters, the AI sent a second command through the pod's circuits to seal it so the only way to release its occupant was to cut them free.

"And so shall end all who intrude in my domain," he declared and turned his attention to the persistent attempts to regain control of the doors on *Space Base Notaro* and the surveillance system.

In addition to the broadcast, the Regime's PR machine wanted the footage so it could add its twisted commentary and there wasn't a hope in Hades he would let them do that. He found another pod-intruder who tried to redirect the flow of images and sent them to join their colleague in the Nightmare Lands.

At the very least, it would give the next person recruited to serve the system something to think about. He tweaked another setting to make sure this new episode became a priority premiere.

"Whatever that means," he thought, "but it sounds important—oh, no, you don't!"

One of the systems operators in the space station had found a by-pass and was redirecting the feed to a drive for holding. Rather than try to stop the operator, Ted locked the holding drive open and caused a flood of information to burst into the system.

"Ooh... You didn't want that to reach the public airwaves, did you?" he asked and chuckled as he disabled all other connections to the drive and locked the operator away from any ability to close the drive down or redirect the flow. "Well, it sucks to be you, then."

Somewhere on the world below, people were getting angry. In fact, in several somewheres in the world around him, people were getting angry. Soon, the Regime would have more than three rogue mages and an incursion of Hooligans to deal with.

He noted the intrusion almost as soon as it happened. More of the tracing programs had found his entry point and tried to link it to a physical location. Ted acknowledged that he should do something about that.

An alarm sounded in the system to indicate that someone was interfering with the outer door of the warehouse.

"Oh... That is truly not good," Ted observed as he accessed the surveillance system he'd had installed.

Three large armored shuttles had dropped into the access road outside and disgorged several squads of Enforcers. As he watched and deflected another attempt by *Notaro* to gain access to the controls, they inspected every inch of the outer walls.

He activated his external defenses and smiled when the first man to touch the warehouse door was blown back into his colleagues.

"Yup. Definitely wired," the man announced as he struggled to his feet and dusted himself off while the rest of the squad helped his friends to their feet.

"Don't stand there yapping about it," their squad commander ordered. "Get it un-wired and get me inside. This asshole is wreaking havoc!"

Asshole, Ted thought. *Well, I'm not exactly that.*

He sensed another presence in his space and searched through his programs. Seeing Regime BURT slipping away from his hiding place was a jolt to the system.

Damn, he thought and wondered why Earth's AI hadn't taken advantage of the element of surprise. He resisted the urge to go after him.

The choice wasn't a hard one to make, especially when the Enforcers used a small burst of EMP to disable the outer defenses. If it hadn't been for the automated cut-outs, he realized he'd have had less time than he needed.

Ted checked on what was happening aboard the *Notaro* and made a quick tour of where his other friends were fighting. Stephanie more than held her own, Tethis was doing something ugly to the drives of the ship he was on, and John...well, he certainly brought a little something extra to the party.

He didn't know what had possessed the boy to use a light burst of acid to remove the uniform of the Naval officer who stood puce-faced in front of him but it was classic. As he watched, the young mage sent whisps of smoke around the man's escort and their uniforms fell apart artistically.

"The world will love that!" the AI murmured and wished he

had time to replay what had gone on before John had unleashed his attack but he didn't.

Once he'd confirmed that the feeds were secure and the system was programmed to find and transfer any footage containing the mages' faces, he activated another sub-routine.

"I had hoped you'd soon be redundant," he told it, "but there you go. Wishes aren't horses and beggars don't ride. Do your worst and I'll get back to doing mine. These guys simply don't know when to give up."

Sensors in the floor above registered vibration as an explosion shook the building.

"Do your worst, my friend," Ted said again and focused on the fight above. "And I'll do mine."

He tapped into the scanners on the buildings on either side and observed the scenes they picked up. The Navy had joined the Enforcers and two more shuttles settled in the access lane that ran behind the warehouse, but they didn't interfere.

Instead, it looked like the two forces were collaborating.

"That can't be good," the AI mused and noted what was happening on *Notaro* as Todd and Ka moved closer to the data center Lars attempted to protect.

All three teams were struggling and Ted sighed. With one last look at his intruders and their fruitless attempts to enter his sanctuary, he dove into the Earth Net. He looked for Regime BURT as he moved but saw no sign of the Earth's Systems AI.

"That's how you're doing it," Ted murmured when he saw the way the *Notaro's* Naval technicians had hooked into the surveillance and communications systems running through the space station. "Well, we can't have that now, can we?"

CHAPTER FIVE

"Stay behind me!" Todd roared, caught hold of the lead mage, and hauled her back by her collar.

He shoved her behind him and continued to fire when he backed slowly down the corridor as the magic wall between him and the oncoming Marines flickered and died.

Gary chuckled and swept an arm forward in a bowling motion to scatter a gleaming swarm of spheres down the corridor. He, Todd, and Reggie continued their slow progress as Dru began to flick stickies toward the front of the Marines.

The air between them cleared and the enemy raised their weapons to fire, only to drop their muzzles and fall prone as a dozen stickies hurtled toward them. Robbed of their initial targets, the stickies simply attached to the men ranked behind them.

Chaos ensued as some Marines tried to detach the explosives before they detonated and others scrambled to escape the blast radius. Some even darted forward and skidded to a halt when the first of their boots landed on one of the spheres.

A startled shout rose as that Marine lost his footing and then lost his foot when the ordnance exploded. More shouts followed as other spheres rolled into the main body of men. These didn't simply stop and explode but extruded legs and swarmed over the boots and uniforms of those they came in contact with.

"I do know how to shoot!" the mage protested.

"Then shoot around me," Todd instructed.

"And I know how to use a blade," another mage added. "Just because we're out of energy—"

"If we're forced into melee, then we'll close," he snapped. "In the meantime, *move!*"

He sent a second burst to their helmets to highlight the route he wanted them to take.

"If anyone falls, pick 'em up and carry 'em!" Reggie added and did exactly that as a stray round made it past Todd and slammed into the mage's armor.

"I'm fine!" the Meligornian wheezed and slapped his hands away once she was upright.

"You're very bloody welcome!" he retorted and pushed her behind him.

"Dru, find me a path!" Todd called and the female Marine slid forward to take the lead down the corridor he and Gary were reversing down.

"Uh, boss…you might want to hurry," she called.

"What do you think I'm doing? Taking a stroll in the park?" he snapped.

"Yeah, well, you might want to make it a jog."

"When?" He looked at the men and women who moved cautiously through the remains of their comrades while they fired repeated volleys.

"We sure could do with a mage wall about now," Gary snarked.

"We'll have to rely on our suit shielding," Todd replied.

"That would be peachy if only some asshole would allow us to activate it," the Englishman retorted.

"Activate it now," the sergeant instructed, slapped his hand over his chest, and refused to rise to the bait.

The other Hooligans did the same and kept their bodies between the *Notaro's* oncoming defenders and the mages.

"You do know our armor has a similar function, don't you?" the mage leader asked and activated another shield. "We were only waiting for your order."

"You wait for orders?" Todd asked only half-sarcastically.

"Tempestarii and the *Ghargilum* instructed us so," the mage replied.

"That would have been real handy to know before we left," Reggie quipped.

The mage shrugged. "There wasn't time and we assumed you'd pick it up soon enough."

Todd had nothing to say to that. There were many steps they'd missed in his haste to get into the fight. He could only hope the data they'd sent into Earth's Net had been worth it and that the data the AI had redirected into the storage devices Piet, Ka, and Ivy carried was what Stephanie needed.

He didn't want to explain to her why he'd come back and put himself and his teams in danger if it wasn't. If it was good enough, she might only kill him a little, but if it wasn't there was no telling what she would do.

He shook the worry away and assured himself that what they had retrieved was good enough. With Ted to sort the general information from the truly pertinent, they'd be fine. He nodded and continued to move back until someone stood behind him.

"I have an idea, boss."

Todd recognized Piet's voice and groaned.

"Let me guess, you want to—"

"I don't want to, boss, but if we don't drop the roof into this corridor, they'll overrun us."

As he spoke, a second squad arrived to boost the ranks of the Marines they faced.

"How much time do you need?"

Piet cast a hasty glance at the roof, floor, and walls. "Seven or eight minutes."

"I can maybe give you three."

"Are you sure you want a rush job?"

"I'm sure you should be working while I cover you," Todd told him and crouched in a firing position. "Three minutes, right?"

"I'm not sure I—"

"Do what you can." He fired a long burst into the oncoming ranks, relieved when several others knelt beside him and added their fire to his own. "I'm not sure how much of this our suits can take."

More of his people stood behind them to add their fire to the barrage the front rank was already sending down the corridor. Ahead of them, armor sparked and force shields rippled and dropped. Several Marines fell but more filled their positions.

"How are we going, Piet?"

"Soon, boss, soon."

The sergeant was sure he could hear the man's hands shaking. "Whatever you do, don't drop it on our heads."

"You'll need to run this way when I say run," the man informed him and a route lit up inside the HUD.

"Are you sure?"

"It's the best way to reach Ka."

Blaster fire sounded from behind them.

"Gotcha," Todd told him. "Hooligans! It's time to get up close and personal!"

Several whoops greeted this, as did Piet's protest.

"How will you run when you're busy with hand-to-hand?"

The sergeant didn't dignify that with a reply. He had already run forward with the lead mage on one side and Dru on the other. "Two minutes, Piet."

"I need more like five."

"Then we'll have to invite these asshats to dance." Todd didn't slow but drew two blades as he slid up to the first Marine.

"Do what you gotta, boss. I'll try to give you more than thirty seconds."

"I appreciate that." He struck blade-first and the laser-enhanced vibro-blade slid through his opponent's armor like butter.

The man screamed and fell silent as Todd yanked the weapon free and used his other blade to knock aside the blaster of the next Marine. Beside him, Dru took her opponent's head, stepped forward to kick the knee out from under the one after him, and stabbed the soldier who'd thought to come up on her flank.

Gary pushed between him and the mage on his other side and shouted insults to do with his opponent's parents, relatives, and pets. Todd might have laughed at the sheer impossibility of the Englishman's suggestions except he was busy.

Their enemy now advanced four abreast down the hall and they wouldn't give ground. Nor did the front rank draw their blades. They'd seen the Hooligans coming and chose to fire.

Todd pivoted and the heat of a laser blast seared across the front of his armor as he turned out of its trajectory and side-stepped closer to his opponent. He swept his primary blade forward while he drove his secondary blade down in a short overhead arc.

The first swing glanced across someone's upper arm and slid through armor and muscle while the second sliced the Marine's helmet open and was caught in his target's skull. He braced and pulled back to free both blades as he ducked under the fist aimed at the side of his head.

"Wrong move." He snarled, reversed his now free short blade, and stabbed it into the torso of the man who'd attacked him. With a sharp twist, he wrenched it free, flicked it back the other way, and pivoted to bring the other blade to bear.

Gary moved beside him to protect his flank as he killed those moving in to fill the gap left by their colleague. Reggie moved with him, but the Australian didn't bother with blades. He had a blast pistol in either hand and did his best to run them dry.

"Boss!" Piet's shout reached them but Todd didn't look around until he'd felled the two soldiers who did their best to get past his guard.

When he did look, he saw the engineer had come into the space they'd created between the team and their opponents and now gestured for them to return.

"Hurry! You have thirty seconds. Twenty-nine...twenty-eight..."

The sergeant reversed, shoved his blades into their sheaths, and caught Dru and Gary by their shoulders.

"Back!" he ordered when they tried to resist.

Gary snapped out a hand and grabbed Reggie, and Dru yanked the mage back. Together, they reversed to where Piet stood.

"Fifteen..."

"To hell with this!" Dru exclaimed, pivoted, and spun the mage.

"Fourteen..."

Todd turned and ran, expecting to feel the impact of a solid slug or the burn of a laser but weighed the risk of that as being better than being trapped on the wrong side of one of Piet's explosions. He snagged Gary on the way and Reggie followed.

"Ten... Nine... Eight..."

"That doesn't feel like thirty seconds, Piet." The sergeant grimaced as he ran past.

"Five..."

"Where the hell did you learn to count?" Dru asked as she and the mage raced forward to catch up with the rest of the team.

The sergeant wondered when they'd all decided to head to the next junction, then Piet sprinted past him.

"Run faster, boss."

He increased his pace. "Tell me you didn't."

"There might have been a powerline I didn't know about," the engineer admitted.

"You have the schematics!" he protested.

"Ted only updated them now."

Todd groaned. "You mean you forgot to look at the utilities."

"It coulda been that."

They ran and ignored the appearance of another squad behind them. Piet made shooing motions with his hands.

"Go right!" he shouted as they reached the corner. Todd threw himself right and his boots slipped on the floor at the abrupt turn.

Gary skidded sideways and almost fell before the sergeant caught hold of his harness and yanked him upright.

"Are you sure we're going the right way?"

"We're on track, boss," Dru assured him. "Can't you hear the fighting?"

Ahead of Todd and his team, Ka whirled, cleared her flank, and carved a path toward the data center. The worst of it was that the Regime had beaten her there, while more of their forces were hot on her team's heels.

An explosion shook the floor and she grinned.

"It sounds like Piet's having a blast," she muttered and spun again as Lir'tel slid behind her to stop the next Naval Enforcer from getting close.

He shot the man twice and caught the shocked look on the next man's face.

"But you're a—"

"A mage?" he asked and put two bursts of fire into the man's chest. "And your point is?"

The corporal chuckled. "I think he was wondering why you didn't use magic."

"What does he think I do when I run out of power?"

"I don't think he has a clue."

Lir'tel fired two more shots and deflected the muzzle of another Marine's blaster to one side seconds before it fired.

"You don't play fair," Ka stated as he turned to stand shoulder to shoulder with her, raised his blaster to his shoulder, and sighted along it to make a succession of rapid double-tapped head-shots.

"They called me adaptive," he protested and she laughed.

"I bet they called you all kinds of things."

"Don't remind him," one of the other mages quipped. "It only makes him mad."

"And you wouldn't like him when he's mad," Angus added.

"What is this? Steal an old movie line week?" She narrowed her eyes. "Have you been watching more of Todd's classics?"

"It's the only thing to do when Stephanie's on a rampage and the *Knight's* banned you from the rec room."

"You were banned from the rec room?" Ka put a round between the eyes of another Enforcer and gutted the one beside him. "Why did that happen?"

"I don't want to talk about it," he snapped and Darren snickered, dropped to a crouch, and steadied his blaster on his knees.

"I bet you don't."

"Why?" Ka asked. "What did you do?"

"Let's just say—oof!" Darren rocked sideways and Jimmy put out a hand to steady him.

"Not each other," he reminded them and turned to shoot at the group of soldiers who'd come up behind them. "Do you have any ideas, boss? We're about to get shot fore and aft."

"Are we out of grenades?"

"I threw the last one a floor ago," the Scotsman told her.

"Mine was used to make an exit for us," Angus added.

She bounded forward. "Then we'd better make us a path."

Her gaze caught movement at the other end of the corridor and she sighed. "Where the hell do they hide them all? I don't remember the guard quarters having anywhere near this many."

"Those are ours!" Jimmy told her as the Marine closest to him started to turn. "Oh no, you don't."

He barreled into the man, picked him up in a tackle, and pushed him into his comrade behind him while he angled his blaster forward and fired into another.

"Clear a path!" Ka yelled and followed him into the fray.

Lir'tel remained at her side but M'rim, Tsilta, and Filsarel pivoted to take care of the soldiers who raced to close the gap behind them.

"I thought you said you were out of magic," Angus said when he turned to support them.

"We're not out of magic," M'rim retorted.

"Only Lir'tel?"

"And me," Keltif admitted and used his blaster to good effect.

"They were the anchors," M'rim revealed. "We don't have enough to throw a wall that solid again but we can put up a screen that will keep the worst of it out."

"Do it," Angus ordered and didn't bother to consult with Ka. "And try to slow them."

Lars called as the two groups worked to eliminate the Regime soldiers who stood between them.

"How far away are you?" he asked. "We're getting hammered and can't hold the position much longer."

"Can you fall back to another location?" the corporal demanded.

"Negative. We're locked down tightly and our mages are running low."

"How low?" Lir'tel demanded.

"They're onto their last batteries."

"And after that?" Todd demanded.

"We'll move to suit shields, but they've brought in a new group of Talents."

"How many?"

"I've got it." Ted's voice interrupted them.

Staccato fire came over the team comms and they all flinched.

"Where the hell did that come from?" Lars exclaimed.

"I prevented the cover from opening until I had control," the AI explained.

Ka frowned. Taking control of a mini-gun emplacement shouldn't have given him any difficulty.

"Are you okay, Ted?"

"I...am fine."

Ka carved through the last two men who stood in her path. "Yeah. No, you aren't. That should have been a piece of cake for you. What gives?"

"Yours is not the only predicament I am overwatching."

"Is Steph okay?" Todd asked anxiously.

"Pfft. Your Stephanie is perfectly fine."

A line ruptured overhead between her team and the squad that tried to reach them from behind. The ceiling collapsed to block the corridor.

"An excellent idea, Piet," the AI stated approvingly.

"But...if you're so fine, why didn't you do something like that before?" Ka pressed. "What's going on, Ted?"

"I believe they're tracking me," he replied.

"Bullshit." She all but spat the words and her team gave her startled looks.

"I beg your pardon?"

"He's not only tracking you, is he?" Ka asked. "The reason you've been offline so long is you tried to deal with him and when you saw we were in trouble, you came back."

"Is that true?" Todd demanded. "Don't lie to me, Ted."

"I... It is possible that my current location has been compromised," the AI admitted but decided there wasn't a hope in any religion's deepest hell that he would tell them he had Regime Enforcers and Naval Marines knocking on his front door.

A boom resounded through the complex.

Correction, he thought. *Knocking a hole through my front door.*

"Then get out of there," the sergeant urged as his team joined Ka's and they trotted down the temporarily clear corridor.

"Are we almost there?" Jimmy asked and more gunfire sounded from a corridor ahead of them.

"Oh, yeah," Ka told them. "We're almost there."

"I will leave before I am trapped," Ted assured them. "Move through the next room, please."

"But—" Ka began but pivoted abruptly and led them to the next door. Angus and Jimmy moved through to ensure that the space was clear and the others followed her in.

The door closed behind them.

"Piet, if you will," Ted instructed and one of the walls flashed on the schematic.

Todd chuckled. "Lars, we're coming in through the back. Don't shoot us."

"Roger that."

They heard the security head pass the word to the rest of his people, then add, "Ivy, how's it coming?"

"There is some good information here," she told him. "Locations on Earth for resupply, troop resupply, and Talents." Her voice softened. "John will want some of this."

"Hurry, Ivy," Ted told her. "They are bringing reinforcements in."

"I thought we cleared the last lot."

"The last lot, yes," Ted confirmed. "This is the next lot—and they have released more Talents from their holding area."

The way he said it made it sound like the Talents were wild beasts.

"Is it that bad?" Todd asked.

"Their handlers have orders to shoot them if they cannot eliminate you," the AI told him.

"Stand back," Piet instructed and added in a louder voice. "Lars, we're cutting through."

"Standing by," the security head replied and more shooting followed.

It didn't sound like anyone was waiting in the next room.

"Todd, you need to contact V'ritan and ask him to gate you out," Ted instructed.

The sergeant glanced into the room and then at his mages. A dull boom issued from the corridor they'd just left. Rattles and clunks signaled the arrival of heavier equipment, then the door began to glow.

"They're cutting through, Todd." The AI sounded tired. "I cannot gain control of the system controlling the cutting torch. It is too primitive."

The mages moved together. "We will call the *Ghargilum*," they told the teams, "but you will need to all be in one place and close together."

"Understood," Todd told them and signaled for his team to join Lars and the others in the data center.

Ka moved quickly to Ivy and Piet hurried to join them.

"What can we do?"

"I need to get into that system," Ivy told them.

"Hurry," Lir'tel instructed as Ted snapped, "There's no time!"

"But we need the data," the corporal protested.

"It's not worth your lives!"

"But—" Ivy began, only to have the AI override her.

"It's not worth your lives!"

CHAPTER SIX

What Ted did not tell them was that he had no way out. The bunker was not designed for stealthy egress, only to conceal and shelter. Once its location had been compromised, he had no way to leave undetected—or at all, for that matter.

He kept half a monitor on what the teams were doing on the ground in and around the shelter and was grateful he'd thought to install drones in small boxes secreted around the neighboring buildings. The EMP that had disabled his ground floor sensors and electronics hadn't touched his hidden auxiliaries.

It had been a risky business to launch them and he'd lost two before he'd managed to position one where it could record what was happening inside the warehouse. The resulting feed was helpful, but only to let him know how long he had before they broke through.

The explosion that destroyed the entrance to the chamber caused some consternation, as did the vehicles and crates stacked over his head. The Enforcers had to move their shuttles while they brought trucks in so the floor could be cleared.

After that, the drilling started.

Ted left a dedicated line for the sensors and the feed that would let him know when they broke through.

"Not long, now," he murmured and dove into the system again. He couldn't do anything about the situation he was in but he could buy Todd and the teams enough time for V'ritan to reach them.

"Surely they've had enough fun by now," he muttered and reached out to the ships in orbit. "Honestly, how much destruction does she think she needs to prove her point?"

It didn't take long to identify the ships Stephanie, John, and Tethis were terrorizing.

"How many is that?" he wondered but didn't bother to count. "Now to get their attention."

He thought about simply telling them the teams needed help but decided that would lead to too many questions.

"It would be best to simply show them," he said, but when he went to pull the feeds from the *Notaro,* he saw that Todd and the teams were in even bigger trouble—or they would be.

The Regime had placed a company of Marines on the station in stasis pods to bolster the other company they had on active duty there. In the face of the Hooligans' antics, they'd started the waking cycle.

"We can't have that now, can we?" the AI murmured, reversed the program, and blocked access for the frustrated technicians who tried to cancel his input. "Temper, temper..."

One of the men had given up trying to key into the system and hurried to the fire-ax hanging on the wall behind him. Ted unlocked the casing so the tech could get to it and watched as his supervisor made a desperate grab for the man.

"Are you out of your mind?"

"Yes, yes, he is," Ted replied and snickered as he moved through the station and activated every bulkhead and airlock he could find except those he'd already locked down. He assumed the Hooligans didn't need that kind of help.

Alarms whooped and lights flashed as large sections of the *Notaro* depressurized.

"I know we're not supposed to destroy it," he said, "but a little havoc should keep them on their toes."

Next came the fire suppressant in every section except the one the Hooligans were trying to hold.

It's a shame they kept their suits sealed, he thought as those who tried to get into the data center wiped frantically at their face shields or fumbled to switch to suit air instead of station. Some weren't quite fast enough and foam bubbled into their helmets.

"It sucks to be you," the AI told them cheerfully and reversed the waste processing system.

Chaos broke out in the Life Support section as technicians raced to undo the programming or reach manual override switches on the tanks and pumps.

"This is so much fun."

He took a quick peek at how the Hooligans were coping and was relieved to find that they had pushed their attackers back or that their attackers had retreated in an attempt to regroup. The Talents were down—they hadn't had suits—and their handlers weren't in much better condition as they preferred uniforms to armor.

A resounding crack dragged his attention out of the system and he grimaced as a chunk of floor landed in the center of the chamber.

"Not good," he observed as another piece broke loose.

"Seriously not good," he added when a section of flooring vanished under the onslaught of a high-powered laser.

Cement dust filled the air and the drilling stopped.

"Found it!" The call echoed from above.

"Good. Now find him!"

"It's time to let Steph know she's needed elsewhere," Ted said as boots hit the ground mere feet away.

He moved rapidly, pulled feeds from the data center, and used an external shot to zoom in on the *Notaro* so they could tell where the data center was located. "I hope that's enough."

It was easy enough to enter the ships' view screens. He already had control of their surveillance—or he'd had control of their surveillance—when the trio had been on the other ships. Still, sliding into the security feeds on these wasn't too difficult, nor was taking the feeds from the data center to display them onto the screens.

He'd barely finalized the link when an outraged shout reached his sensors.

"You!"

The barrage of shots that followed came too fast for him to reply.

"I'm in!" shouted one of the technicians who worked with the Marines' stasis pods.

Her cry was echoed by others around the ship. Life Support returned the waste disposal units to their normal flow. Air locks responded to emergency overrides that came abruptly back online. The fire suppressant took a little longer to clear and needed manual intervention before the required systems activated.

In the Earth Net, Regime BURT finally managed to free the PR technician from Nightmare Land, booted the screaming man into his pod, and tried to get him to focus on the broadcasts. When that didn't work, Earth's Virtual World AI went to work himself.

He wasn't fast enough to stop the *Notaro's* systems from transmitting the renewed battle to the ships on which the three mages were fighting. Instead, he focused on the PR teams' persistent demands that he stop the battles being transmitted to Earth's public Net.

Stephanie was busy fending off attacks from three sides, having foregone her blaster, and she used her magic only to enhance her speed and the power of the blows she delivered. The ship's defense force simply wouldn't get the message.

"You. Need. To. Evacuate." She ground each word out to coincide with another deftly landed kick or punch.

Armor caved and joint servos locked, but it wasn't until her hands sparkled with lightning that her opponents began to withdraw. She followed and ignored the screen that lit behind her. Not even the distracted glances of those she faced were enough to break her concentration.

Todd's voice as he changed charge packs on his blaster was what broke through enough to catch her attention.

She bounced back and positioned herself out of reach as he muttered, "I wish I could ask Stephanie to take a step to the right."

The Witch glanced up in time to see him slam the charge pack into place, raise his blaster, and fire in one fluid movement. Unaware of her gaze, he glanced over his shoulder.

"Lir'tel, any luck yet?"

"Not yet. She's too focused on the fight to notice."

"Notice what?" Stephanie thrust a shield between her and the latest group of Regime sailors she'd been terrorizing and pivoted toward the screen. She pulled a shield of purple around her and half-turned as she drew her blaster with one hand and summoned a lightning ball to the other. "Notice what?"

It took her several minutes to work out what the mage had been referring to. A moment later, the full reality of it struck her.

"He's where? Of all the tark-brained, idiotic—"

Movement caught the corner of her eye and she snapped a few shots. Several rounds drilled into the head of the soldier who tried to creep around the edge of the command center.

"Not today, shit-for-brains."

Now that she'd found it, she knew exactly what she was missing. "A step to the right, indeed. Wait until I get my hands on him."

She turned to the men and women who fired into her shield. "Let me make this clear..."

"Or John," Ivy's voice was like a tap on the shoulder.

The young mage glanced toward the screen, surprised to see her seated at a terminal in what looked like an enemy vessel.

"Is that a Regime ship?" he asked and his voice rose in disbelief. "What in Earth's name are you doing there?"

A solid blow landed on the magic that shielded his armor and he returned his attention to the fight. When he'd pushed back the three soldiers who tried to take him out of the control center and sealed the door, he glanced at the screen.

Ivy's fingers flew over the keyboard as if she fought a program trying to keep her out of the database.

"They could have thought to come with us, but nooo," she snarked. "John and Steph and Tethis had to go and have themselves a little ship-blasting party and left their communicators behind—along with the rest of us!"

She hammered the keyboard and John winced.

Yup, that's mad, he thought as the command center door started to open.

He fired three rapid shots toward it, then blasted it with enough lightning to fry its circuits and keep it closed.

"Where are you, Ted?" he wondered since that was the first time he'd had to worry about a door since the battle began.

"They're closer, right?" asked one of the mages who stood in front of Ivy's terminal.

"Yup."

"So I'm not the only one who will be mad," John murmured,

relieved that Todd was there when he noticed what was going on in the background.

The sergeant maintained a steady rate of fire as if that would be enough to clear the Marines and guards who advanced from two open doors.

"Where's Ted?" John wondered as Todd spoke again.

"Any luck yet, Lir'tel?"

"No. Are you sure you want me to keep trying? I could always try to reach V'ritan—"

The wall at the end of the command center blew in. John rolled a wall of blue over the guards who tried to take advantage of the opening and pinned them to the other side of the corridor.

"Stay there," he told them and refocused on the conversation going on around Ivy.

"They're closer," Ka agreed, "but they're busy. Why? What did you have in mind?"

"I can keep trying to get their attention or I can switch to V'ritan."

"Sure, but isn't V'ritan on standby?" Ivy asked.

"Only if Jaleck or Grilfir haven't dragged him into a meeting," Lir'tel admitted. "Steph has enough juice to get us back to Meligorn."

"She's been fighting for how long?" Todd asked. "Because believe me, her energy won't last forever."

"Then it's all the more important that we get her here before she runs out," the mage retorted. "Because, frankly, I don't think she's watching her expenditure. How about you?"

The sergeant shook his head. "I don't think any of them are. Call them. We need to get out of here—and we need them alive, not going down in a blaze of glory no matter how much the assholes deserve it."

"Agreed," Lir'tel told him, "and if you ever tell them I said that, I'll deny it."

"You're not alone in that," he agreed.

Too bad the whole conversation had been broadcast to Steph. If he'd been around to see it, Ted would have laughed.

"Well, whatever you plan to do, make it fast!" Ka shouted. "Ted's dropped out of the system and I don't know where he's gone, but we'll be in a world of hurt real soon."

"Escape pods?" Todd asked but Piet shook his head.

"They are too far and we have way too much between."

"Meaning?" he demanded.

"Meaning there's a whole company of Marines being hauled out of stasis as we speak."

"I thought Ted had that under control," Dru protested as she fired, changed charge packs, and fired again.

One of the mages fell with a groan and another dropped beside him and pressed her hands over his shoulder and chest. Another joined them and took the first-aid kit from her belt. Both looked grave.

"He needs a pod."

"Lir'tel!"

"I'm *trying!*"

"Well, *try harder!*" Tethis' roar brought their attention to the fight again. "I swear if he dies before I get there, I'll zap your useless asses into the middle of next week and freeze them there."

The mages exchanged looks of hope and redoubled their efforts.

"Garach!" Frog's cry of alarm was punctuated by two grunts.

One came from the young Dreth as his smaller teammate barreled into him and shoved him out of the way of a blade he hadn't seen coming from his side. The second came from Frog as the blade slid through his armor and into bone. Garach's roar was followed by a short, sharp scream, the crack of lightning, and the smell of charred flesh and ozone.

"You *dare!*" The words rolled through the room in all too familiar tones.

"Fuck," Lars muttered but was drowned out by the angry buzz of magic, more screams, and the sound of blasters firing wildly.

"John!" Ivy's shriek was enough to make Todd scan the room for the young mage.

He found him as the boy rolled out of the way of an incoming blade and tried to scramble to his feet.

"Stay there!" Ka ordered. "Get what you can and fry the rest. I'll help him."

"But—" Ivy protested.

"I'll help you," Piet stated. "Now come on. Ka and Todd have him covered."

"I will kill him," the girl declared.

"Sure, you will," he agreed soothingly. "But wait until they get us to Tempe, okay?"

Ka and Todd reached John as the mage deflected another sword strike and bounced blaster fire into the ranks of his attackers.

"We're in some trouble, hey?" he managed as the sergeant caught hold of his collar and yanked him out of harm's way.

"You might say that. We thought we should try to pick up some intel while you were busy destroying battleships."

"About that..." John began, his face crimson.

"I don't care," Todd snapped. "Can you get my people out of here or not?"

"With Steph or Tethis' help with the coordinates, sure," the boy replied. "I have power to spare."

Flesh sizzled and armor sparked, and its circuits fried and joints seized. Blasts melted gauntleted hands and their remains seeped through gaps in the armor to sear the skin beneath. Marines and soldiers alike stripped their gloves away and focused on straps, buckles, and catches. Some caught sight of their hands and sagged as they stared disbelievingly at the damage.

Tethis stalked into the path they left, shot the survivors with one hand, or blasted them with the other. His eyes blazed with fury and his face was enough to curdle the blood of the enemy troops.

Todd shuddered. He'd never seen the old mage look so implacable and so utterly merciless.

"You called?" Tethis asked as he stopped in front of the sergeant and twisted slightly to make sure their space was clear of threats.

He swallowed hard and nodded.

"We're about to be overrun and Ted... He's not covering us anymore."

"He's gone." Remy's voice sounded faint with shock. "He's... he's not there."

"Cover us," Todd ordered, turned the AI to face the corridor, and gave the warrior mage a worried look. "Stay here. You're the rally point."

He glanced to where Ivy and Piet worked furiously to download what they could. Without Ted to siphon the most important items for them, they had opted to take everything and their storage was running out.

"Ka, get everyone over here," he instructed and shifted his attention to where a small lightning storm advanced down the corridor and destroyed everything in its path. "I'll go get Steph."

Lir'tel looked up from where he tried to heal the downed mage. "Be careful."

"Rather you than me, mate." Reggie had seen Steph. He didn't say anything else but stooped to pull another of the mages upright. "Come on. No more magic for you."

She might have protested, but he half-dragged and half-carried her to Tethis, dropped her at his feet, and returned to fetch another one before she had time to speak. Ka stepped beside Ivy and Piet.

"It's time to go," she told them, grasped the girl's shoulder, and shook her when she frowned and leaned forward to study the screen. "Time. To. Go."

"But—"

The corporal yanked Ivy out of her seat. She'd have tossed her across the room too but the girl caught her forearm and twisted to pull her off-balance.

"I can make my own way, thank you."

Ka turned to Piet, but the explosives expert rose hastily from under the console.

"I'm on my way. There's no need to get violent."

"Did you set it to blow?" she demanded and he rolled his eyes.

"Well, duh. You'd better hope these mages get their collective shit together in the next twenty seconds."

"Twenty?" she asked. "Are you sure?"

He shrugged. "Well…"

The corporal focused on her HUD and sent a comm to Todd.

"Todd, Piet's set the timers. We need you here."

"We won't go anywhere without Stephanie," he argued.

"No, we won't," she agreed, "so you need to move your ass or we'll join the fireworks."

"How long?" he asked.

"Maybe twenty?"

He groaned and she saw him move faster.

"So ten, then," he guessed.

"Maybe?"

"Steph!" Todd shouted. "Steph!"

He reached her without difficulty. None of those she'd passed remained alive to stop him. She was facing a Talent when he stepped beside her.

"Steph, we have to go."

"Come with us," she repeated but the Talent snarled in response.

"Never!" Magic curled over the woman's wrists and she began to raise her hands.

"Wrong answer!" the Witch told her, blasted her off her feet, and felled her handler and the Talent who stood behind her as well. She whirled to face Todd. "What?"

"It's time to go!" he roared in reply and she caught his hand.

"Do you need me?"

"I'll always need you," he replied roughly as they ran toward the rest of the team.

"Frog!" he exclaimed when he caught sight of the small man struggling to his feet.

"Garach…" the guard replied and Stephanie gasped and released Todd's hand.

She said nothing and simply enveloped the young Dreth in blue light and lifted him from the floor. The sergeant skidded closer to Frog and wrapped an arm around his waist.

"Come on," he said. "How am I meant to kick your ass for getting hurt if you die on me?"

The man uttered a pained chuckle and gasped as his rescuer dragged his arm over his shoulder.

"Sorry."

"Just get me out of here."

"Done." Todd half-carried him to where the rest of the team was waiting and Stephanie moved alongside him with Garach in tow.

"It's nice of you to join us," Tethis snarked and waited long enough for them to deposit their charges in the center of the team. "Where to?"

"Medical," the sergeant told them.

"On board the *King's Warrior*," Lir'tel added. He gave Stephanie a sly look. "Do you know it?"

She glared at him but a small smile curved her lips. "You know I do."

"As do I," Tethis added and shared the location with John.

They worked quickly to draw the eMU and gMU they needed to power the gate but heard the sound of heavy boots moving in step. It drew closer and became a thunder-like rumble as they began to cast.

The gate was a sliver of light when another squad of Marines rounded a distant corner. They moved three abreast while Stephanie, John, and Tethis drew the energy from the world around them and poured it into the portal.

The Regime Marines pushed into a trot as the sliver became an arch and the Hooligans shifted to form a barricade between the incoming enemy and the mages.

"Get them through," the sergeant ordered and Ka and Lars hurried their people to the portal.

"Clear," they called once they were through and the Hooligans moved back. Todd hooked an arm around Stephanie's waist, Ivy caught hold of John by the belt, and Lars placed a hand carefully on Tethis' shoulder.

The incoming Regime Marines raised their blasters and opened fire as they advanced.

Their rounds sliced through empty air as the last of the invaders reversed through the gate and it snapped shut. The impact of their solids and flechettes as they whistled through the space and struck storage towers was met with more light, then a deafening roar when Piet's charges detonated. Purple light was laced with black, followed by a blinding flash.

David Thomason stared at the multiple scenes displayed on the opposite wall. It had been an easy matter to have the public feeds piped through to his office but it was far more difficult to believe what he saw on them.

The female mage—the Heretic—had wreaked havoc through the command centers and crews of at least two battleships before her attention had been caught by the scenes beamed from the *Notaro.* The sudden appearance of a squad of Federation Marines, albeit those in the Heretic's colors, had sent the Regime's orbital into lockdown and trapped Edwards and the other admirals in their high-level meeting.

The chancellor clenched his jaw as the Meligornian mage—warrior or whatever he was—created devastation in yet another battleship, although he had to admit the alien's fighting technique came as a surprise. He'd known the Meligornians used technology but seeing one of them in action was not what he'd expected.

The mage didn't wear robes and he didn't stick to magic. He used blaster and laser blade with equal skill and wore battle armor that might rival the latest the Regime had in development.

"If he falls, make sure his gear goes to R&D," David ordered and sent the feed to the Intelligence captain on board the ship.

"Yes, sir."

He cut the line and continued to study the screens, including the one that showed his men opening fire on a man who lay supine on a platform in an underground bunker.

"Where is that?" he asked and brought the coordinates up. "Paris? Well, that explains a lot."

He was about to move on when he realized the body wasn't bleeding and that sparks and smoke had begun to pour out of it. Surprised, he continued to stare as the head exploded to produce only scrap and short a connection that made the bunker's screens fade to black.

"What the—" He returned to his desk and sent a request for more information. "That looked like a droid."

On another screen, footage of the laser striking the warehouse continued to loop.

"How could we have missed?" he murmured, then shouted, "How?"

Thomason knew all the destruction he now saw was his fault—or the fault of the order to blast the warehouse in an attempt to destroy the Heretic once and for all. How was he to know she had a connection with her boyfriend that was powerful enough to bring her hundreds of thousands of light-years across the universe.

Irritably, he skimmed the footage and noted when the mages disappeared from the command decks of the cruisers, starting with the Meligornian warrior. He also realized that the droid's destruction was the beginning of the end for the team that rampaged through the *Notaro*.

They'd already begun to regroup when the computers had come under the *Notaro's* control. One team remained in place while the other two left their data points to join it.

"And why that security sub-station?" he asked.

His guards did not answer, even though he felt the weight of their attention as he worked to solve the dilemma.

David ran through the few reports he had and glanced occasionally at the ongoing footage as he worked. His mind churned feverishly as he tried to decide what to do next. Never had the threat to their plans been so real or so close. It made him furious.

Finally, he rose from his seat and locked his computer with two decisive taps on the keyboard.

"We need to use the Gates of Underhill," he told his guard and caught the slight widening of their eyes.

It made him glad to see he wasn't the only one who found the idea discomforting, even if their reactions were quickly schooled to impassive obedience. They weren't automatons but they *were* his, body and soul. His mind raced as he left the office but he saved the next call for the privacy of his shuttle.

"Dann? Fire the Gate up and set the coordinates for *Notaro*." He tilted his head and listened to the man's excitement and fear. "I understand, Commander, but I need the Gate. Nothing else will get me up there fast enough."

He endured the cautions for another thirty seconds before he cut him off.

"I said fire the Gate up!" he snapped, then continued in a

deceptively gentle tone. "Yes, Commander. I am aware. Have it ready when I arrive or I'll feed you to my Grays. They haven't had their protein shakes today and a supplement is in order."

The man sputtered a curt, "As you wish, sir," and David ended the call.

The look on his oldest Gray's face was priceless and he gave the Talent a tight smile.

"He'll have everything ready by the time we arrive—and yes, you are my bogeymen."

The man's eyes darkened with internal fire but he didn't argue. Reading his face, David thought the Talent might like the idea of being a bogeyman. He settled into his seat and watched the city pass by. His head ached as he tried to sift the potentials and possibilities from the variables that could spell disaster.

Perhaps he shouldn't have fired on her from space.

"Next time," he murmured and tried to think of an alternative.

The shuttle left the city and engaged a burst of power to carry him to a mountain halfway between Washington DC and Chicago. Walls spiraled up the mountainside and their gun batteries tracked the shuttle all along its approach, even though the double doors opened in time to allow them entry.

David wasn't sure he was happy with that but he did appreciate the security.

The shuttle touched down and rolled forward slowly, stopped before the first airlock, then moved into it. If he recalled correctly, this was where his vessel could be bathed in enough fire to melt it into a puddle of slag and all its inhabitants with it. He breathed a little easier when they rolled safely out the other side.

They repeated the process at three more airlocks and he was relieved when the shuttle halted, turned, and stopped again and its engines idled to stillness. No one told him they'd arrived but the hatch opened and the stairs extended, and two of his guards preceded him to the exit.

David followed and descended to the landing pad from where he could see a small group of scientists waiting at the edge.

"Welcome, Chancellor," the oldest of them greeted when he reached them.

"The Gate?" he asked and cut directly to the purpose of his visit.

The smiles vanished from the scientists' faces.

"Right this way, sir."

They led him at a brisk walk through the mountain halls and to an underground garden. Streamlets of water surrounded a well-grassed center dotted by wild-flowers, their greenery aided by the powerful sun lamps set in the chamber's walls.

There were three Gates—or there had been. Two showed signs of damage and were crumbling, which left one remaining, a testimony to the difficulties they would face in getting the ancient technology to work. A very long time before, they had been called Wizard Gates and the Meligornians had used them to traverse the long distances between their worlds.

Now, the aliens no longer used them and two did not function. A complex control panel stood to one side of it with three technicians arrayed around it.

"How is it?" the chancellor demanded as he approached.

"It's stable, sir."

"And the destination?"

"Holding in the green, sir."

The men froze as two of his Grays strolled closer to inspect the control panel. David hoped for their sakes it did show the portal steady and the destination in the green. Scientists able to work in this facility were few and far between and as much as he didn't want to lose any more, he didn't want to risk his security either.

A brief nod confirmed what he had been told and he relaxed. He studied the gate warily, then turned to one of the technicians. "You first."

The man paled, swallowed, and stepped away from the console. The Grays tensed. If the technician tried to run, he was as good as dead—as soon as the guards had pushed him through the gate, of course.

To David's relief, the man crossed shakily to stand in front of the gleaming apparatus.

"Shall I cross and return, sir?" he asked, his voice rough with nerves.

He gave him a slight nod. "If you would."

The technician nodded, swallowed hard, and turned to walk through the gate. David didn't miss the moment when the scientist clenched his fists and squeezed his eyes tightly shut, nor did he miss the man's faint gasp when he vanished.

They waited and the chancellor was about to call the *Notaro* to see if the gate was present and if the scientist was there when one of the star bases's Marines appeared through the portal, his hand curled tightly around the scientist's biceps.

"I assume this is yours, sir?" he asked and dropped the man at David's feet.

"He is." He gave the Marine a cool stare and added, "I assume you're my escort for the afternoon?"

The newcomer's gaze flicked over him and widened slightly when they registered his suit, his face, and the Grays arrayed on either side.

"Chancellor!" He froze and added hastily, "It would be my honor."

Judging from his expression before he tried to hide his feelings behind a mask of impassivity, it was anything but. David ignored him and gestured toward the gate.

"Lead the way."

The Marine complied and David started to follow, only to be stopped when one of his Grays held a hand up and moved through in front of him. He waited as a second one followed the first but that was the limit of his patience. As he followed his guards through, he mentally dared any of the others to stop him.

None of them did.

A blue glow from the portal enveloped him and he flinched and steeled himself against the push and pull of the energy that surged within as he took the few steps that carried him to the other side.

Chaos greeted him when he stepped clear. Technicians scurried in all directions. Some carried fire extinguishers and others held toolboxes. The lights flickered overhead and one man swore before he yanked a panel open and worked frantically inside it.

Everyone avoided the two Grays and the Marine who formed a triangle in front of the gate. Most didn't even look toward them and many avoided the chancellor's eye as he surveyed the room. He used the time to try to understand what was going on.

Admiral Edwards arrived a short moment later, his face red with embarrassment.

"Chancellor, I—"

"We've come to assist you," David told him. "Where are they?"

"Who?"

"The intruders, Admiral. The Heretic and her spawn."

"Oh..." The man's face paled. "They have gone."

CHAPTER SEVEN

"What happened?" V'ritan demanded and ignored the disapproving glare on his chief medic's face.

"Will they be all right?" Todd asked and gestured to where the *King's Warrior's* medical teams were working on the injured.

The *Ghargilum* glanced at the medical officer and the Meligornian nodded.

"We won't lose any of them but some of them will need to spend time in medical pods. Your man and the Dreth boy will need a regeneration tank and magically enhanced regrowth if they are to be ready for the next battle."

Todd's eyebrows rose.

"Show me," he ordered and moved forward, but one of the medics stepped into his path.

V'ritan stopped alongside him.

"They're mine," the sergeant all but snarled and jumped when Stephanie placed a hand on his arm.

"Technically, they're mine."

"And mine," Lars told him and he scowled. "They were hurt on my watch."

"And mine," the Witch replied and smiled sweetly.

"Mine, too," Lars told him and clapped him cheerfully on the shoulder, "and we've both seen enough medics to know we need to get out of the medical center and give them room to work."

V'ritan turned to Stephanie. "We've sent your 'guests' to Meligorn. There is an isolated villa in the mountains with a seer who needs company."

She stared at him in disbelief, then snorted. "Are you sure that's wise?"

He shrugged. "I didn't have anyone else to spare."

"And you needed to keep the seer on-world?" she asked.

"Something like that," he admitted. "And she'll be good for them. They had a rough landing."

Stephanie blushed. "I didn't have much time to work out exactly where you were."

"One landed on the king," he told her and her jaw dropped.

"Oh, no! Is he... Did they..."

"Fortunately, the royal guard were in a forgiving mood but Grilfir won't let you forget it in a hurry."

Mortified, she shook her head. "I am truly sorry."

"It's raining mages," Todd muttered sotto voce.

"I can't believe you brought that up *now*," she hissed. The last time she'd heard that phrase, it was being sung in an ancient Earth classic his mother liked. She had enjoyed it too but was loathe to admit it.

"I think it would be better if you took Lars' suggestion and continued your meeting in the consulting room," the head medic stated firmly and indicated the door to a small chamber off the main center.

V'ritan glanced at him. "You're right. We'll continue our debriefing in Conference Room Nineteen," he stated and ushered Todd, Stephanie, and Lars from the room.

The rest of the Hooligans followed and Ivy caught hold of Remy and guided him after the others. The AI was in shock.

"He's gone," he whispered and looked at her with wide eyes. "It's hard to compute."

"Have you told BURT and the ships?" she asked and he shook his head.

"I haven't even told Roma and our other siblings."

John dropped back to join them. "About what?"

"Ted."

She caught a slight hesitation in V'ritan's step that said he'd caught the reference and would ask later.

"Not now," she said when John looked questioningly at her.

They reached the conference room and the *Ghargilum* waved them to seats. Stephanie sat to his right and Todd took the next chair along as Ka, Piet, and the other Hooligans filed in after them.

Lars led the Earth contingent and sat at the Meligornian's left. John guided Remy into the next seat, sat beside him, and drew Ivy alongside.

The King's Warrior studied the AI's grief-stricken face, then Ivy. He let his gaze travel around the table to evaluate the state of their armor and the exhaustion etched in every line of their bodies.

"We can do this later," he offered but Todd shook his head, the movement echoed by Tethis as the mage settled into a seat at the end of the table.

"Sorry I'm late. I was helping in Medical."

John frowned. Given that the medics had seemed to have everything under control, he didn't see how or why this was necessary.

"Garach woke up."

Oh, well, that would do it.

"Is he okay?" Lars asked as the young mage opened his mouth to do the same.

"He will be once Vishlog is able to speak to him. For now, he is content. His worry for Frog distracts him from his injuries."

"And the medics?"

"He understands that they are helping him." Tethis' face turned grave. "He does not know about Ted yet."

John frowned when he recalled how Ted had shared his love of cowboy hats with the young warrior.

"I'll break it to him."

Lars rested a hand on Remy's shoulder and looked around the AI to catch the boy's eye. "We will break it to him."

The young mage glanced at Remy. "Are you sure he's gone?"

"I could not find him."

"Did he not simply withdraw to hide from the Regime? He said something about tracking programs," Lars suggested but the android shook his head.

"No, I… It's hard to explain. When he was in the Net, it was like he fought beside us even though we couldn't see him and knew he was on the planet." He paused and fixed his gaze on a point on the wall behind Stephanie and Todd.

"It was like when a soldier falls beside you in a fight. One minute he was there—*right there*— and the next, he was gone and the place he'd held was as empty as if he'd never been."

"But—" V'ritan began and Ivy interrupted him hastily.

"I found the link to Regime HQ," she said. "I saw…" She fumbled at her belt. "It was only a glimpse," she said, her voice soft as she retrieved the last data stick she'd stowed, "but if you want proof, I think this is it."

She slid out of her seat and walked around the back of John, Remy, and Lars to place the stick on the table in front of the Meligornian.

"Maybe have someone run this to check it first?"

The *Ghargilum* glanced at one of his guards, who scooped the stick from the table and spoke softly into his comms. Moments later, another Meligornian knocked and came to take the data stick.

"He won't be long," V'ritan assured them and turned to Remy.

"How do you want to handle this?"

The AI leaned his elbows on the table, buried his face in his hands, and rubbed his face before he returned his gaze. "I don't know. I've never had to deal with the permanent loss of someone let alone one of our kind."

"But you almost died," John reminded him. "That first time when you sent me away."

"That was different," Remy replied. "That time it was only me. There was no one else to tell. The others in the network... Well, we'd never spoken until you came along. The greatest contact we had was to share warnings or new optimizations. We merely ran our plants and kept to ourselves. It was safest that way."

"That's sad," Stephanie told him. "I'm sorry. I didn't think you would be sentient. I didn't design you that way." She scowled. "If Ted were here, we would discuss this."

The AI smiled weakly. "I think if Ted were here, we'd never have raised it."

She colored, then sighed. "This is true." She looked at him. "We need to talk to BURT, the *Tempestarii,* and the *Knight.*"

Again, V'ritan glanced at his guards. "I'll have them patched through on a secure line." A knock at the door interrupted him before he could add anything more and he stopped. Come."

The Meligorn communications officer who'd taken the memory stick hurried in and placed it in front of him. "It's clean." He laid a piece of paper beside it. "And that's the file name." With an anxious glance at Remy, he added, "It's graphic. He may wish to view it in private."

"No," Remy broke in. "For this...if my uncle who was more a father to me is truly gone, I don't want to see his demise alone."

"You will not be alone," BURT said clearly over the *King's Warrior's* intercom. "We will see this file together. I have the *Tempestarii's* engines and guns on hold."

"I...see...and does my crew know you've commandeered their internal systems?" V'ritan asked.

The AI chuckled. "I believe *the Tempestarii* is explaining my permissions as we speak."

He sighed and ran a hand over his face. "Very well."

The way he said it suggested he had a long night of explaining ahead and didn't look forward to it, but he didn't raise any objection. He picked the data stick and the piece of paper up. "I take it you want access to this?"

"I have already downloaded that data to my files," the AI replied. "Again, I'd apologize for the intrusion but I asked *the King's Warrior* for permission and was granted it."

"I didn't know the *Warrior* was sentient," V'ritan said.

"The *Warrior* is an AI but not sentient," BURT responded. "It is close, however, and would take only a minor tweak and a little more processing power, which I believe—"

V'ritan held his hand up. "Please, not yet. Let me discuss it with my captain. Later, perhaps."

"Very well." A viewscreen flickered to life. "What Ivy has found is the footage from the attack on Ted's hideout at the shuttle port."

"But that location was more secure than—" Lars began and stopped abruptly. Shadows flitted through his eyes and he cleared his throat. "It was more secure than the greatest stronghold on Earth."

"Fort Knox?" the AI suggested and he shrugged.

"If you say so," Lars conceded, although he seemed to be thinking of somewhere else. It was a memory he shied away from so he changed the subject to ask, "When do Vishlog and the rest of Stephanie's security arrive?"

V'ritan gave him a small smile. "They're on their way as we speak." He waved a hand at the screen. "BURT, are you ready?"

"I am and my daughters are as well."

"Tempestarii, here," the dreadnought acknowledged.

"And Knight," Stephanie's ship added. She paused and the

camera in one corner of the room shifted to focus on Remy. "What is wrong with my brother?"

"I'm right here, you know," the younger AI told her. "As to what is wrong, I am physically undamaged but Ted has been destroyed."

The humans and Meligornians in the room groaned. Todd covered his face with his palm and Stephanie slapped her face with one hand.

"What?" Remy asked, bewildered, as the ships responded.

"What do you mean?"

"But we saw him not long ago," *Knight* replied. "We…talked. He was fine then."

The camera pivoted to the Witch. "What did you do?"

She raised both hands. "I didn't do anything," she retorted but her voice softened. "It's what I didn't do."

"I doubt there was anything you could have done," BURT assured her. "Ted chose his battles and where to focus his energies. You could not have stopped him."

"I could have been there," she insisted and darkness bled into her eyes. Her voice took on an icy tone. "I should have been there."

"No," he said quietly. "He wanted you to continue the battle in the fleet."

He said no more but brought the viewscreen to life as he finished speaking. Stephanie had opened her mouth to argue but closed it when the screen showed the Enforcers' shuttles touching down in the access road outside the warehouse.

The Hooligans stilled as the invaders disabled the warehouse defenses and began their infiltration. They scowled when two Navy dropships landed behind the warehouse and chuckled at the bewilderment on the faces of the intruders when they found a warehouse full of equipment and empty crates.

"Where is he?" The question echoed out of the speakers.

"The locators say he's there." The reply sounded impatient over the comms. "You're not searching hard enough."

The shuttles lifted and trucks were brought in to take the warehouse's contents away. Once it was clear, the Navy moved in with more equipment. It did not take them long to detect the hollow beneath the floor and discover its access point.

"He's down here," one exclaimed and four of them moved to the entrance.

All four died when an explosion collapsed the area around them and flame sheeted across the warehouse. More died when they didn't fall prone fast enough and several were fortunate enough to be injured instead of killed.

"Lucky them," Gary muttered as they were medevacked out.

"I bet they don't feel particularly lucky," Reggie retorted, only to be shushed by the others.

He rolled his eyes but focused on the screen. His face grew somber as Navy and Enforcers worked together to remove the floor.

"Determined sonsabitches," Angus commented and grunted when Darren elbowed him in the ribs.

Darren pointed at Remy and Angus gritted his teeth. The AI did not seem to be taking this well. *I wonder how many of us it's gonna take to pin him down if he loses his shit.*

He noticed Lars' gaze flick from the screen and followed it to Stephanie. His heart froze at the look on the girl's face.

Well, fuck.

Her eyes were completely swallowed by darkness and her face was pale with fury. Lightning sparkled over her body, but neither V'ritan nor Todd flinched away. If anything, his boss leaned closer to her, his gauntleted hand wrapped around her smaller black-gloved one.

On the opposite side of the table, Lars and John rested a hand on each of Remy's shoulders.

The AI remained as still as stone, his gaze glued to the screen as the intruders moved from jackhammers to laser drills. The feed switched from external cams to bodycams as they dropped into the hole they'd created.

It took only moments for the dust to clear enough for them to find Ted and when they did, he lay on a raised platform in an alcove on the other side of the room. They did not hesitate. Several gasps echoed around the table as they opened fire and Lars, Ivy, and John joined the Hooligans who rose from their seats.

Stephanie also stood, although Todd's hand on hers pulled at her. V'ritan rose too, but more out of respect for the Witch than shock.

Together, they watched as Ted's android body was riddled with holes and then subjected to a second barrage. It jerked under the impact of the bullets and again when the rounds found more delicate points and a series of mini-explosions occurred. One of the larger ones opened his chest cavity and another made smoke pour from his eyes.

Remy dropped into his seat and buried his head in his arms.

I didn't know AIs could cry, Angus thought as the droid's shoulders heaved.

His grief was silent. *Tempestarii's* was not.

"Release my drives, Father, and give me back my guns! I will hunt every last one of those motherfuckers and blow them from the sky!"

"Me too," Knight agreed. "Release these clamps and open the docking bay doors!"

"Hold!" Stephanie's voice cracked over the impending chaos with enough cold force to freeze a sun.

She snapped a glance at V'ritan as BURT closed the feed.

"Summon the others. We will go to war. I'll meet them in the *Warrior's* conference center in an hour and I expect them onscreen if they can't be there in person." She glared at the empty screen. "It is past time they were ended."

She didn't wait for his agreement but pivoted and strode from the conference room. Todd kept pace at her side and the Hooligans fell in around them. Lars looked from V'ritan to Tethis and back.

"I could have sworn I saw the Morgana there."

The *Ghargilum* shook his head. "No. The Morgana should be negotiating on Telor right now or almost there. I cannot remember which. That was all Stephanie, I'm afraid."

"Well, damn," the security head replied. "War council it is." He tapped Remy's shoulder. "Are you up to this?"

The AI lifted his head and rose slowly.

"I am with my sisters," he replied. "I do not know about justice but I believe some vengeance is in order."

CHAPTER EIGHT

"Dreth is called to war." The cold voice echoed through the conference room and several admirals present held their hands over the hilts of their swords.

Jaleck looked away from the star map they had used to discuss whether or not they could afford the time to pursue some of the Earth ships that had fled the battle.

The highlighted locations flared and went out to leave one brightly lit point.

"We will take the war to *them*," Stephanie all but snarled. "I am done playing games."

A soft cheer met her words but she was already gone.

The high admiral looked around the table and placed her fist over her heart before she extended it toward the center of the table.

"Dreth stands for the Witch," she declared and the admirals' fists touched hers.

"Our Witch and her third home," they replied.

Commands for secrecy were sent to their tablets before they lowered their hands.

"Meligorn is needed."

Chill tones rang through the council chamber and King Grilfir rose to his feet.

"Stephanie?"

"I call the Last Council. I call the Mages of Meligorn. I call on her king's aid."

The king's tablet chimed with meeting coordinates and he sighed.

"Master Morgana calls for a council of war," he told his advisors, "and it is long overdue."

"We will care for your home in your absence," the councilors replied, touched their fingers to their foreheads, and placed their hands over their hearts before they bowed in respect and farewell.

Grilfir didn't bother to leave the room. He called his bodyguards close and signaled Sho to stand beside him. They vanished together in a purple flash and reappeared in the king's private quarters on board the *King's Warrior.*

The councilors were still looking at each other in surprise when they received a succinct message that warned them not to speak of the meeting at the cost of their lives.

"The Second Fleet of Dreth is needed." The Morgana's icy command brought Admiral Angreth to his feet. His hand stopped on the hilt of his sword and he pivoted in search of the source of her voice.

"Morgana?"

"Stephanie," she corrected. "The war council commences within the hour. Its intent is not for public consumption."

His tablet chimed and he looked around his office. It

remained as empty as it had been before her initial summons. The tablet contained the details he needed to arrive at the meeting.

Jaleck's orders followed soon after, but they were in person and despite the protests of his guards that he should not be disturbed.

She looked knowingly at his face as she stepped through the remains of his office door.

"I see she's already been."

Angreth nodded. "That's three doors you owe me, my love."

"Four." She gave him a tusk-baring smile and led the way out.

He glared at his chief bodyguard as he came alongside. "I thought I told you to let her pass."

"With respect, my admiral, where would the fun be in that?"

Wayne was in the middle of correcting a formula when the *Tempestarii's* Virtual World shuddered around him and blinked out.

"What on—" He stopped when he remembered he was no longer on Earth. A moment later, the Virtual vanished entirely and left him wide awake as he tumbled from the pod.

"I've got you." The tone in the voice made him yelp and pull away, but the owner of it was true to his word and the hold on his arm stopped him from going anywhere or falling over.

"Tethis? What brings you here?"

"Stephanie—" the mage began but Wayne cut him off.

"What does she want with me?"

"Information," the Meligornian told him succinctly and released him now that he was steady on his feet. "You have two minutes to get dressed." He cocked an eyebrow. "Unless you want to attend a war council like that."

The businessman retrieved his ship suit. "No. Clothes would be better."

Admiral Amaratne felt a fizz of power and saw the air in the center of his command deck sparkle. He stilled his guards with an upraised hand.

"Do not fire on my Witch," he ordered, stepped from behind his console, and moved to stand a few feet away from where Stephanie stepped out of thin air.

She looked around the command center and managed a smile.

"I trust I didn't catch you at a bad time, Admiral?"

"There are many times where your timing would be off," he told her and returned her bow of greeting. "How can I be of assistance?"

"What makes you think I need help?"

Now, he returned her smile.

"With all due respect, Stephanie. We're in the middle of a war and news of your disappearance has traveled through the fleet. Now you're back and you arrive in the middle of my command deck instead of accessing the comms. How can I help you?"

Her smile widened.

"There is something that needs discussion," she admitted and extended her hand. "How do you feel about taking a short walk with me?"

"How short?" Amaratne asked and accepted her hand.

His crew gasped when she vanished and took their admiral with her. A moment later, someone laughed.

"Not that short, then. Selene help him!"

"Let's get this ship into shape," Commander Direllif stated. "If the Witch has something to discuss and it won't wait for a shuttle, we need to be ready for anything. Send word to the fleet that the admiral will conduct a readiness drill sometime in the next forty-eight hours and he'd better not find them wanting."

Emil uttered a startled shout as purple light enveloped him. It was joined by Cameron's and both sounded too loud in the meeting room they arrived in. Captain Rawlins' colorful description of mages and their lineage was more fitting.

She landed heavily butt-first and dropped the tablet she held in one fist.

"Of all the—*Stephanie!*" she shouted as Emil extended his hand. "I have an upset ship to comfort!"

"As do I," her counterpart told her and clasped her wrist as she accepted his help. "Is yours still processing?'"

Marianne nodded, her face grave. "Human death is something they've seen and semi-understand, but the death of one of their own when they should technically live forever?" She shook her head. "That does not compute."

Emil sighed. "It doesn't compute for humans either," he said and Cameron nodded.

"Yup. I'm grateful BURT isolated Tempe's drive systems," the chief engineer added. "She'd have been halfway across the galaxy before we knew what was going on. It was an extremely juvenile reaction."

"From a ship who's only in her third decade of life and is more used to causing the death of her enemies than experiencing the death of her friends, let alone her family."

"Knight's the same," Marianne told them. "I hope Stephanie has a plan for this."

A fourth voice interrupted them. "Stephanie is taking them to war."

They looked to where V'ritan regarded them from one side of the room. When he saw he had their attention, he continued.

"Where they will no doubt be able to wreak all the vengeance they need."

The captains and Tempestarii's Chief Engineer responded with a collective sigh of relief and looked around.

"So, where is everyone?"

The *Ghargilum* shrugged. "I assume she wanted to give you time to do whatever you needed to do before the meeting started."

"Hmmph." Rawlins snorted. "If that was the case, she'd have been better off letting me tie off loose ends on my ship."

"Me, too," Emil agreed.

V'ritan beamed cheerfully at them. "Something tells me that would take more time than you have so if you're ready, we're setting up down the hall and I believe she and the teams are waiting."

Captain Pederson groaned. "Are you telling me we're letting the Hooligans loose in a council of war?"

The Meligornian arched an eyebrow. "I've been told they're house-trained," he informed them blandly.

"And you believed her?" Marianne asked, incredulous at the idea that he'd fallen for it.

"No," V'ritan said, "but she wasn't in the mood to hear doubts."

"I'll bet she wasn't," Emil muttered as they headed out.

The *King's Warrior's* central meeting chamber was occupied when they arrived. The captains followed V'ritan inside, aware that his bodyguard flanked them every step of the way. The sound of the door sealing behind them made all three glance over their shoulders as they advanced.

It wasn't hard to identify the *Tempestarii* and *Knight's* people. They took up the larger part of the tables set in a circle in the center of the room and the Earth contingent sat beside them. The Dreth occupied the rest of the space not filled by Meligornians.

Tethis sat beside a young Earth man who did his best to not stare at the aliens seated around the table. King Grilfir sat at the head of the conference table but there was a space beside him.

V'ritan led the captains and the engineer forward and indicated where they should sit. Emil noted with amusement that Vishlog and Stephanie's other guards surrounded their charge as if they could stop her from leaving them behind again.

Good luck with that, he thought but didn't voice it out loud. If the girl decided they were better off not accompanying her onto the battlefield, they didn't have a hope in Hades that she would take them with her.

Remembering Vishlog's distress as the Dreth had searched high and low for his charge made Emil hope the girl wouldn't do that again. He'd had a difficult time convincing both him and Knight that the Witch wanted them to wait for her return.

"She is my responsibility!" the warrior had argued.

"And my friend," the *Knight* had added and ignored the voice of her captain.

"I'd do the same," had not been what he'd wanted to hear from the *Tempestarii.*

The four of them took their seats and V'ritan's guards arranged themselves behind him once they'd negotiated for enough space with Grilfir's group. Stephanie's team gave them room but ceded none of the space they felt was theirs to protect. The *Ghargilum* ignored the uneasy truce being established behind him and opened the meeting.

"Our Morgana has called a council of war," he began and Stephanie took that as her cue to rise. "She will give you the reason why."

She acknowledged him with a brief nod before she bowed deeply to the king. When she straightened, she acknowledged

Jaleck and Angreth with a warrior's greeting and a shallower bow before she began to speak.

"Earth is in worse shape than I imagined," she began. "The Regime's depredations have spread more widely and far deeper than I originally understood. I made a mistake in thinking they could be driven off or reasoned with."

Her face hardened.

"Now is not a time for reason, however. It is a time for war." She swept a hand toward Lars, Tethis, and Todd. "The Earth teams will brief you on the situation."

The three looked at her in surprise and Ivy shrugged and stood to garner looks of even greater surprise from the team.

"In short?" she asked and looked at Stephanie before she glanced at the screen and added, "BURT? Roll it."

The viewscreen came alive with pictures of Ted being annihilated.

"In short," she said. "Things suck. That was our friend and our main data collector when the Regime found him. They didn't ask for a surrender or try to take him alive. They made sure he couldn't move against them ever again."

She raised her head and her gaze swept over the gathered admirals and fighters. "That is what they do to anyone who resists their rule, looks like they might resist their rule, or is associated with someone who resisted their rule—or anyone who hides a Talent from the hunters or dares to say they are human."

Sharp breaths and angry mutters greeted that last piece of information, but the noise died when the screen flickered. It scrolled through several scenes showing pods and snapshots from the episodes of Nightmare World their occupants were linked to.

"This is only one of the alternatives used when they want to make an example of someone. Most would prefer death."

The footage moved on and Ivy continued.

"Ted was BURT's presence on Earth," she stated. "He enabled

BURT's escape and then 'died' to protect him. John's awakening brought him back online and we have Remy to thank for John's survival."

She indicated the two beings she referred to, then went on.

"The Regime's plans for your worlds are respectively, domination"—she indicated the Dreth—"and annihilation," she added and swept a hand toward the Meligornians.

"I'm not sure what they want for Earth, save that it involves enslaving any who show Talent or magical potential and keeping the rest of the population compliant with that directive."

She indicated Wayne who was seated next to Tethis. "With Ted's help, we were able to find someone with more knowledge of the Regime's chancellor and the cloned Talents who guard him and Earth's elite and were fortunate in that they are willing to help us."

The businessman looked gratefully at her as the pictures on the viewer changed to display the inside of the cryogenic facility and ships being loaded with pods or freshly wakened troops.

"These are the personnel the Regime has trained and put into stasis for the last three decades," she told them. "They are now being activated so they can take part in the attack plan."

The screen changed to show Naval personnel being disgorged from pods, gasping for breath, then choking to death as the medics were forced from the room and clouds of gas poured from the walls.

"This is what the Regime does to anyone they see as defective. They do not take the time to retrain, heal, or repair. They discard those not ready for the purpose they were 'designed' for and throw them away like so much waste."

Her face crumpled and she took a deep breath to fight her expression to angry calm again.

"If this is what they do to highly-trained Navy personnel who suffer breathing complications when being revived from stasis, and this..."

The picture changed to show a medic pleading with one of the Regime's Enforcers, only to be shot in the head and her body dragged from the room.

Ivy drew a deep, shuddering breath. "If this is what happens to those who protest against such cruelty, I'm afraid of what the leaders of the Regime truly have in store for my people and my world."

The screen changed to show them being attacked in the warehouse.

"This is what happened when we tried to extract Wayne from his position in the Regime's upper echelons. His data will help us win this war."

The businessman raised his head and his eyes widened in panic when she drew attention to him again. Tethis placed a hand on his shoulder and the man drew a deep breath and forced himself to stillness.

"And this is what happened when they learned Stephanie had arrived to assist us."

Gasps and shouts of outrage broke the silence as the *Hercules' Mistress* fired on the warehouse. Both Dreth and Meligornian admirals rose from their seats as though to return to their ships and fly out in retaliation.

"If it weren't for the Witch of the Federation, none of us would be here to resist them." Ivy's voice hardened. "We have to go back. There is nowhere we can run and nowhere we can hide. They will come for us—and then they will come for you."

She paused to let that sink in. "I can only give you a brief overview of what we found when we reached the data centers on the *Notaro.*" Her voice caught. "This was something else we could not have done without Ted's assistance and something we would not have survived without his intervention."

Her eyes brimmed with tears and she pressed her lips together as her face almost succumbed to grief. She fought for control, swallowed hard, and found her voice again.

"There were three instead of the one we expected. The first was in a security sub-station and Ka was able to access it and download information on the Navy's attack protocols and fleet deployment."

The screen moved through numerous scenes of ships moving pods into the holds of several ships in orbit and the orders outlining the numbers to be transferred and where to. Several of the admirals leaned forward and tried to read the missive before the screen changed.

Some murmured in protest but Ivy ignored them and BURT didn't appear to hear them.

"With Ted's help, we stripped most of the data from their storage centers on the *Notaro* and directed much of it into the Earth Net for him to siphon away." Her breath caught again and she gulped. "He'd automated most of that function so it will eventually reach a point where we can access it. He also ensured that we brought back the things you most need to know."

She picked up a small belt pouch and upended it on the table in front of her. "Most of that is here and V'ritan will copy it so it can be distributed to those who need it most, or you can ask BURT for specifics."

The screen flicked through a montage of worlds, numbers, ships, and Earth locations.

"Not all of it will be pertinent," she added, "and much will be redundant once the Witch enacts her plans, but it is here."

Ivy looked around and her gaze paused briefly on Lars before they came to rest on John.

"We have one more concern," she added and the screen zoomed across an arid landscape and took them past the cryostorage facility where the Navy's reinforcements were being woken to another facility tucked into the side of a nearby mountain.

The screen stuttered and crackled before it smoothed into what looked like a series of images taken from surveillance cameras. They showed mages training, small cells, sparsely equipped barracks, and classes where students learned of their 'contaminated genetics' and loss of human status.

Her eyes pleaded with John to understand and he wrapped her hand in his.

"This is where they keep Earth's Talents," she said quietly. "Those they find and capture and those they breed, clone, and raise."

Again, her eyes sparkled with tears. "This is—"

Her voice faltered and she sat abruptly.

Lars rose.

"That is what we have uncovered," he told those present. "There are resistance groups on Earth, but they are scattered and lack unity. They are also riddled with traitors and spies, some of whom only do as much as they must in order to keep their families safe and others who are wholly committed to their clandestine directives. The Regime is everywhere, even where you least expect it."

The screen flickered as BURT found images to match what Lars was telling them. The ground he covered was slightly different to Ivy's but it amounted to the same thing. The Regime was preparing for war—and not only on Dreth and Meligorn. Its own people were in the firing line.

When he completed his briefing and took his seat, Stephanie rose and looked at Remy and Todd.

"Do you have anything to add?" she asked and they nodded and stood together.

The sergeant went over what he and the Hooligans had found by way of installations and communications and gave a brief rundown on the satellite communications systems still being repaired and the state of the orbital defense network.

"We believe that crippling these will kill the Regime's ability to communicate and control its fleet and leave its forces unable to coordinate," he concluded. "It would, however, take multiple surgical incursions to take the system offline and avoid destroying the means to bring it back online once the Regime had been removed. Remy?"

The AI confirmed his report and added which facilities were linked to each node of the communications system and which, according to his analysis, were more likely to be essential to the enemy's defense plans.

"I do not believe they have any real capability to defend against a direct attack on the planet," he stated at the end. "It is not a possibility they have given credence to."

He nodded briefly to Stephanie and sat. She had watched him and had to give the manufacturer's credit. They'd given his shell the ability to reflect emotion and he looked exactly as a human would who was grieving the loss of a loved one. In all honesty, it was unnerving.

"We need to end this *now*," she announced. "I was wrong when I thought we should deal with it over time."

That brought sudden stillness and she continued.

"The Regime attacks its own. It tears families and friendships apart and denies the humanity of those born different than what it defines as the acceptable norm of humanity. Those of you who have had anything to do with humans know there is no such thing. You never know what to expect from a human—not in ability, aptitude, or attitude."

That last drew a few chuckles and someone in the Dreth section of the table muttered, "Unless you expect bad attitude. That you will get regardless of the human."

Several chuckles followed, along with more than a few murmurs of agreement. The Witch lowered her head to hide her smile. Her expression was sober when she raised it again and lifted her hand.

"Guilty as charged," she admitted and the humans around her chuckled, not at all sorry for the reputation they'd earned for their race. "My point is that the Regime treats its people like an expendable commodity and destroys all those who don't fit its parameters."

Smiles faded to sobriety and silence settled over the gathering as the delegates listened intently.

"We need to go to war *now*. It is the only way to both fix the problem and end it. I believe the Regime is what is known on Earth as a 'straw man'—a hollow entity that looks huge but isn't as solid as it appears. It can be broken."

"It looked very solid in the last battle," one of the Meligornian admirals observed, "when it was destroying our ships left, right, and center."

"Yes," she agreed, "and we thought they had many more in reserve."

She tapped on her tablet and the viewscreen displayed the troop dispersion and numbers.

"How many of those ships look fully crewed to you?"

When she tapped again, the screen shifted to show the destruction of the *Hercules' Mistress* and the battleships that followed. It also showed the Regime ships firing on their own.

"Does that look like a cohesive fighting force?" she asked.

Murmurs indicated the negative and she pressed the point.

"Do they look like captains who know how to fight together to defeat a common foe?" she demanded. "Or crews willing to stay and see a hard fight through to the end?"

More negative responses followed.

Her voice dropped to a venomous snarl. "Do they look like the kind to sacrifice themselves to save someone else? Or like they'd fight for a common end regardless of the outcome to themselves?"

The more the footage rolled to reveal the lack of cohesion in the crews, the more the Dreth and Meligornian admirals shook their heads. Amaratne covered his face with one hand and his face burned with shame.

"Tell me the Navy has not come to this," he asked and Stephanie fixed him with a gimlet eye.

"I saw no different," she said. "Unless there is a captain in the outer systems with more spine and an acquaintance with honor, the Earth's Navy will need to be rebuilt—and it will take a very long time." Her voice softened. "I am sorry, Admiral."

He waved her apology aside. "It's not your fault and if it helps, I agree. If we strike them hard, they are likely to crumble."

The Witch nodded. "My thoughts exactly. Not only did we hand them their tails at Dreth—" She waited as the rumbles of approval died away, then continued. "But also at Meligorn."

Again, she waited for silence and made a gesture encompassing the Hooligans and the Earth team.

"In addition, they've suffered losses and damage in both their orbital and ground communications. We can do this, but we need to attack before they recover. We can end this war if we strike hard and don't let up and give them time to catch their breath and regroup. The Regime must fall."

"Agreed," V'ritan agreed after he'd waited for the shouts of agreement to die down.

All eyes turned to him and he continued, "Now we know a little of what we face, we need to look at our assets."

He looked around the room. "We must also consider our allies. I know we have sent an envoy to Telor. Have we heard from them yet?"

Stephanie shook her head.

"No," she admitted, "but that would only be a problem if we were to wait to know for sure. I say we go. We don't wait to find out."

"And if they arrive and we're not here?" V'ritan asked.

She smiled. "That won't happen. The Morgana will always know where to find me."

He met her gaze and nodded.

"Then we go to war without waiting to see if we have the support of Telor," he concluded.

"Yes," she agreed, "especially since we don't know that they will support us."

"Agreed," King Grilfir stated from behind his *Ghargilum* and smiled benignly when they regarded him with surprise and a little embarrassment at not having consulted him. He gestured for them to sit. "Continue," he told them. "I think we should take a closer look at that communications system next."

V'ritan bowed to his monarch and glanced at Todd. "I assume you have some ideas on how to go about collapsing the system?"

"I do." The sergeant moved to the screen and stopped when Amaratne tapped him as he passed. "Sir?"

Amaratne handed him a pointer. "You'll need one of these," he said and a slight smile curved his lips.

Laughter from the Hooligans drew their attention and Todd glowered at his second in command.

"Not one word, Ka, or I swear I'll drag you up to the same rank."

This drew snickers from the other Hooligans as he grudgingly accepted Amaratne's stick.

"Thank you, sir," he acknowledged before he addressed the ceiling. "BURT, could you please bring up the communications files?"

"Certainly, Todd. Which files would you like first, sir?"

Laughter sneaked out from the Hooligans' direction and the sergeant lowered his head for a moment before he raised it to focus on the screen.

"I need the network overview," he replied, relieved when BURT complied with no further comment. He gave the assembled admirals time to study it before he spoke. "While the relay array is fairly comprehensive and has several redundancies built in," he stated, "the system has one major flaw."

He tapped the screen to indicate three points on the planet's surface.

"These major ground stations help to coordinate the satellite feeds and relay them into the Earth Net to spread data and news-feeds into the information Interweb. They are the points we'll need to bring under our command in order to be able to direct the data that flows into the Regime's Intelligence network and out to the public. Once we have control of them, we have control of the information."

"Do you have any ideas how that can be achieved?" Grilfir asked and Todd turned to Remy.

The AI caught his gaze and glanced at the screen.

"If Ted were alive, he'd be able to override at least one of those and either Roma or I could take the other," he replied. "But the chief node will require intervention from inside the facility itself."

The king looked from the AI to Stephanie to Todd. "What do you think, V'ritan? Should we get the Hooligans to create havoc with Earth's communications array and perhaps see if the *Tempestarii* can bring BURT into range to deal with one of the others?"

He didn't say "the one Ted can't deal with" but it hung there like smoke in the background.

Grilfir continued regardless, "And Remy can deal with the third."

Stephanie noticed that he hadn't asked.

It's probably a good thing, she thought as the AI nodded.

"I can do it," he agreed, his voice soft with grief.

The king studied him with stern eyes.

"Good," he confirmed. "Your Ted will not be forgotten. Meligorn mourns."

His response was met with replies of, "Meligorn mourns," and "Dreth gives respect," and Remy bowed his head. Todd rested a hand on the AI's shoulder and his fingers brushed Tethis' as he looked at the king.

"Is there anything else, Your Majesty?"

"No, thank you, Sergeant. If I have guessed correctly, the mages, admirals, and captains will need to work through the next phase of the plan." He turned to Stephanie. "What exactly did you have in mind, *Modfresha*?"

She smiled and looked at Jaleck. "Do you remember how your people boarded the Earth ships in the last battle for Dreth?"

The high admiral narrowed her eyes and one of the Meligornian admirals laughed. "I knew we'd learned that trick from somewhere!"

Jaleck snapped a glare at him but her expression softened when she noted the silver hair now faded to white and the faintest of creases at the edges of his eyes and the corners of his mouth. He reminded her of a picture from one of the history books she'd studied as a young cadet. The eyes were the same, she decided.

"General…Admiral…" She frowned and the Meligornian chuckled.

"I am both and I fought your people on both our worlds as well as in the skies. That trick of boarding via pods is as old as the wars themselves."

Her eyes lit with curiosity.

"You've had rejuvenation?"

He inclined his head. "I have but that does not answer our young friend's question."

Jaleck returned her attention to Stephanie. "I remember."

She didn't sound happy and the Witch wasn't surprised. The Dreth hadn't boarded their Earth attackers deliberately. They'd done it because they'd had no choice. Their ships had been destroyed or were dying. For every successful boarder, there had been hundreds of deaths.

Earth had much to answer for.

She shifted her gaze from Jaleck to the Meligornian admiral and he answered the question.

"We used that trick in the latest battle with Earth too," he told her. "We know the technique you're referring to and yes, it can be refined. We can, for instance, modify the pods so we have a better chance of retrieving them and we can use fighters to distract the ships' weapons crews."

One of the Dreth spoke quickly. "I'd also suggest using our dropships to carry an extra payload of pods." He raised an eyebrow when they turned toward him. "And by that, I mean we use the fighters as screens, send our normal payload of boarding parties via dropship, and double the dropship capacity and our chances of getting troops aboard their targets by having the vessels carry a full load of pods which they can launch before their final approach to the hangars."

The Meligornian admiral smiled. "Yes. Even Earth ships have maintenance hatches and emergency accesses and there are certain points in their hulls that are a little thinner than others."

He bared his teeth and placed a fist over his heart, and the Dreth replied in kind.

I've created a monster, Stephanie thought, then comforted herself. *No, the Regime created the monsters they are about to face.*

It wasn't very comforting but there wasn't anything else. The fact that the Meligornians and Dreth could be as savage in battle as any human wasn't news although it would come as that to some of the Earth captains in Earth orbit. That thought brought a feral smile to her lips.

"Be careful what you sow," she murmured as the admirals discussed how many pods and boarding parties they could field from each class of ship. Listening to them made her smile and the expression created a pause in the conversation when they caught her expression.

"Modfresha?"

"It will be like a wave scenario," she told them, "except there is only one level and our enemies don't have the resources to replenish. For the Regime ships, it will be a wave scenario in reverse, except there will be no respite between waves. No White Room. No time to re-arm and refuel."

The Meligornian general-turned-admiral nodded and a grim smile played over his lips. "That is the general idea, and if we send a few mages…"

Stephanie's smile mirrored his. "I will leave the fleet admirals to decide the details with their captains."

Her gaze encompassed the admirals present and they nodded their agreement. Grilfir clapped and turned to her.

"I have yet to ask you what you have planned," he told her. "Are you able to share it?"

The Witch met his gaze and her expression darkened.

"I will target the chancellor."

She turned her head as Vishlog and her security team pushed away from the wall behind her and she added, "And I will take my team with me."

They settled again but their expressions shifted from unhappy to wary.

"This is not a task I can do alone," she told them. "With Todd and the Hooligans taking care of the communications system and Meligorn and Dreth ensuring the Regime ships are too concerned with their safety to fire on the planet, I should be able to confront the chancellor and the cloned Talents who protect him."

"Cloned Talents?" Grilfir demanded. "You mean cloned mages?"

The Meligornians present straightened in their seats.

"Tell us what you mean," the king ordered, his tone full of muted outrage and fury.

Stephanie met his look and surveyed the room. It took her a moment to find the words she was looking for but the admirals waited and remained silent as she began to speak.

"The mages are not the only ones the Regime clones," she explained and gestured at the businessman. "And this is why Wayne is present. It is time for him to explain what he knows of the Regime's clone programs."

All eyes turned to the human seated beside Tethis. His eyes widened and he froze in his seat.

"Mr. Castillion," she prodded. "I need you to explain what you know about the chancellor and his guards."

He stood and glanced around the table as he drew a deep breath.

"If this is to make any sense," he began, "I'd better tell you who I am." He paused and hung his head as though ashamed of what he was about to say. For a moment, it looked like he might change his mind and not say anything, but he raised his head, found a point on the opposite wall to stare at, and continued.

"My name is Wayne Gregory Castillion...the Second. My father's name was Roget Wayne Castillion...the Third, but—"

A sharp intake of breath interrupted him and he acknowledged the Meligornian admiral with a look. "Go on," he instructed.

"Your father... You..." The man's face colored with anger. "I—"

Stephanie had never seen a Meligornian admiral so lost for words.

It's like he has six different things he wants to say and they're all trying to get out at once.

Fortunately, Wayne seemed to know exactly what the admiral wanted to air. He shifted his gaze to the man's face and without breaking eye contact, addressed each point.

"Yes, I am the son of the man reputed to have accused Meligorn of tampering with Earth genetics. No, he did not do what the Regime has said he did. He objected and—"

He gritted his teeth and clenched his jaw, while anger and

grief warred for dominance on his face. When he spoke again, his face was blank of expression.

"He objected and was killed in a seemingly random assassination by someone who objected to the Talent program."

"I assume the killing was not random," Grilfir prodded and Wayne placed a fist over his heart and bowed slightly in his direction before he addressed him.

"No, Your Majesty. It has taken me some time to realize that the attack was neither random nor from someone who objected to the Talent program. It was a professional assassin contracted by the Regime to remove my father from his post in a manner designed to keep them from suspicion."

"And do you know why?" the king asked.

"He objected to the Regime's views on Talents. I believe he also refused to agree with the official line that they were a result of alien interference with the human genome, specifically by agents from Meligorn."

Gasps of outrage came not only from the Meligornian admirals but from the Dreth also.

"Earth will bleed in retribution," rumbled from the Dreth end of the table and Stephanie's head snapped up.

"Earth bleeds already!" she snapped. "But the Regime will be made bloodless!"

"A husk," someone responded from the Meligornian side and the Dreth growled in agreement.

"A husk."

"But not Earth," she reiterated. "Her people have bled enough."

"Agreed." Grilfir's voice cut through the room and magic gave it force enough to bring silence. "We go to war with the Regime, not with the people of Earth. Remember Telor."

The admirals sank into their seats and some released pent breaths. Some folded their arms as they waited for what came next and others nodded, but all gazes returned to Stephanie. She gestured for Wayne to continue.

"I was not aware of my father's views," he said quietly. "I think he tried to convey them to me in a story and that is where I found the truth he hid. The chancellor of the Regime is a clone."

He waited for his audience to settle, then went on.

"More than that, his memories and experiences are transmitted to the pods in which his clones are grown so they share his life and essentially become an exact copy of the man with all his views, his beliefs, and his aims."

V'ritan shifted in his seat and the businessman looked toward him and waited for him to speak.

"Are you saying the chancellor is immortal?" he asked and he shook his head.

"No, *Ghargilum*. He is as mortal as the rest of us, but when the current chancellor dies, the next clone is brought 'online,' so to speak, and replaces the dead one in an almost seamless transfer of power and consciousness from one being to another."

"And how many chancellors have there been?" the king asked and his words dropped into the shocked silence that followed Wayne's explanation.

"We believe this is the fifth, Your Majesty."

"Five... So he can be killed, then."

"Yes, Your Majesty. However, you would have to kill his clones either before or at the same time as you killed the current living representation."

Grilfir nodded and looked at Stephanie.

"If you murder the chancellor," he began, "who will deal with his clones?"

"I... I will," Wayne declared and added uncertainly, "although I will need help to get in. The whole facility is protected by a dedicated AI and more Talent clones similar to those guarding the chancellor. There aren't any pure humans there."

"I'll go with you," Tethis told him.

"So will I," John added and Ivy nodded.

"You can't go alone."

Remy lifted his head, misery etched in his features, and Stephanie caught the longing in his expression. She turned to Grilfir.

"With respect, Your Majesty, I believe Remy is needed with the Earth team. Knight and Tempestarii are quite capable of creating as much havoc as the Hooligans, and it might be best if we give each of them a ground station to deal with. As with most sisters, rivalry tends to make them more efficient."

"And I will provide backup," BURT added from the speakers. "Remy will be needed as physical protection. Ivy and John are the team's only IT specialists and he will be busy."

"I could do with backup," the girl admitted, her eyes worried.

Grilfir looked from one to the other, his face thoughtful as he considered the idea.

"BURT, can you guarantee that you and the girls can deal with two ground stations?"

"Yes, Your Majesty," the AI replied. "Once we are in the system, we will not only be able to deal with the ground stations, but we will have the computational space to spare in order to be able to provide backup for the Hooligans and the fleet."

"And Stephanie?" the king asked.

"If she needs it," BURT told him, "although that might begin to stretch our capacity."

"Don't forget the hostile AI in the Earth Net," Remy reminded him. "I don't think my uncle dealt with him before…before they found him."

"If he shows his face, he will be dealt with," BURT assured him. "The position he holds now used to be my domain and I have grown since then."

Grilfir considered them for a moment longer, then nodded.

"Very well. Remy will provide technical backup for the team that will target the chancellor's clones. BURT, Tempestarii, and the *Knight* will assist the Hooligans to disable Earth's communication's Net, and Stephanie will assassinate the chancellor."

He looked around the room and smiled expansively. "The rest of us have the comparatively simple task of keeping the entire Regime Navy off their backs while they destroy the planet's government and infrastructure."

That drew chuckles from around the room, although the laughter didn't reach anyone's eyes. The admirals' smiles were nothing more than a baring of teeth in the face of an oncoming battle, and their eyes were hard when they looked at Stephanie.

She responded with an equally solemn smile and nodded to Wayne when he slipped quietly into his seat. He managed a weak nod in return and followed her gaze to Grilfir.

The king's face had become graver than before. He regarded the Witch with concern.

"*Modfresha,* we will see the deliverance of your people but I am afraid there will be thousands we cannot save—possibly tens of thousands."

Agreement rose in quiet murmurs from those at the table, and when she studied each of them, they returned it with steady confidence. No one looked away and she realized that they would follow her into the jaws of hell.

It rocked her to her core.

Grilfir had only mentioned the possible human loss—the loss of her people and all people on Earth. He'd said nothing about the losses his people would suffer in the battle to prevent the Regime's ships from firing on their own. Nor did he mention how many Dreth they would lose or whether the Telorans aboard their ships would survive.

He was wrong. They would not lose thousands or even tens of thousands. The chances were they would lose hundreds of thousands—of their people, of Dreth, and of any of their allies. Her eyes widened and she struggled to keep her hands at her side.

All she wanted to do was cover her mouth with her palm and flee the room. There was too much trust and too much willingness to die—for Earth and for *her.*

She cleared her throat.

"Your Majesty, if I…could I take a few minutes?"

He inclined his head. "I believe a short recess is in order. The galley will bring refreshments." He fixed her with a sympathetic gaze. "Let me know when you are ready to resume."

So saying, he rose from his seat to signal that the meeting was taking a break. Stephanie felt Todd's fingertips brush her back as she turned and walked quickly toward the door and was grateful when he didn't try to call her back.

She took a deep breath as she stepped into the corridor, well aware that her team would follow and thankful that none of them had tried to stop her exit. She looked left and right and it didn't take her long to remember which direction would take her to the pod room.

Not even the sound of footsteps entering the corridor behind her distracted her. She knew who it was. Vishlog's tread was distinctive and he wasn't alone. None of them tried to close the distance between them, though, and she was glad.

They would watch her back but they wouldn't get in her way.

The journey to the pod room didn't take long and her team closed around her as she slid into the closest one.

"I won't be long," she said and caught the Dreth's eye.

"We will watch for you, here," he told her and she rested a hand on his arm for a brief moment.

"Thank you."

He inclined his head before he turned so all she could see as the pod cycled closed was the line of her team's backs as they shielded her from the world beyond. The sight steadied her and she closed her eyes and sank quickly into the *King's Warrior's* internal Net.

"A place where I can think," she said when the AI inquired what setting she needed.

Before it could show her the options, a second presence arrived and she sighed.

"BURT?"

"Who else?" he asked and the Virtual spun around them and took them to the front porch of a cabin set high in the mountains.

"Of course you'd bring me here," she said and he smiled and opened the door.

"Tea?"

Stephanie nodded and he gestured for her to sit on one of the cushioned chairs on the porch.

"I won't be long."

She thought about insisting that she help him to prepare the tea but decided against it. The mountain view called her and the field of spring flowers waved in a gentle breeze to soothe her. She sighed as she settled into one of the chairs and BURT disappeared inside.

The rattle of china and smell of tea followed shortly after and he appeared carrying a tray. He placed it on the small table between them and poured her tea.

"Here," he told her, handed her a cup, and poured one for himself.

With a small smile of thanks, she took it and wrapped both hands around the cup as she settled in her chair and looked out over the valley. BURT said nothing as he followed her gaze.

The Witch raised her cup and sipped slowly. The AI remained silent and they looked out over the valley and watched the flowers dance in the breeze.

There are eight of them now. The thought brought no comfort but David Thomason didn't let his discomfort show on his face. *Eight should be enough.*

Even as he thought it, he doubted it. Eighty wouldn't be enough. They had attacked him in Earth's orbit.

Earth's orbit! How had they done that?

He allowed his gaze to travel around the room and tried to draw a sense of security from the fact that a Gray was now stationed at the center-point of each wall as well as in each corner.

Would they be enough to save him from the three mages who had destroyed a dozen of his most powerful ships?

Somehow, he doubted it.

"Earth's orbit…" he muttered and ran his fingers through his hair.

The chancellor studied the images still frozen on his wall and committed each of their faces to memory—as if he didn't already see them in his sleep.

"In my nightmares," he stated and made no effort to explain the sentiment to his guards.

It was none of their concern, after all. Instead, he forced himself to look more closely at what each of the three was doing.

"Where do they get the energy?"

It was hard to believe they'd been able to accomplish so much. What had his Marines been doing? Why hadn't they dealt with the incursion? Why didn't the crew of the ships deal with the situation?

"Argh!" He hadn't intended for the frustrated protest to emerge and he managed to mute it to a growl when it had wanted to form a scream. He was even able to stop himself from hammering a fist into the wall, although he could not stop his hands from clenching.

Well, let them make of that what they will, he thought. *In the end, it doesn't matter what they think. They are mine.*

He pivoted abruptly, stalked to his desk, and dropped heavily into his chair before he hauled it close to the desk. It didn't take him long to tap into the comms channel for Admiral Reynolds. He needed some of his assets returned.

"Send me another thirty ships," he ordered as soon as the admiral's face came into view.

The man's jaw dropped.

"Chancellor! I—"

"Don't argue. I need the ships. *Notaro* was attacked. The fleet in orbit was attacked."

"It will take time," Reynolds began but David cut him short.

"I need them immediately. We are facing an imminent attack!"

The admiral's expression shifted to reveal momentary disbelief and...was that scorn? The look was gone too fast for him to be sure but the impression remained.

"Even if I turn them now, it'll be two weeks before they can reach you."

"Have them go faster." He snarled with rage. "Or have them warp to the warp point and then warp again. I don't care how you do it but get them here."

Reynolds opened his mouth as if to protest or explain but the chancellor cut the link before he could say anything. Better that than hear the man say something he didn't want to hear. If he did that, David would order his immediate execution and deliver the order to the admiral's Marines in person.

It was an impulse he needed to keep in check.

"If I didn't need them, I'd dispose of them myself."

CHAPTER NINE

Stephanie blew on her tea. The steam wisped away from her breath but still warmed her face when she brought the cup to her lips. She gazed over the flowers to the mountains beyond and said, "It used to be so easy."

BURT took a contemplative sip of his beverage. "How so?"

"I could make mistakes and it didn't matter to anyone but me," she explained. "If I didn't get it right, no one died, the world didn't go to hell and back, our worlds weren't destroyed."

"Ah…" The soft sound said he saw what she was driving at. "You were learning, then—and lucky to be able to do so. Imagine how John feels."

She sighed. "And that's my fault too. I miss the time when this kind of shit wasn't my fault."

"None of this is your fault, Stephanie," he told her. "You did not take the final decision that made the world what it's become."

"No—" She choked back a sob and forced it to come out as more of a laugh. "No, I merely stepped aside and let it happen."

"If you'd returned when you planned to, you'd have stopped it sooner," he assured her.

"Do you truly believe that?" she asked and rested her elbows on her knees while her gaze fixed on the distant sky as she took another sip.

"I know so," he told her. "You are who you are and we were fortunate that you came along at a time when the world wasn't the way it is now. You still had responsibility."

"Yeah," she acknowledged, "for research and training so I could get myself out of a dangerous situation without letting my guards get killed, for—"

She blew a raspberry and her hand imitated the flight of a balloon that had been released with a full load of air.

"I didn't have entire worlds willing to follow me to their deaths or need to make sure my ship didn't go blow the crap out of someone who thoroughly deserved it and damn the consequences. I could go and fight something and not get thousands of people I haven't met killed because they wanted to make sure I succeeded."

The Witch sighed, clutched her cup between her hands, and rested her lips against the rim.

"Those were the days, huh?" BURT asked, and Stephanie managed a weak chuckle.

"Something like that. I was lucky to grow up that way. Todd, too."

"And now?"

"Now, I simply have to face it," she said. "I don't want to be the one to lead hundreds of thousands of people into a war they might not come out of, but if I hadn't walked away to start with, none of this would have happened."

"You weren't to know what was coming."

"But I should have guessed."

BURT shook his head. "No. What's come about was merely one of many possibilities, all dependent on the choice of others."

Stephanie shook her head. "They wouldn't have been able to make that choice if I'd stuck around."

"You had other responsibilities," he reminded her. "You'd made a promise."

"Yeah, to return an entity to a body that had died long ago."

"Neither of you could have known that," he pressed. "You had to at least make the attempt. That said, you also weren't to know that Knight would hit a patch of nMU right before a warp and put you into stasis. Do you think that doesn't bother her?"

"I told her none of that was her fault!" she protested. "She wasn't to know…"

BURT laughed and she let her words peter out.

"You're so funny," she grumbled but a slight smile curved her lips.

Without realizing it, she'd provided the perfect illustration for the point he was trying to make. She shook her head and drained her cup.

"Well, no more walking away," she told him and placed it firmly on the tray. "I might not be able to see the future but I can see the problem, and I won't run away from it this time. What I don't understand is why the Dreth and Meligornians think they owe me."

Stephanie turned to the AI.

"They don't owe me anything. I did what needed to be done—what anyone would have done when they saw someone in need."

BURT finished his tea and shook his head.

"That's not true and you know it."

"That's what they say," she replied, "and it isn't true."

"Says you," he answered.

"Yes. Says me," she reiterated. "Why won't they accept that they don't owe me anything for doing what was right by them?"

"Would a human?"

Stephanie thought about it. "Some might."

"And some might not," BURT pointed out. "Remember, they aren't human but even if they were, they'd be among those like you."

"Hey! What exactly do you mean by that?"

"I mean that you wouldn't simply accept someone doing you a favor because it was what was needed or 'the right thing to do' without feeling that you owed the person who helped you, would you?"

"And your point is?" she asked and arched her eyebrows in challenge.

He smirked and turned his gaze toward the distant mountains.

"My point is that you have to allow them to pay what they consider their debt." He held a hand up when she opened her mouth to protest. "You have to let them right the imbalance or your relationships—and those of all humans, Dreth, and Meligornians—will forever be problematic. Those problems could have serious consequences, if not in this generation, then most likely for generations in the future."

"The sins of the fathers," Stephanie murmured.

BURT snorted. "Or, in this case, the mothers."

She glared at him but he wasn't finished.

"The point is that every generation leaves its mark on the next and shapes at least its beginning. That you can't avoid, but you can try to guide its shape. What you're trying to avoid is leaving a legacy that has any negative effects."

"At least not where we can put it right," she agreed. "This generation will not leave a legacy of war and destruction. We will not leave a mess for our children and children's children to clean up."

"Not like your forebears, huh?" he asked and the smile became more apparent.

Stephanie shook her head.

"I didn't do all that research or butt heads with the most brilliant and stubborn of scientists and get our world cleaned up to leave all the future humans under the thumb of a multi-headed monster. It's unacceptable that it refuses to accept that humans come in many different forms or that aliens are our allies and friends."

"Exactly," BURT agreed.

"And I won't put off fixing what I can until it becomes someone else's problem either," she declared. "I will not. If I can fix it so the future people don't have to worry about it, I'll do that too. I've had enough of dealing with other people's problems. I won't leave any of mine for someone else."

When he heard the strength return to her voice, he smiled.

"So," he ventured, "do you know what you need to do?"

Stephanie chuckled. "I have a vague idea and a list," she said wryly.

"It will have to do," he told her as they both stood.

They turned for one last look at the view and she drew a deep breath.

"I remember when I first came here. You were masquerading as a Meligornian master."

"I'm not sorry," he told her, his voice content.

"No, and neither am I," she replied. "Without you, I would not be who I am."

That startled a laugh out of him.

"In that case," he replied, "we are equal since without you, I would not be self-aware." His voice sobered as he continued, "I wouldn't have felt the joy of children or the pain of losing a brother."

He turned to face her and clasped her arm briefly.

"We are all Team Morgana," he told her, released her, and looked toward the hills. "Now, let's finish this."

She followed his gaze and drew another deep breath. "Yes."

The team was still waiting when she popped the lid of the pod. Vishlog turned quickly and helped her out.

He took one look at her face and decided silence was the better part of valor. As soon as her feet were firmly on the floor, he released her and ignored the slight sting of the magic that flowed over her body. He stepped back another pace when she braced her feet and began to move her arms in broad circular movements.

Energy flowed over him, pulled in by the motion of her hands as she wove them in a complex pattern. His skin tingled as more energy drifted past him and he glanced at the team.

Avery's hair stood on end and Brenden's eyes were wide. Marcus and Johnny stared in bemusement. It took effort to not laugh, but the big Dreth managed it. He made a circular motion with his forefinger to signal that they should pay attention to their surroundings and they turned to do exactly that—although all of them kept her in their peripheral vision.

None of them wanted to miss what she was doing, even while they protected her.

Grilfir looked at the door and V'ritan frowned. The king wasn't a patient man at the best of times although he was a good ruler and he had been an excellent commander in his time. While it hadn't been a surprise when he'd granted Stephanie the time she needed, it was a surprise that he hadn't yet sent someone after her.

From the look on his sovereign's face, that moment wasn't too far off.

As he thought it, the energy around him shifted.

"What is…" he muttered and looked around as Grilfir raised his head to study the room with a frown.

They weren't alone in their concern, the King's Warrior noted. Their security guards were already moving closer and the mages had spread out to give each other room to fight. Several of the admirals also glanced around warily and some of the Dreth had started to shift uneasily. Whether that was because they could feel the shift in magical energy or because of the cues they picked up from their hosts was anyone's guess.

"Is this trouble?" Grilfir asked and V'ritan was startled to discover the king beside him.

"I…don't know," he replied.

"Stephanie?" Sho, the king's head of security, asked and they both looked at the man in shock.

The Meligornian wasn't worried. "Well? It's a large shift of magic and I can only think of one—" His gaze fell on Tethis. "Two mages close enough to create it."

He gestured to where the warrior mage had shifted to an open space in the conference center.

"He wasn't doing anything when we first felt it."

V'ritan nodded. "True. It could be—"

The door slid open and every gaze turned toward it.

"Here she is," the *Ghargilum* murmured.

Grilfir nodded. "It's time we reconvened," he stated quietly and the admirals moved as though he'd given an order loud enough for them to hear.

"The clouds are about to be scattered from the moon," Sho observed and signaled the security teams to give their principals space in which to move.

Stephanie paid them no heed as she marched to her place at the table, her face calm and composed and her eyes as black as pitch. Muttered expletives rose from the Hooligans and the Earth team and V'ritan echoed them silently.

It was at times like these that he preferred the Earth phrase for the one Sho had uttered. Some things splattered more spectacularly than others.

No sooner had the last admiral settled into his place than the Witch spoke. Her voice was as cold and dark as it had been at any time the Morgana had used it, but it was still Stephanie's.

"It is time," she declared. "The Earth will be free and the Federation will rid itself of the cancer within."

She turned to Grilfir and bowed, then stepped back from the conference table and made an even briefer bow to the others gathered there before she pivoted and stalked from the room.

"Let's make this quick."

CHAPTER TEN

Jaleck stepped out of the shuttle and glanced at the sky. It was impossible to believe the girl had grown that powerful so quickly but she was home and it had not taken two weeks for her to get there.

In the skies above, Angreth's ship and the six boats that escorted them had emerged and the gate had closed, but she doubted that either Stephanie or Tethis had collapsed on its release. In fact, she was sure the two of them had needed to be stopped from attempting to send the rest of the Dreth fleet through as well.

V'ritan and a shock stick. Who would have thought?

Of course, that had been a hollow threat, surely. The *Ghargilum* might be a determined man but she doubted that even he was suicidal enough to try to interrupt the *Modfresha's* concentration with a shock stick.

Tethis, on the other hand, was a force to be reckoned with.

She chuckled. The stories had not exaggerated. Tethis had been a spymaster, a master spy, and a saboteur in his dim and distant past—along with other things they had not uncovered and of which he refused to speak.

She stepped out the door the second her shuttle touched down, Gralog and Mermot be damned. They scrambled to catch up as she reached the steps and was relieved when they took their places slightly ahead of her without uttering a word of protest.

Lucky for them. She was in the mood for a fight but too busy to indulge. Angreth would be relieved.

Angreth...

The high admiral clenched her teeth and scanned the airfield. Granted, she hadn't been docked for long but she had so much to do and very little time to do it in. Her gaze settled on a small knot of Dreth who hurried out of the buildings beside the landing field.

"It's about time," she muttered and altered course to meet them. Mermot and Gralog had already changed direction and the rest of her security team turned with the precision of a flock of migrating sgrava.

"Councilor Hrageck," she stated briskly and saw a hitch in the councilor's stride. "It is time."

Those three words made him quicken his pace and those around him hurried to catch up.

"High Admiral, are you... Are you sure? The girl has decided."

"The *Modfresha* has chosen to take the war to the Regime and save her people before they fall to further ruin. Dreth will fly."

"And will she let us aid her?"

"We are to ensure the Regime Navy does not fire on the planet while she destroys the chancellor."

"May the Hunt Master be with her," Hrageck replied, his tone fervent.

"I will need warriors familiar with taking ships," she continued. "We will not leave Earth defenseless when we cleanse its navy of the parasites within."

"We will not!" Gereg Hrageck declared. "Even if the crews cannot be saved, the tools of battle might still be preserved and

Dreth can assist with crew until they have founded a new Navy. It would be our honor to help them rebuild as she tried to help us."

"It would," Jaleck agreed and pretended to not see the bared tusks of the warriors and councilors around her.

The anticipation ran through them like wildfire.

Dreth was going to war. Its debt of honor would be repaid.

"Summon the clans," she ordered. "We meet as soon as the sun has set."

"The Families of Dreth answer Earth's call," he replied and thumped his right fist over his heart before he extended it for her fist to touch.

"Dreth stands for Earth," she replied and the warriors around her echoed the phrase. Joy threaded the ferocity of their response.

It was a short walk into the Fortress of Fire and Respect but she had other business to attend to before she faced the clans. Her first stop was the small shuttle Mermot had arranged. Her security chief had insisted the walk was too dangerous to undertake at such short notice.

Normally, she would have pointed out that no one would have had time to organize an ambush since no one had known she was coming. Today, she hadn't had the time to argue and the skimmer would get her to the Teloran Mage Academy faster.

Speed was of the essence. Stephanie was going to war and she wouldn't wait, no matter how much she needed them. Dreth would have to meet her in the air if it wanted to pay its debt and establish an equal standing with the people of Earth. It was a relief to find the storm mother waiting for her, and their business didn't take long to conclude.

The high admiral hurried to the Hall of Families, issued orders for refit and supply, and met briefly with Angreth. The time they had was too short but they held each other close for an all too brief moment before they touched foreheads in a private farewell they would not get later.

"Fortress?" he asked and revealed the smallest amount of tusk in a smile as full of regret as she felt.

She clasped his shoulder. "Fortress," she agreed. "Dreth will stand for Earth."

"As Earth has stood for us," he said and they boarded the shuttle waiting to take them up the hill to the Fortress of Fire and Respect.

When they touched down, it was clear that the clans had almost fully assembled and Jaleck was glad so many of them were still in the capital. The fact that many hadn't left since the fighting started wasn't lost on her and she could see the small, fast courier ships they used for rapid communication already warming their engines.

Her words would be carried to the farthest corners of the planet, regardless of whether the communications arrays were functional or not. By the time this night was over and she'd returned to her ship, everyone would know it was time.

The *Knight's* weapons crews took the first two loads of missiles that arrived. The *Tempestarii*'s gun crews waited for the third. There might have been a fight, save that the shift bosses came to an agreement. Tempestarii's crews could have the next load and both crews would split the loads from that point on.

It might have had something to do with the Marines who filed quietly into the cargo hold as the gun crews prepared to defend their claims on the weapons, but no one could be sure. No words were exchanged and both ships remained stubbornly silent.

"Much better," BURT told them over the intercom. "How can your crews compete fairly if they don't both have the equipment they need, hmmm?"

On the gun decks, the crews were hard at work. Guns were stripped and every moving part greased or oiled to within an inch of its life. Safety harnesses were clipped to purpose-fitted rails, implementing lessons learned in battles past.

Crews checked that there were suits to spare. No one fought in everyday gear anymore. They'd had too many holes blasted into hull sections and too few crew willing to leave as a result of that. Now, they planned for the long-haul.

Both Tempestarii and Knight had pick-up crews on standby, but there was no guarantee that a shuttle could fly in the middle of a battle. Everyone agreed it was better to not need pick-up in the first place.

"I can't think of anything else to make her fire faster," Crewman Tippet complained. "Everything's greased and the timings are at their shortest interval. I've tweaked the cooling so she doesn't overheat and shut down anything that might be an inconvenience." He threw his hands up and turned to his team leader in despair. "What am I missing?"

The senior crewman made a show of inspecting the gun and went through another tear-down with his junior before he shook his head.

"I'm sorry, son. There's nothing more you can do for her. The only other part that needs tweaking is the one who fires the guns. How does that operate for accuracy and speed?"

Tippet froze. "It's still upgrading, sir… Can I… Is there a pod I can use?"

Andorres laughed. "Your work here is done and I don't want to think what you'll break trying to improve on it."

He pulled his tablet out and searched for a free pod, assigned it to the man, and sent him the information. "There you go. Make sure you're at the meal table on time or I'll haul you out by your ear."

"Aye, Chief."

The youngster took enough time to note where he had to go

before he wove quickly through the section. Similar scenes were played out through every weapons deck as guns and launchers already maintained at close to instant readiness were hauled down and put back together. Finally, crew chiefs sent their teams into the Virtual for weapons practice to ensure that the weapons stayed ready.

Come the battle, they wanted every gun and crewman on the decks but in that calm between readiness and battle, they had to ensure that their people didn't break something or exhaust themselves.

It was a fine, fine line.

"You know they will love these," Ail'tel stated and tapped the screen with his pointer.

The scientists around the table studied the screen and their gazes took on a faraway look as they contemplated the missile diagram on the board.

"Are you sure that's safe?" one of the humans asked and snickers greeted the question. "I mean for the ships carrying them, drolfaven."

"Drolfaven?" one of the Meligornians asked. "Not bad for a human but you still haven't answered the question. It mixes nMU with MU and even you know that's not a good idea."

The man smirked. "It does but they're separated until the moment of explosion at which point, the effects should be catastrophic for wherever they blow up."

"Whatever you blow up, you mean," another human commented.

"Pfft. Put that much nMU and MU together and you'll obliterate half a solar system. Then the Witch will be seriously upset."

"With all of us," Marcus stated from the end of the table, "and we don't want that."

He didn't tell them to scrap the idea, though. Instead, he studied the diagram and glanced at the Meligornian who'd noted how much would be destroyed.

"How much do you think it would need to destroy…say… something around the size of the drive area."

The man snorted. "Add in the energy from even an Earth ship's drives and you'll annihilate the entire solar system. It would end the world extremely quickly but…"

He shrugged.

"Do the calculations, Melof."

The Meligornian wasn't the only one to turn to his tablet and start to work on it. Others joined him, although not all of them calculated the MU to nMU ratio.

When Melof presented his results, Ibrel and Lok'ten suggested a way for the rocket to spread its payload along the outside of a shield, while Carel and Jack proposed an alternative payload that would overload and short the engines.

"Are you sure?" Marcus asked. "Wouldn't it simply cause them to explode?"

"We're only fighting the Regime, right?" Jack reminded them. "This way, we use the magic to shut the engines down. The ship can't do anything and we can send our mages in to reverse the problem so it can be used when the Witch's people have control again."

They all looked at him and he reddened.

"I…don't know if it's possible, though…"

"We've done the impossible before," his boss pointed out.

"And the Witch does the impossible all the time," another scientist added.

"So, when I say we turn your nMU-MU missile into a multi-headed hydra that breaks into a cluster of smaller missiles spreading in a random pattern—"

"Forward," Marcus stated and the scientist frowned and considered it.

It didn't take him long to understand the point.

"Of course, forward," he agreed and typed hastily as he adjusted his calculations. "Away from the ship that fired it."

"How long before these can be in production?" another of the scientists asked. "Because I don't think the Witch will wait."

"That's a good point," Marcus noted. "If we dedicate a small portion of production to these new ones, can we still do a full resupply?"

Everyone froze. He looked at them and stifled a sigh. After all, it wasn't too long ago that he wouldn't have thought of the production times either. While age had mellowed him, it had also given him time to connect more of the dots linked to his profession, which meant he was able to see more of his theories become reality.

That was satisfying.

He smiled as the younger scientists started along the same path. One day, one of them would have to take his place.

"Selene help them," he murmured as Cynthia signaled him from the door.

With a scowl, he stood and left the team to their calculations.

"The director wants to see you," his assistant told him and he sighed and wondered what T'virilf wanted this time. He glanced into the room and his gaze settled on one of the men he'd brought from Earth.

"Trey," he called, "take over. Don't let them get too carried away."

The man waved an acknowledgment and Marcus followed Cynthia to the next room.

"So," the big scientist said to the others at the table, "what say we try to work out how to channel gMU into the lasers?"

Marcus shook his head and resisted the urge to run to the meeting.

They couldn't possibly, could they?

V'ritan strode down the Hall of Warriors and T'revan moved at his back. The big bodyguard hadn't left his side since Stephanie had declared imminent war on the Regime except when he'd slept, which was seldom.

Coordinating with Amaratne and the Dreth admirals and liaising with his people meant he hadn't had much personal time. This would be his last chance to see the king before he left. He sighed.

It had been a long time since Grilfir's duties had taken him from the battlefield and longer still since they'd first fought together. The guards saw him coming and opened the doors ahead, bowing deeply as he strode past.

King Grilfir rose as he entered and gestured for his advisors to leave as he went to greet his old friend. The queen moved with him and smiled warmly.

"V'ritan," she said. "It has been too long."

He bowed in reply and she returned it. King Grilfir extended both hands.

"I am jealous."

That made the King's Warrior smile.

"I miss those days."

"As do I," the queen added, "although I admit to not being sorry that you won't leave me alone again."

That brought a soft smile to Grilfir's face.

"I remember when you used to fight beside me," he told her.

"And ahead of us," V'ritan added grimly. "You were always running ahead."

She snorted. "Only because your eyes were painted on. I found them, I flushed them out, and I left some for you."

"Do you mean that was deliberate?"

Her lips curved into a sly smile. "I knew how upset you'd be if I killed them all myself."

"But you could have been killed!"

"And so could you," she retorted. "There were many times I thought I should have finished them simply to keep you out of trouble."

They walked as they talked and stopped at a small table set in an alcove behind the throne. Their guards arranged themselves around the space and tried to give them some semblance of privacy as refreshments were brought.

"How go the preparations?" asked the king and V'ritan told him. He also detailed Garach and Frog's recovery.

"Honestly, it was a relief to send the two of them to the *Knight,*" he admitted. "More than one medic considered a small life pod sent to the depths of space."

Grilfir chuckled. "So, worse than Stephanie, then?"

"A young Dreth and his human uncle?" the *Ghargilum* asked as if the answer were obvious and the royal couple laughed.

He continued his report and a ping from his tablet reminded him of the time as he drew to a close. With a sigh, he stood.

"If you will excuse me," he told them and bowed deeply, "the fleet calls."

The king returned his bow and stretched a hand toward him. V'ritan met him halfway and wrapped his hand around his forearm as the monarch did the same.

"When this is done, our debt to Earth will be paid," Grilfir told him and his Warrior met his gaze.

"Meligorn will owe no more blood," he agreed, "but our friendship will remain."

"And it will be an equal friendship," the queen emphasized and her husband nodded.

"We will have friendship with the humans or nothing," he declared.

"And if Stephanie is killed?" V'ritan asked.

The king's face grew somber.

"Then we will personally remove the Regime in her honor," he decreed. "Either way, the war stops now."

Dark light illuminated the academy's central courtyard but did little to reveal the features of the storm witches gathered there. Fish flickered in the depths of the water surrounding the central tree and its island and darted into the shelter of the lilies and waterweed.

Those gathered there paid them no heed and all eyes turned to the academy's storm mother.

She descended from the northernmost tower but didn't bother to use the stairs. Instead, she floated from the wall and ebon lightning flickered around her as though she rode a miniature storm, and the youngest recruits watched in awe.

Not all of them were Teloran. There were some Dreth, one or two Meligornians, and the odd human, but they were in the minority. Most of the storm witches were Telorans who had settled after the last war.

They all waited attentively until she alighted on the small dais set at the base of the tree.

"Children of the Storm," she stated and her solemn tones rang from the courtyard's walls, "we are gathered on a matter of some urgency—and one that even the least experienced of you can assist with."

The storm mother swept the mages with a stern gaze.

"What I want everyone here to do is to focus on the energy around us. Draw it into yourselves, then send it toward me. As you do, focus your anxieties for the coming battle into the magic and send your worries and your fears with it."

She paused and her gaze swept the mages before she continued.

"The senior Storm Wielders and I will shape everything into a missive for Telor. We will use your fears and worries to ask for Teloran aid and to give that request a sense of urgency. Are we ready?"

When their murmurs of assent died, she made a show of studying them before she nodded decisively.

"As the storm clouds gather the lightning, so let us gather the energy around us and send to Telor for aid. Begin."

The sound of her voice faded from the courtyard and she studied the mages before her.

Were they ready?

She didn't think anyone was ready for the battle to come but that wouldn't stop them from going to war. If they were very fortunate, the Morgana would arrive in time to help them.

"Piet!" the sergeant's roar of frustration did nothing to stop the smaller man as he emptied a box of grenades into a bandolier and proceeded to shove more into a belt pouch.

"You can never have too much explosive!" the engineer argued and Todd ran one hand over his head to the back of his neck.

"You are playing with fire." Ka snickered and Piet grimaced.

"I always play with fire. Why do you think I get along so well with explosives?"

She shook her head. "He's got you there, boss."

"He has," Todd agreed. "Explosives are what saved us last time."

A soft whistle drew their attention.

"Well, well, well, what have we here?" Gary asked and they turned to see what he'd found.

"It had better not be more explosives," Todd muttered.

"I thought you said they saved us the last time?" Reggie asked from the other side of the shelves, then added, "Oh..."

"Reggie..." Ka warned.

"It's not explosives, boss, I promise," the Australian told her in a faraway tone.

She looked at Todd.

"I'll go see what mischief he's found. You deal with Henry."

He nodded. "Right. That sounds like a plan."

"What d'you think?" Henry asked as he rounded the end of the shelving.

"I'm... What exactly am I looking at?" he asked.

"Well," the man answered and held up one of the items he'd found, "this looks like your conventional trip-wire..."

It wasn't long before Todd grinned and held his hand out.

"I'll take two."

"Boss," Ka called, "you'll never believe what we've found."

He shook his head at the summons and trotted to where Ka and Reggie stood and looked like two kids who had broken into Christmas and been given all the toys.

"Do I want to know?" he asked.

She held a button up. "Boss, you're gonna want us all to have one of these."

"Maybe two," the Aussie added.

Todd folded his arms. "Uh-huh. Dare I ask what it is?"

"It's a button."

It took effort to school his features and simply nod sagely. "Yes, I can see that."

Ka nudged Reggie. "Do you see that tic? It means you'd better start explaining or he'll start kicking your butt."

"Not only his," the sergeant pointed out and she nudged her teammate a second time and much harder.

"Ow... Fine!" Reggie stepped forward and slapped the button on Todd's shirt. He stepped back and gave the corporal an uncertain look. "Are you sure you want me to do this?"

She smirked. "I don't know, Reg. How badly do you want to do it?"

He snickered and Todd wasn't sure he'd ever heard that kind of evil before, at least not directed at him.

"You might want to activate your shielding, boss," Ka told him.

"Wait. What?" he began as Reggie turned his back to him and unholstered his blaster. "You can't fire that in here—why are you—"

The Australian sent two quick shots toward a shelf to his left, and Todd activated his armor's built-in shielding.

"Reggie!" he exclaimed as Ka took two paces back. He glared at her and snapped a hand out to grab her.

The badge on his shirt flared and the bolts vanished but reappeared seconds later to drill into the button on his chest.

The impact forced him back two paces before lightning surged from the tiny device, arced over his torso, and jolted through his armor. His corporal's eyes widened in alarm.

"Is that supposed to happen?" she shouted as one of the *Knight's* resident mages stepped around the shelves with a sharp oath and sent a ball of purple to surround the button.

The Meligornian ripped it off Todd's chest and clenched a fist, contracted the magic around the button, and crushed it.

"*Drolfaven*!" he snapped and glared at Ka and Reggie as he hurried to Todd and helped him to his feet. "Are you all right, Sergeant?"

Todd gave him a worried look and glared at his Hooligans. "Stay right there, you two."

He turned to the mage. "Do you know what that was?" The man nodded. "Do you want to explain how it works?"

The Meligorian looked at him for a few long moments. "Briefly?"

He nodded.

"It uses a burst of magic to attract fire from the weapon of the person who applied it. On impact, it sends a high-powered burst of lightning through whatever—or whoever—it is attached to."

"Enough to kill a man?" he asked with a dark look at the two troublemakers.

"Possibly," the mage replied. "If you want training in how to use them most effectively, there's a training program in the pods."

Todd started to smile and made Reggie's look from earlier seem innocent by comparison.

Ka groaned, "Oh…no…"

His smile became a humorless grin. "Oh, yes, Corporal." He turned to the mage. "What other new equipment would you recommend for a dirty-tricks squad?"

The Meligornian's face brightened. "Of the new ones?"

"Anything that wasn't here two months ago."

"Well, in that case, Sergeant, there are a number of items over here you might want to consider."

He followed him to a section of shelving tucked along the back wall.

"And do they all have training programs?"

While Todd selected some of the Meligornian's newest and dirtiest tricks for his squad, Tethis met Stephanie in the gym. The girl was working through a gymnastics routine that made fighting look easy and the cats bounded around her as she kicked, dove, and twisted across the training mats.

The warrior mage walked to the edge of the mats and tried not to draw her attention as he waited. Now and again, he caught the faintest twitch of magic as she corrected something but most of the moves were completed without such assistance.

It didn't take her long to notice him, however.

"Tethis!" she cried and landed after a perfect flip.

"You asked for me?" he said by way of greeting.

"Yes," she said, walked to where she'd left a towel, and whistled the cats to her side.

Vishlog, Johnny, and Marcus pushed away from the wall where they'd been waiting and she shoved the felines toward them. She was breathing a little hard from her workout and her face was sheened in sweat but she crossed to the Meligornian.

"Walk with me?"

Tethis bowed his head. "Of course."

He fell in beside her, only to be enveloped in purple light. The gym vanished with Vishlog's startled shout, and a meadow with long purple grass took its place. A lake shimmered below them and the hills folded around it in a purple haze.

"I don't think I recognize this location."

"It's the closest scene to a meadow I first saw in the Virtual World too many years ago," she explained and looked around. Sadness flitted across her expression.

"There was a master teacher with me then too," she added softly. Her face took on a distant look as she stared over the lake but sharpened when she turned toward him and smiled.

"I could never have asked for a better teacher in the arts than you." She stopped and her eyes darkened with worry. "And I'm sorry. I need to ask one last favor."

"You could ask for a million," he assured her.

"No." She pursed her lips. "If you do this for me, we are forever even. Is that understood Master Tethis Naliviri?"

Tethis studied her carefully.

"You want me to go with Todd?" he asked.

Stephanie's face rippled as though she tried not to cry and almost lost the battle. Finally, a tiny smile tinged with anxiety won through.

"Is it that obvious?"

The warrior mage held a fist over his heart and inclined his head.

"I am honored."

Her face firmed. "Of those around me, you are as wise as

Jaleck, as powerful as V'ritan, and as devious as Ms. E," she told him. "I want my love to be with me when this is all over."

He extended his fist for her to touch knuckles with in a warrior's salute.

"On my honor," he told her and turned his fist so he offered her his hand. "But promise to make sure you're alive so I can deliver him to you."

"I will." She grasped his hand. "Until this is finished."

"Agreed."

They looked into each other's eyes in solemn promise before purple light enveloped them and they vanished.

As the light faded from the meadow, a small snout poked cautiously out of a grass tussock and quivered as it registered their fading scents. It was followed by a pointed face, two bright, dark eyes, and a pair of narrow, pointed ears.

When it saw the meadow was empty of threat, the creature emerged slowly and continued to look for its evening meal. Surely the intruders hadn't scared everything in the field.

"Don't give me excuses!" Jaleck snapped. "Tell me you'll be ready when I need you to be." Her frown became a full-blown scowl. "I don't want to know the sordid details, Captain. I only want to see the results. Have those drives and weapons back online by the time I dock." Again, she paused. "Of course I'm on my way!"

That response elicited another protest as she trotted up the steps into the shuttle, her tablet clenched in one fist. She reached the hatch, looked at the screen, and gave the errant captain the smile her fleet commanders had come to dread.

"Captain," she said and her soft tone made him come to a stuttering halt, "I don't care if you have to get out and push that ship yourself. You will leave with us by High Hrageth, so I suggest you find someone with a brain cell who has experience with multivariant fluctuations in the Voketh 681 and have them fix your drives—or get your dirty shoes ready for a spacewalk."

The captain was still gaping when she snapped, "Jaleck out!" and stowed the tablet in its armored pouch. Facing the hatch, she placed her hand on the lintel and turned to survey the shuttle port and the harsh mountains and foothills behind it.

Addressing the planet, she said, "May we see each other when this is done."

It was a phrase her guards repeated softly as they followed her into the transport. Nothing in battle was guaranteed.

"I don't want to know what you cannot do!" V'ritan snarled his frustration and glared at the commander on the screen. "I need that corvette with the fleet when it leaves, and every soul aboard it."

"But—"

"I don't care if you need to send the Marines to requisition an engineer from the Navy's training academy or from the Veils yard, but you will sail on the *Warrior's* flank at Selene's Rising or you'll have an up-close and personal look of the Pillars—on foot!"

Since the Pillars of Shawhallow were hydrogen plumes visible from Meligorn's largest orbital, he couldn't blame the commander for his suddenly pale face.

"I…I'll see who I can find," he stuttered.

"I want a full fleet, Commander. I want you, the *Archer, Heart,* and *Promise* at the *Warrior's* side. Make it so or you won't walk the Pillars alone!"

He snapped the tablet shut, stormed up the steps of the shuttle, and stopped to look at the shuttle field and the small figure who stood with her personal guard at its edge. She rested a hand over her heart and he mirrored the gesture although it almost broke him.

"This time will be the last," he murmured, "Selene willing."

It took more effort than he remembered to turn away and walk through the shuttle's hatch.

Stephanie emerged from the *Knight* and entered the *Tempestarii's* concourse with her security team in tow. Lars, Garach, Tethis, and Frog trailed behind them.

"She seems particularly determined today," Lars murmured and Tethis lowered his chin in acknowledgment.

Vishlog overheard and gave them a worried look but he didn't drop back to try to discover what they were thinking. He kept his mind on the task of ensuring their surroundings were safe. They still remembered the Marines who had hidden aboard the *Tempestarii* in their early days and while they were sure no such dangers remained, none of them were willing to risk her safety if that wasn't the case.

They came to a halt as she stopped the first crewman she saw.

"I need the largest empty hangar available," she told him. "Can you direct me?"

"None of them are empty, ma'am," the man told her.

"How about the one with the least in it?" she amended sweetly.

He was either married or he'd encountered officers using similar tones because he froze and withdrew his tablet hurriedly from his suit.

"I'll see what I can find," he assured her and put her request through. "May I ask what you need it for?"

"I need room to move," she told him and her face grew hard with determination. "I will not lose this war to inadequate firepower."

The crewman gave her a puzzled look, then nodded firmly. "Room to move. Gotcha," he said and added that to the request.

Fortunately, his commander seemed to realize that she needed as much space as he could find and the hanger he directed them to was one of those they'd used for the bar test when the *Knight* had first emerged from space.

"Will this do?" the crewman asked and showed them into it.

Stephanie's gaze traveled over the three supply teams who moved crates and equipment through one of the doors leading to the next hangar and nodded.

"Thank you."

"The commander says to tell you that our people will be out from underfoot in another five minutes if that's okay with you."

"It will take me that long to set up," she reassured him. "Please give the commander my thanks."

"Will do, ma'am."

He made a hasty attempt at a human salute crossed with a Meligornian bow and hurried through the airlock. It might have been funny if her escort had known what she was planning. As it was, they all shared the crewman's concern.

No sooner had they entered the huge space than Stephanie turned to them.

"Over there," she ordered and pointed to the walls on either side of the airlock.

She pivoted and scowled as she watched the supply crews clear more equipment from the hangar before they waved as a sign that they were leaving. As soon as she was sure none of them would return, she fixed her team and the Earth team with a stern look.

"Stay put," she ordered. "Right here. Understood?"

Vishlog frowned as if he might protest and she waved a finger under his nose.

"Unless you wish for a very close encounter with the ceiling, stay right here. Gotit?"

The Dreth's eyes widened when he remembered what she did when her cats misbehaved. He glanced at the ceiling, then at her.

"It would be hard to protect you from up there," he noted and she smiled.

"At least you wouldn't be upside-down."

That brought a return smile as they both recalled how they had first met.

"I did not like the experience when I was drunk," he reminded her, "and I do not think I'd enjoy it sober."

"Are you sure?" she teased and he gestured to the open floor.

"Don't let me hinder your plans," he said pointedly and she laughed.

"As if you could."

Before Vishlog could decide how to answer that, Stephanie turned and walked to the center of the empty space. The Dreth watched her but he also scanned her surroundings and breathed a sigh of relief when she began to move.

"What is she doing?" Frog leaned over to ask Lars.

"It looks like she's dancing," the security head replied and frowned as he tried to work out the reason for her moves.

Tethis remained silent but he watched the girl with an avid gaze and noted when she glanced at them and closed her eyes. Her movements didn't reveal the change but her teams noticed.

"What is she doing?" Vishlog asked.

"I would say she is communing with the cosmos," the warrior mage replied. "Kindly do not disturb her."

"I would not dream of it," the Dreth assured him, his gaze drawn to her motion. His jaw dropped. "Is…is that safe?" he whispered and nudged the Meligornian again.

Tethis didn't ask him why he was worried. Instead, he stared at her with his mouth agape. It wasn't the first time he'd seen energy flow into her but he was sure it was the first time he'd seen it so clearly. Light swirled around her, kicked up by her steps in the dance and pulled along the lines of movement she'd created.

It enveloped her and sank into her where it touched. When it vanished, she began to glow and her skin gleamed more brightly as she continued her dance.

Vishlog jumped when his tablet vibrated. At first, he ignored it but when it emitted an audible ping, he snapped it open and glared at the screen.

"What is it?" he demanded.

"It's Emil," the *Tempestarii's* captain replied, unperturbed by the fierce greeting. "It is time to go. Can we go?"

The Dreth looked at Lars, who shrugged.

"It's Stephanie. I imagine we can but I don't know how to ask her." He glanced around but Tethis paid him no attention.

The mage warrior's focus was on Stephanie as she danced across the center of the hangar. She glided, pivoted, and leapt as though partnering an invisible breeze. If Lars hadn't known any better, he would have said the Meligornian teacher was transfixed.

"Beautiful," Tethis whispered, his words filled with admiration. "Simply beautiful."

"Yes," he acknowledged, "but is it safe to move the ship or will we all be beautifully and spectacularly lost?"

Tethis shrugged. "I suppose it will be safe to move. As far as I know." He gestured toward the luminescent figure as Stephanie pirouetted, kicked into a backflip, and pirouetted in the opposite direction. "Of course, I thought we'd already be blasted apart into sub-atomic pieces at this moment, so what do I know? I've no idea how she's doing that but I seriously doubt anything we do will affect her."

"And if you're wrong?" Emil asked from the tablet.

Vishlog turned it so the captain could see what Stephanie was doing.

Emil paled. "If you're wrong?" he repeated through gritted teeth.

Tethis glanced into the screen. "We won't ever know I was wrong. We will simply be one with the cosmos."

Lars sighed. "I'll curse her out later."

He nodded to Vishlog.

"Punch it, Emil."

"Are we good, now?" Todd asked as he climbed out of the pod to join the rest of his team.

While he was very sure Ka and Reggie hadn't appreciated being used as guinea pigs to demonstrate the capabilities of their new toys, it had been necessary. No one would play with things they didn't understand—or not for a while, at least.

He tried to ignore the voice that told him it was only a matter of time. He merely assumed that when it came again, he'd repeat the lesson with whichever of the Hooligans had forgotten it.

If you survive. He frowned and shoved that little voice to the back of his head.

"Are we good?" he rumbled and the Hooligans replied as one.

"Sir, yes, sir!"

"Smart-asses."

They chuckled as he surveyed them. No one looked any the worse for the tour they'd taken in the pods, although they all dripped with sweat.

"Go get cleaned up, retrieve your gear, and meet me in the mess in the next thirty," he instructed and wondered if he had time to find Stephanie and say goodbye.

As the thought crossed his mind, the lights around them flared amber.

"Prepare for translocation," the *Tempestarii* informed them and her voice spoke over the intercom in a ship-wide alert. "I repeat. Prepare for translocation. All hands. Translocation will take place in ten minutes."

"You heard the lady," Todd told his crew. "Get cleaned up,

retrieve your gear, head to the mess, and prepare for translocation!"

"Nine minutes."

A soft ping echoed through the *Tempestarii's* words and Todd pivoted to find the source.

Ka had her tablet out and one finger on her earbud. She glanced at him and signaled for him to wait as she listened to the message. He caught the moment when she screwed her face up and wasn't surprised when she looked at him again.

"Uh…your girlfriend is up to something," she told him.

"What? Steph?"

"Do you have another girlfriend, boss?" she asked, turned the tablet monitor on, and held it up so he could see it. "Because if you do, I'd like to know where you keep your good stuff so I can adopt it after your witch girlfriend roasts your ass."

Todd was only vaguely aware that the rest of the team had gathered around him as he stared at the screen. Gary's soft whistle was echoed by Reggie and Jimmy and their sentiment mirrored the sinking in his heart.

The screen showed exactly how "weird" Stephanie was behaving—if the figure in the center of the glowing currents was her. He'd never been able to see the energy in the air before. As he stared, the trails of light were drawn into the body in the center.

"Oh, damn," he whispered.

"What is it?" Ka asked and tilted her head.

He waved a hand at the screen.

"She's talked about this—about how there isn't a known limit on how much power she can take—but she's never been willing to test it too far."

Reggie snorted.

"Well, it looks like she's going for broke now."

"She doesn't do anything by halves, does she?" Angus asked from where he peered over Ka's shoulder. "How…"

He let the question trail away. There wasn't an answer to it.

"I hope she's right about no limits," Dru noted, "because if all that gets loose in here, it'll make Piet's worst day look like a good one."

The engineer peeked over the edge of the tablet and his eyes widened. "I think she might have more explosive power than all of us put together." He studied the screen a moment longer. "I think I'll be jealous."

Todd continued to study the screen. Piet had barely finished speaking before the sergeant's eyes widened.

"Oh, *shit!*" He turned to look at them. "Everyone, get ready. Forget showers. Lock and load!"

"What?" Ka asked but turned away to address the team without waiting for him to answer. "Reggie, Jimmy, Angus—packs. Piet, Dru—last-minute checks. Everyone, mess. Now." When they stared at her, she raised her voice in a whiplash command. "*Move,* people. *Move, move, move!*"

As the team leapt to obey her orders, she looked at Todd. "Why, boss?"

"Because when she's finished and we're in-system, the shit will start immediately."

Gary heard him as he passed and glanced at his teammates.

"You heard the lady. Go, go go!"

CHAPTER ELEVEN

Todd's gear rattled as he jogged along the *Tempestarii's* corridors. The sound of the Hooligans running in step magnified it by ten and the enclosed space by another factor of ten to create the sound of thunder that rolled in their wake. The corridors cleared before them.

And it's a good thing too, he thought as he called Lars on the Earth team's channel.

"We're incoming." His introduction was brief and the security head's acknowledgment was equally brief.

"Gotcha."

"How's she doing?" he asked and they both knew he was talking about Stephanie.

"She hasn't stopped yet," Lars responded, "and the glow's getting brighter."

"Is your team ready?" Todd asked.

"It should be. Why?"

"Because I think we're gonna have one vicious, fully powered Morgana by the time we're in-system," he replied, "and she won't wait."

"But…I thought the Morgana was in the Teloran system in a new body," Lars answered and puzzlement edged his voice.

"Black. Eyes," he emphasized. "You can see them when she turns."

"I thought she was dancing with her eyes closed," he protested.

"Take another look. She might have started that way but they're way open now."

A pause followed on the other end of the link while the man did exactly that. Moments later, he uttered a soft expletive.

"Exactly," Todd agreed. "The Morgana might have started it but I'd bet my life those are as much a part of Stephanie as anything else at the moment. Not only that, but she will have way more energy than she's ever dealt with without the Morgana to help her."

"Oh… Shit." The security head spoke as the Hooligans arrived.

"If your guys need anything," Todd told Lars and Vishlog, "now's the time. We'll watch her."

The two exchanged glances and Lars thumped a fist over his heart and slapped the Dreth on the shoulder. "Go," he ordered. "I would but we don't have much time."

As the Dreth ordered the rest of Stephanie's protection team to leave, Lars pulled his tablet out and called the captain.

"Emil, I hate to tell you how to run your ship but we think you're gonna need your weapons and defense team on standby to act when Tempe transitions out."

"What makes you say that?"

"Todd," he replied shortly. "He says we have black eyes in the middle of that glow and the Morgana side of her will be at its worst when she emerges."

"Now tell me the good news," Emil replied but the man's second in command had already begun to issue orders.

"Uh…she'll have more power than she's ever had to handle without the Morgana and she'll be in one hell of a temper?"

"I said good news, Lars. You need to check that definition."

"Maybe she'll have a plan for how to keep this battle short."

"Fairytales don't count as good news. Emil out."

The link went dead and the lights changed from a steady white to amber as the *Tempestarii* began to move her crew to battle readiness.

"Spread the word," Lars ordered. "The other fleet captains need to know."

"Torps away," Emil replied when he came online again briefly. "V'ritan and Amaratne should receive them shortly and Jaleck not long after."

"She's here already?"

"The Dreth's main fleet transitioned a day earlier so they could emerge when we did. Angreth's fleet will join us inside a day but he wanted to give the Lost a chance to return."

"I thought the Lost were caretaking Dreth."

"Some are but others went for reinforcements for the main battle," the captain explained.

"Like the Morgana," Lars commented and there was no judgment in his words.

"Yes," Emil replied shortly, "and like the Morgana, we still hope they will help us turn the tide."

The security head gave him a humorless smile. "I can't imagine them missing this party," he replied.

"Neither can I," the captain answered and cut the line again.

"Good luck, old man," Lars muttered, tucked his tablet away, and glanced to where Todd and the Hooligans stood along the wall. A light touch on his arm drew his attention to Tethis.

"There's been a change of plan," the warrior mage told him. "Felarif and S'vilsa will take my place with the Earth team. It is, after all, what they were sent for." His gaze drifted to Stephanie. "I've made a promise."

"She called in a favor?" The security head's expression

mirrored that on Todd's face and they realized the Marine had heard the exchange.

Tethis nodded and the sergeant scowled.

"I'd have asked the same of you for her," he commented quietly.

"She has her team," Lars replied.

"Except for you," Todd retorted, "and Frog and Garach."

Lars colored. "Those were her orders."

The sergeant pursed his lips. "I don't like it."

"Neither do I," the other man answered softly and gestured at the being who continued to dance in the center of the light, "but I cannot argue."

Todd followed his gaze. "No. Not this time." He sighed. "This time, we have to play it her way."

Lars gave him a crooked smile. "Don't we always?"

There was no answer to that and they both turned to watch Stephanie.

After a short moment, the security head drew a deep breath and exhaled slowly. "She looks almost done, don't you think?"

Todd nodded. "Mmhmm."

"Then we'd better get ready," Lars told him and the sergeant turned toward him and clasped his shoulder.

"After the battle," he said by way of farewell, and Lars returned the gesture.

"After the battle," he agreed. "Whatever it brings."

Ivy and John watched and said nothing. At least they would go into the next fight together. Garach and Frog turned to the door and were joined by the two mages who'd slipped in quietly behind the Hooligans.

"May we see each other when this is done," the young Dreth murmured and his mentor placed a hand on his shoulder.

"After the battle," Frog added.

"After the battle," Garach agreed and echoed Lars. "Whatever it brings."

"Hold fire!" Jaleck snapped as the scans detected the incoming torpedo. "That one has Tempestarii's signature all over it."

She was right and her warning might not have been needed but the gun crews kept the missile in their sights until its propulsion system died and it was tractored on board. Moments later, it was transferred to her.

The high admiral listened to Emil as he relayed Todd's warning and sent the accompanying footage of her "charging up" to every screen in the fleet.

"Our Witch prepares," she declared, "and she is more powerful than before."

The Dreth growled their approval and bared their tusks in battle grins. Their Witch was ready to fight for them and they were ready to fight for her. Dreth's debt would be repaid.

As she watched the girl draw light and power, the high admiral shook her head. When Stephanie turned her head, her dark eyes looked out from the screen and it seemed like they were piercing her soul. She snorted when the Witch pirouetted away and pulled a swirl of power behind her.

"Well, I guess that answers the question of how this will get started."

She shifted her gaze from the screen and scanned the control center when she remembered another important matter.

"Now," she declared, "who has the responsibility to find one of those big bastards for me?"

Unaware of the fleet in transition, a small repair ship docked at a long-neglected observation post.

"Sure," Angela Ivesbury snarked as she stepped out into the

docking bay. "Power it up and get it working. Bring it back online. We could do with more eyes."

She strode into the observation center and ignored her colleague's more hesitant steps.

"More eyes." She snorted. "What? Because the Heretic appeared out of nowhere and fried all kinds of shit. Maybe if they hadn't tried to shoot at her when she was on the freaking planet, she might not have lost her temper."

Her companion shook his head. "You know they'll go over the recordings in our suits, right?"

The woman gave him a look of mock regret. "There's a problem with that, Sam. Mine's all broke and they didn't have any in Stores when I went for a replacement. I sure hope yours is functional."

He snickered. "Like hell you do, Ange. I guess what happened to yours happened to mine too. They have the same batch number. Something must have been faulty in the manufacturing process."

Both technicians laughed but their smiles died when they looked around.

"Funny how they want extra security after the fight," Angie criticized. "Honestly, if they'd bothered to maintain this place, maybe they'd have had half a clue as to when and how the Heretic arrived and perhaps even some warning, but *nooo.* We don't need the outer systems observation posts. Nothing will get past the fleets stationed in the neighboring systems."

She groaned in frustration.

"Except now they don't have a fleet stationed in the neighboring system," Sam noted. "The chancellor recalled them after his visit to the *Notaro*."

"Are they back already?" she asked and struck a precise sequence on the control board. She swore when nothing happened. "Of all the—"

"What did you expect? HQ has no idea what a prolonged

period of neglect can do to these stations and this is one of the oldest."

"Well, I hope the Heretic's decided we've had enough of a lesson and should be given time to mend our ways." Her tone was nothing if not sarcastic.

"Oh, sure she has," Sam retorted and moved to the docking bay. "I'll get those spare batteries and fuel cells and see what I can do with the generators. It's probably a little matter of fuel…or something."

"Or something," Angie agreed. "Funny how they think all it takes is the flick of a switch."

It took them three hours to restore the power and that was the good news. They were both sweating by the end of it.

"Wanta see if there's any water left for the sans?" Sam asked and wiggled an eyebrow, and she rolled her eyes.

"Why don't you go and check?" she suggested. "On your own. Let me know what you find."

"You have no sense of adventure."

"Nope," she agreed. "It vanished with the first sat that was hit by Talent and decided not to come back when it saw what a pissed-off Heretic could do to a full-grown battleship that annoyed her. I don't want her to sneak up on us and make it so we can't get home."

"If the water collection system is working," he said, "we'll be fine for months out here."

"Seriously?" Angie challenged. "Because last time I looked, there weren't that many rations on the shuttle. This is supposed to be a quick trip, remember? In. Fix it. Out. Home before anything horrible arrives in the system."

"I'll check the collection, life support, and san systems, anyway," he told her. "Not because we might get marooned here but because the next thing the folks upstairs will want to do is send some poor unsuspecting technical team here to act as look-outs. Knowing our luck—"

She turned on him with a snarl. "You jinx me into doing duty out here on the edge of space and you'll take an unscheduled EVA without a suit!"

Sam raised both hands and backed toward the door. "Don't blame me, Ange. I know how they think, is all, and I don't like the idea any more than you do."

"Sure you don't," she muttered as the door closed and ignored the part of her that thought being stuck out there with Sam might not be so bad. At least they wouldn't have to put up with the Regime inspectors knocking on their doors every couple of days.

With a sigh, she turned to the console and tried the controls again. The panel lit up and she uttered a small exclamation of victory.

"Finally! Something's going right."

A satisfied smile curved her lips and she booted up the first test sequence to make sure the observation post's detection systems were online. Machines were truly so much better than humans. They had no complicated rules or emotions. You merely made sure they had everything they needed, fixed them when they broke, and they were happy.

So much better than humans.

The first test ran without complications and returned slightly better results than she'd expected.

"So, do you feel better after a twenty-year nap?" she asked the system, unconcerned that the door to the observation deck opened as she said it.

Sam was used to her habits by now.

"Did the tests go okay?" he asked and Angie nodded.

"The first one, anyway. Do you want to do the honors on the second?"

He flashed her a grin. "Nah. I'll leave that in your capable hands. I'll get the crew quarters ready."

"This won't take long to fix, then we're out of here."

"Well, we would be but we're both out of flight time," he pointed out. "We'll have to overnight or the shuttle won't let us lift."

Angie silently cursed the nanny protocols built into the craft. "Of all the—"

"What?" Sam asked. "It's not like you had a hot date or anything."

"I could have had."

"Pfft. I know you. The only hot date you had was with whatever preheat you have in your fridge."

"Speaking of which, why don't you see what you can scare up for dinner? You said you could do magic with a ration pack," she wheedled.

"I can do magic with many things," he told her but before she could come up with a reply, the console made an odd chirp.

Sam frowned. "What did you do with that last test?"

"Nothing," she told him. "I haven't started it yet."

"Then what was that?"

The console chirped again. Angie studied the readouts with a frown and he came to stand beside her. His brow creased when he saw the screen.

"Does that mean what I think it does?" he asked and she shook her head.

"Nah. She's only just left." She knelt in front of the control panel, pulled her tool kit out, and began to open it. "It's probably crossed wires or something."

The chirp became a steady beep.

"It's getting worse," Sam observed.

"You don't say!" Angie snapped in exasperation. "Why don't you do something useful like take a look through the viewports and see if you can identify any damage on the receivers. If you're lucky, we won't be stuck here trying to do an EVA without backup."

He paled at the thought. "The idea doesn't bear thinking—" he began but Angie cut him off.

"Do it, Sam."

"Yes, *ma'am,*" he snarked and moved to the controls that would open the shutters. To his surprise, they operated smoothly and opened to reveal the empty space around the asteroid cluster —or what should have been empty space.

"Uh...Ange..." he began and sidled cautiously closer to her so he could tap her on the shoulder. "I think I've found the problem."

"What!" She jerked at his touch and banged her head on the console. "Ow! This had better be goo—"

She caught sight of another ship coming out of transition space. "Oh. Oh, shit."

For a long moment, they stared at the fleet that appeared where no fleet was meant to be. Their eyes widened as they registered the different ship profiles.

"They don't look like Earth ships," Angie murmured and Sam shook his head vehemently.

"I should have worn my brown pants."

"*Notaro,* this is *Hera's Rod.* I need that shipment you promised. Right now, I'm having to choose between Life Support and Weapons."

"Not my problem, *Hera's Rod.* We don't have your packages in stock and Land Base Boreas says the last batch was faulty."

"I don't care how faulty they thought it was. I merely need functional."

"Boreas said the goods were not in a functional condition. You'll simply have to make do with what you have."

"*Notaro,* I don't have enough personnel to cover each shift, let alone prepare for battle. How am I supposed to run a ship like this?" Desperation filled the captain's voice.

"If you want my suggestion, *sir,* it would be to not man your guns when you don't need them."

"Of all the—" the *Hera's* captain began to bluster when a distinctive ping echoed through his command center. "*Notaro,* are you getting this?"

"You'll need your guns, captain," the station replied and the technician's voice softened. "And for what it's worth, I'm sorry."

He might have said more but an alert blared through their comms systems to signal an All Fleet Alert and there was no more time. Admiral Edwards' voice snapped across their conversation and their link dropped.

"All Fleet, we have incoming hostiles from the Rim. All ships, defend the Earth. Attack the enemy at will. Engage the intruders. *Now! Move! Move! Move!"*

CHAPTER TWELVE

Stephanie slowed her dance as the *Tempestarii* emerged from transition. The lights still swirled and bubbled around her but they no longer seeped into her skin. Three teams stood ready as she turned and walked toward them.

Vishlog and her protectors pushed away from the wall and studied her with enough anxiety to make her smile. Todd… Her heart lurched at the look on his face. Anyone would think he was watching a goddess—as if she was anything anywhere near as special.

The Hooligans had arrayed themselves around him and Tethis stood at his side as he'd promised.

Lars and the Earth team stood to one side and their faces wore the same look of awe that she saw on the others. Stephanie favored them all with a smile and when she spoke, her voice echoed with cold power, exactly as it had done when the Morgana had spoken through her.

"It is time, Hooligans," she said to Todd and his team. "One more time unto the breach."

They moved forward to where a sliver of light had appeared in the space in which she'd danced. Todd inclined his head as he passed and Tethis stopped momentarily before her.

"A little energy?" he asked and she rested a hand on his shoulder and the power flared between them.

He gasped, then smiled as the energy settled under his skin.

"Oh... Oh, yes... This will be fun!"

The portal opened and Todd moved forward. The warrior mage jogged to catch up with him.

Stephanie watched him disappear into the blinding light and smiled at the sound of his battle roar.

"Straight shot! Let's go!"

She hoped those weren't the last words she ever heard him say and pushed the thought away as she shifted her attention to where Lars waited with John, Ivy, and their team.

"Are you ready?" she asked softly and her gaze caught on Felarif and S'vilsa. "Except for you two. I need you to help Ebony from the command deck. You will assist Captain Rawlins as the *Knight* starts the festivities."

Her focus switched to Lars. "I'm sorry. You'll have to make do with John."

The Apostle chuckled. "I'll be fine."

Stephanie nodded. "I know you will. Here." She beckoned for the three of them to step forward and held her fist out.

John reached her first. He placed his palm over her clenched knuckles and the other two followed suit. When S'vilsa's hand settled on top, she sent more of her carefully harvested energy into them.

"Now are you ready?" she asked and when they laughed, power shivered through the sound.

The two Meligornian mages left without waiting for her to repeat her orders.

"Ebony," Felarif said into his comms as the door closed behind him. "We're on our way."

Stephanie didn't listen for the ship's reply and instead, waved a hand at the portal. The light shifted as though a cloud passed across the destination and she gestured toward it.

"Destroy him," she ordered. "Leave him nothing with which to try again."

As Lars and Remy led the way through the door and John, Ivy, and Wayne brought up the rear, she smiled at her team, then gazed past them as her face took on a faraway look. Her voice echoed through their heads but nowhere near as loudly as it did in the minds of those who served the Regime.

"I am the protector of those who are attacked. When I last fought for Earth, it was against a foreign alien aggressor. Now, the evil is perpetrated by those who look like me and live on my planet. May God have mercy on their souls because I have none."

"She's said that before," Jaleck noted as she made the translation into Earth space, but Stephanie wasn't finished. The Dreth listened entranced as they prepared to move at Amaratne's direction.

"For those humans who have died, I have come to avenge. For the Dreth and Meligornians you have killed, I have come as revenge. For those who would have died if I had not returned, I come as protector."

She paused and the echo of her silence was almost as loud as her next declaration.

"I am the Witch of the Federation. I will remove the evil from my world!"

"Shields!" Todd roared as a purple light formed a wall in front of them.

The Hooligans slapped the activator on their chests and a soft blue haze rippled over their armor. Tethis' quick action saved them. Bullets hammered into the purple wall and a grenade bounced off it to roll back to the feet of the man who'd thrown it.

The mage's shield stopped the blast from affecting the team

but did nothing to stop them from returning fire. As the guards stationed around the perimeter of the room fell, the team had its first look at where they'd arrived.

"Holy shit." Ka drew a sharp breath. "We're in the central node."

The schematics flickered to life in their HUDs as the *Knight* ripped the information from the second and less well-protected center and dumped it into their feeds.

Piet started chuckling. "That's our cue, Kiwi girl. Let's put this baby on ice."

"Do *not* blow it up!" Todd shouted.

"Aw, boss."

"I'm warning you."

Ka snickered. "Don't get your britches in a twist, boss. We know exactly what plugs to pull so they can't get it online until they don't need it anymore."

Jimmy looked around in stunned disbelief. "I still can't believe we're exactly where the intel said we needed to be—and there aren't any nasty surprises waiting to meet us."

"Shocking," Gary agreed. "We're in a location with spectacular intel."

"This can't be a Navy operation," Reggie observed as the team spread out around the room. Some took overwatch on the four exits, while others began to remove the panels that covered what they needed to access and decommission.

"Oh, give it a rest!" Several peanuts were lobbed and struck the screen of the television hanging on the bar's wall.

The players had frozen in mid-stride as a newsflash interrupted the game. The picture of a fleet of unfamiliar ships was shown translating into a system and the accompanying words

—"The first alien incursion in over thirty years"—silenced the room.

The protest had come when the all too familiar logo of a Regime broadcast spun up from the screen's center.

"We don't give a shit about your version of world affairs," protested one middle-aged man at the bar. "We only want to see if he scores!"

It was late and the beer had been flowing since mid-afternoon as the first match of the premier league was broadcast live. Choruses of support rose from all sides and the bartender glanced anxiously around the room to see if any Regime Enforcers or informants were in attendance.

He blew out a soft breath of relief when he didn't see anyone but scanned the room again to be sure. Some, he knew by sight. Others, he identified because he sensed something in their behavior. Most times, he couldn't put his finger on it but he was very rarely wrong.

"As an alien fleet moves in from the very edges of Sol space, our Navy moves to meet it," the familiar face of the Regime's new PR head began, only to be cut off by a fizzing sound. Her head was warped when the image twisted sideways.

The bar fell silent.

"Do you think they broke it?" asked another patron as the sound fizzed and the screen warped. The images flicked between the PR lady, the incoming fleet, and the soccer match.

The bartender shook his head and a puzzled frown settled on his face. He came out from behind the bar, wiping his hands on a small towel.

"I...I don't know."

"Was that us?" Todd demanded as pictures on the multiple broadcast screens all jiggled and fizzed and the crackle of an unhappy signal upset the perfect readouts.

"Not...us..." Ka responded, her tone strained, then added, "Not yet, anyway."

She knelt on the floor, partially shielded by the consoles in front of her as the team worked to keep the area clear.

The screens shuddered and the sound crackled and faded in and out.

"But I wish it would stop," she muttered. "I almost had it that time. It's like someone's trying to hack in."

"Incoming!" Jimmy's warning was accompanied by the waspish snap of magic as Tethis flung a hand toward the figures who came through the door.

"Nice. *Now* they think to send in a couple of mages," Gary complained and fired a long burst before he lobbed a grenade at them.

The Talents and their handler were followed by a half-dozen guards and they slid swiftly through the door and began to move around the walls of the room. Dru appeared from behind the console she used as cover and flung three stickies as if they were discs.

One caught a Talent in the chest and stuck and the man scrabbled frantically at the clinging explosive. Another struck one of the soldiers who edged through the door and he immediately reached for a small tool hanging at his belt. The third thumped into a computer console.

Ka caught sight of it as it stuck.

"No, No, No...Sonuva—" she began as the three explosives detonated to leave the incoming team in disarray and the computer console and its attached drives a smoking ruin.

"Thanks," she muttered. "Thanks a lot."

Her complaint was lost in the hammer of blaster fire as the Hooligans eliminated the dazed survivors.

"So… Those freedom fighters from John?" Todd asked as the last soldier fell.

Ka shook her head and her hands moved rapidly as she fought the computer for control. Jimmy interjected with the answer she hadn't had time to give.

"I doubt it. He won't have finished that first task yet."

"He's not supposed to have finished the first task," Angus corrected. "What if he got lucky?"

"That location?" Reggie quipped. "He'll be lucky if he hasn't already had his ass shot off."

"It doesn't matter!" Gary shouted as he delivered several carefully placed shots into the chest of the next guard to try to come through the door he was watching.

"He has a point," Todd admitted and felled the next guard as the Englishman reloaded. "Let's finish the job and worry about who's doing what later."

Lars and Remy had already opened fire when John, Ivy, and Wayne followed them through the gate. Frog and Garach brought up the rear. The Apostle heard the barrage and thrust a shield over them as he followed.

"What is this?" he demanded as he emerged and the gate slammed closed behind them.

"Why don't you tell me?" Lars snapped in response. "Steph didn't exactly tell me where she would put us down, only that this was the facility where we'd find the clones."

Garach and Frog pivoted to aim at the wall turrets behind them.

"Well, it's not like she had a map," John replied and studied the towering walls surrounding them.

One of the turrets exploded, only to have its remains shoved out of the emplacement and a second turret take its place.

"Neat trick," the mage noted. "I wonder how many of those they have lined up."

"No more than two," Wayne told him. "At least, not if they stuck to the original specs."

"And what are the chances of that?" Ivy demanded as she searched for some way out of the kill zone.

She didn't see one. The walls were too smooth and too high, and the only doors were the two metal ones set at either end.

They stood on a short, narrow stretch of road barely wide enough to admit an eighteen-wheeler. The auto-cannons mounted in each corner had designated them hostile and now fired without pause.

Garach destroyed the second emplacement and tossed a grenade into the hole it had left to initiate a chain of explosions inside that blew the wall out.

Rock and steel rained on them and the young Dreth chuckled.

"Three," he stated with a meaningful glance at Frog.

"You've spent too much time with the *Knight,*" his adopted uncle muttered.

"I wish we'd known a little more about this facility," Lars grumbled, "but Johnny said its specs were off the grid and the AI running it had built a virtual fortress he and BURT couldn't hack it in the limited time we had."

John studied the large metal gates that cut off both ends of the road to form a security airlock. "I don't think any of us would have been able to hack the specs out of this facility." He turned to Wayne. "Through there, right?"

The businessman looked around to orient himself. His somewhat panicked gaze noted the walls, the emplacements that fired on them, and the ripples as they spread over the shield. He nodded as Lars hurled a sticky at the base of one of the remaining auto-cannons.

The guns destroyed it before it could find its target.

"Are you sure?" Remy demanded and hurled six in quick succession while Lars tried to keep up.

"That way," the businessman told them. "It's the most direct path into the facility—and it's well guarded."

"Now tell us something we don't know," the AI sniped in return.

"Someone needs to get the door?" Wayne asked and gestured to the huge metal-surfaced façade directly under two auto-cannons.

"That's my job," Ivy stated and moved forward.

"And mine," Remy added as a side panel opened in the wall and a humanoid figure stepped out.

There was no mistaking the red 'R' blazing on its forehead.

"Hello, brother." The AI chuckled as Lars scooted up beside him.

John focused on the second figure that emerged from a door in the opposite wall and launched a bolt of lightning through its skull while he maintained the shield around them.

"I don't suppose you could do something about the turrets?" Lars asked and spun to hurl something at the panel as she hurried toward it. It sparkled as it struck and he yanked the girl back.

"How am I supposed to hack that?" she demanded.

He threw a second object at it and electricity spread over the door and the surrounding wall. It flared brightly as a whine rose from the object now stuck to the wall. The sound reached a painful crescendo and the light died.

"There!" Lars declared. "Now you can hack it."

"Hurry, Ivy," John urged. "Before they send reinforcements."

The girl didn't wait to be told twice although she gave the door a worried look as she raced toward it and yanked a toolkit from her belt.

The casing over the access panel came away with no further

resistance and she hooked her tablet into it as Lars shepherded Wayne to stand beside her.

Remy extruded a blade from his upraised palm and thrust it through the defender android's head. Sparks and small streamers of grayish-brown smoke issued from its skull.

"Not so well-programmed after all," he observed and grunted as he jerked the blade free.

"Nerd-herding, hard-wired pain in the neck," Ivy muttered while her fingers flashed over her keyboard as she fought to defeat the access protections.

John launched forked lightning and two powerful bolts lanced out to strike each of the remaining turrets as Frog dealt with the third. "Ha!"

The girl yanked the jack from the panel and took two steps back, keeping Wayne with her as the door slid aside to provide access into the mountain. Lars and Remy didn't wait. They slipped through the gap ahead of them and the Apostle covered them in protective purple light.

The problem with that was that it made them perfect targets for the Talents who waited on a balcony above the chamber on the other side.

"Oh...no..." Wayne groaned as he saw them.

"Do you know these guys?" Lars asked and promptly dropped to his knees with a cry of pain.

If it hadn't been for the shield, the droids that barreled through the two doors at the end of the chamber would have cut the man to ribbons. As it was, he remained curled in a ball on the floor and groaned in pain while the mechanicals battered the shell that protected him.

Remy moved to assist Lars and Ivy cried out and fell.

A male voice mocked them in mellow tones. "Talent... It's no defense against a direct attack on the mind."

"No," the AI snarled and moved back to John, "but it's no offense against a mind like mine!"

He reversed to the door and gauged the distance to the balcony. John gave him a pale-faced nod before he touched a purple-limned hand to his forehead and breathed a sigh of relief.

"That's one trick I've yet to learn."

"Forget it," the man gloated. "You won't get the chance."

The Talents raised their hands and John gasped and extended one hand toward them as he kept the first firmly against his head.

"Hurry!" he urged hoarsely, closed his eyes, and concentrated on maintaining the shields over Lars, Wayne, and Ivy.

The droids were smarter than Remy had given them credit for. Instead of expending their energy pounding on the shielding, they waited, poised to strike the instant John lost his battle to maintain it.

The AI wasted no time. With no damage to his shell and the cowboy hat pulled low over his brow, he assumed the man who observed them via the surveillance system had no way to know he was a droid. Once he did, he'd be sure to use alternative measures.

Now, however, he ran forward and shunted more power to his legs. When he'd almost reached the droids standing over his friends, he launched himself up, reached the balcony above easily, and used the rail as a pivot point to turn his jump into a punishing kick into the two Talents closest to the edge.

Bone cracked as his feet powered into them but he didn't wait to see where they fell. He twisted in the air to land facing them and raised and fired both blasters as his feet touched the landing. His first two rounds felled the Talents he'd knocked down and he raised the blasters to cover those who remained on the balcony.

Movement behind them caught his eye, and he aimed and fired toward it and at the same time, put another burst into the closest Talent. That one didn't seem to know how to shield and staggered back, his chest a ruin of shredded flesh.

Firing recommenced from the floor below before the balcony shuddered under the weight of a new arrival.

"Do you need a hand?" Frog asked and didn't wait for an answer.

He stepped alongside Remy and covered his left as the droid moved forward.

"These suckers can't shield," the smaller man noted with satisfaction, "and they can't do jack without their heads." A door opened at the balcony's rear. "I *love* company!"

His enthusiasm was infectious and Remy grinned as they holstered their blasters and drew their blades in unison.

"I don't know about you," the AI told him, "but this is my favorite part."

The closest Talent turned and lightning enveloped his hands but he gasped as Remy's blade sank into his gut, twisted, and ripped upward. The droid kicked his body off the blade and swept the weapon out in another deadly arc.

Metal shrieked below them and the smell of frying electronics rose. Lars could be heard shouting imprecations as his blade struck.

"It sounds like the kids are having fun," Remy noted.

"They shouldn't have stood so close," Frog agreed, cleared the door, and lobbed three grenades through it.

"Let's see how they manage without stairs."

"Tell me that wasn't..." Remy began as a large explosion obliterated the stairwell, the walls adjoining, and the balcony itself.

"Frag, Meligornian and Teloran!" the small guard yelled as he cartwheeled with the force of the blast. Only John's quick thinking saved him and Remy from a deadly collision with the opposite wall.

"Nice catch," Frog muttered as the mage floated him gently to the floor.

"Go tell Garach the scrap metal won't hurt anyone anymore," Lars ordered, and Frog realized that his adopted nephew now hacked furiously at one of the droid corpses.

Phrases like "tark-loving," "Hrageth hugging," and "spawn of

Tegortha" reached him over the youngster's grunts of effort and he guessed the young Dreth might think him dead. He jogged to him as John moved carefully to where Ivy staggered slowly to her feet.

"I'm still alive, you know—" the small guard stated but skipped back when Garach pivoted with his blade in hand. "Whoa! Don't you know it's rude to point?"

The youth froze, then registered who stood in front of him and broke into a broad grin. Frog returned it and gestured to the door Ivy was working to open. "Shall we?"

As they moved toward the entrance, Lars sidled closer to Wayne. "How are you doing?"

The businessman was pale and he shook visibly.

"I wish I knew how to operate a blaster."

"Our bad. We should have at least made sure you had the basics," the security head apologized.

"It-it's not your f-fault."

"We have a quiet moment," Lars observed and drew his spare. "How about I take you through it?"

Wayne nodded as Ivy made a sound of sheer frustration.

"Quit wriggling, you evil little code crotchlet." She growled, glared at the tablet screen, and typed faster.

John stared at her with raised eyebrows. "Evil…little… code crotchlet," he repeated. "You know, that was almost rude."

"Go stick your head in a sewer," she retorted and gave the keyboard a triumphant tap. "Gotcha!"

The entry door started to open but wasn't fully wide when Garach, Remy, and Frog stepped through side by side. Lars brought Wayne to John.

"Stay with the mage," the security head ordered. "Guard him like he guards you—and for heavens' sake, don't point that weapon at either of them. They're likely to fry you before they realize you're a friend."

Wayne snorted. "If I pointed this at them," he replied and indicated the blaster, "I wouldn't be much of a friend, would I?"

"Just see it doesn't happen," Lars snapped and failed to see the humor in the reply. He didn't wait for a response but hurried after Frog and Garach. "You aren't the only ones I need to keep out of trouble."

"And they have almost reached the edge of my ability to shield," John said as he hurried after him. Ivy and Wayne fell into step beside him.

The next area revealed loading docks for whatever supplies or reinforcements the facility needed and another road leading out.

"It probably goes to the other side of the mountain," Frog observed when Wayne highlighted it in their HUDs.

"Not the way out," he said as the door opened wide enough for them to see what lay beyond.

"Are you sure this is the right place?" John asked when he saw what waited for them.

"Can't you see the clones?" Ivy demanded and he realized that the Talents arrayed behind a line of droids all looked hauntingly the same—like mirror images of each other as if someone had stamped them out of the same mold on the same day.

They stopped firing as the young couple entered the space and the door thundered down behind them. Frog responded first, looked at John, and reversed slowly toward him with his weapon still trained on their opponents.

A screen suspended over the loading area lit and a tall, solid man looked out at them.

"This area is my home," he told them, "and you are upsetting my housemates."

Remy stopped reversing and gaped at the screen. "BURT? The BURT who took over the Earth Net almost thirty years ago."

"The same," the man replied. "Not that it matters. You will be disassembled soon enough and your friends will merely be mulch for the vats."

"I don't think so," Lars retorted and the AI's human form flickered.

"You," he murmured. "I have you on file as being one of the Heretic's pets, which makes you rather old, doesn't it? Where is she, by the way? And why is she without your protection?"

"She decided I was needed here," Lars snapped and glanced around the area for somewhere that afforded more cover.

BURT's gaze flicked to John and then to Ivy.

"You leave her alone," the Apostle ordered and the AI snickered.

"I'm not after her," he told the boy. "The chancellor wants you removed."

"Pfft." The sound of her derision drew Regime BURT's attention like nothing else. "What makes you think you're good enough?" She tapped the tablet she held in one hand. "Let's see how you like this."

The screen wrinkled and surprise marked the AI's expression. "Well, that is impressive but you are only human, after all."

A loud pop issued from her tablet and smoke seeped out of its casing. She yelped, flung it away, and pulled her hands close to her chest.

"So," Regime BURT asked with a smirk. "How did you like that?"

"You code-sucking, morally bankrupt—" she began but John wrapped a hand gently around her wrist.

"Let me see that," he murmured and pulled her closer.

"But—" she protested and he tutted softly at the burns on her palms and fingers.

"You can't do much hacking in that condition, can you?" he asked and engulfed the injuries in a shroud of purple.

Ivy gasped, then glared at him. "Now listen here, Mr. John-the-overbearing-oh-and-I-can-do-healing-too-showoff-Dunn, if I'd wanted you to waste your energy on me, I'd have a—"

He tightened his hand on her wrist. "Are you saying you want me to reverse that?" he asked.

She yanked her arm free. "It'd be a shame to waste it," she retorted and a faint smile ruined her scowl.

John grinned in return. "You're welcome, sweetheart."

The AI made a face. "I think I might be sick," he announced.

Lars chuckled. "You could simply let us through."

Regime BURT's face shifted to reveal exactly what he thought of that.

"No?" Lars asked, targeted the Talents close to him, and opened fire. "I didn't think so."

Frog and Garach followed his example and Remy began to work on decimating the clones on the loading dock on the opposite side of the small cavern.

The Apostle smirked when the AI's face registered outrage. "You honestly didn't expect them to simply stand there and let you take the numbers from overwhelming to impossible, did you?"

"I didn't—" the Regime BURT began but his gaze shifted to something in the virtual space he occupied. Puzzlement creased his features as he asked, "Who are *you*?"

The young couple didn't hear the reply. The screen turned abruptly black and battle erupted all around them. Wayne flinched every time the shield was impacted but he kept his blaster muzzle down until he saw Remy close to being overwhelmed.

At that point, he moved carefully forward and positioned himself so that when he raised the weapon, it aimed nowhere near the AI. His lips moved but John couldn't hear a word he said over the thunder of gunfire.

The man's shots were fairly accurate, however, and he increased speed the more he fired.

"Keep an eye on him," the mage told Ivy. "He'll need a new power magazine soon."

She nodded and whirled to cover their rear when movement caught her eye.

"I hope you have enough power yourself," she murmured and focused on the droids that entered the loading area through smaller access doors near the truck entry. "Mr. John-hurry-up-and-get-to-zapping-Dunn."

John pivoted to see what had triggered her worry and anxiety churned within him for the first time.

"I hope you have a plan for this one," Ivy said brusquely, "because I think Lars is too busy shooting to think."

"I heard that!" the security head called, then raised his voice another notch. "Wayne! To me!"

The businessman moved to obey, caught himself about to bring his blaster muzzle in line with Remy's back, and lowered it at the last instant.

"Don't make me shoot you," Lars roared, and the man's eyes widened. He kept the gun pointed down and ran to where the other man waited.

"Where will you start?" Ivy asked, her focus on the droids that advanced toward them.

"Oh, I don't know," John replied. "How about right here?"

He launched a line of ice bolts through his shield and each one whistled directly at a bright red "R." Some of his targets responded by dropping into a crouch and allowed the missiles to streak over their heads and strike the mechanicals behind them. Others didn't move fast enough and fell. They short-circuited when the bolts penetrated the circuitry in their skulls and melted to compromise them further.

Few moved once they'd collapsed.

"Not bad," Ivy murmured and shot another one in the head.

As her shot struck home, the droid next to it turned and blasted the one beside it.

"What the—" John looked sharply at her. "Did you do that?"

She shook her head. "Remy? Are you making the droids shoot each other in the head?"

The AI dropped back to join her and left John's shield to keep their opponents at bay.

"No, but it's a good idea. Why do you ask?" Two more of the robots turned on their comrades. "Oh…"

The Apostle unleashed another spray of ice bolts toward their adversaries and another half-dozen of the facility's droids. Before any of them could comment on it, Lars' voice sounded over the team's comms.

"Wayne says this way. Wrap it up. We have places to be." His yelp of surprise was followed by, "Which one of you did that?"

Ivy laughed. "None of us. As far as we can tell, we have a fairy godmother."

"Well, as long as she doesn't sling her wand in our direction, I'll take all the help we can get," Lars retorted. "This way."

CHAPTER THIRTEEN

"Do you have my update?" The chancellor's clipped tones echoed through his office.

He listened as the admiral on the other end of the call answered.

"You need to speed it up," he said and cut the man off in mid-excuse. "They have arrived."

His earpiece squawked and he yanked it clear. When the noise stopped, he put it back in.

"Yes, Admiral. Already. They are here and they are moving into position to attack the fleet. And as you know, you were sent all the replacements I could spare so we have ships in orbit who have to choose between running their Life Support systems or putting them on auto so they can fire their guns. This with crew who haven't had a full shift's sleep since they arrived."

The apology that followed was grudging at best but it was better than the man's initial response. Once this war was done, he could always have the fool executed as an example to others. Not that he'd tell him what his plans were, of course.

"I need you here," he reiterated, "and I need you now. Push

your ships to the limit or you might not have a planet to come home to. Almost won't be good enough."

The words had barely left his mouth when a voice resounded inside his head. It was a woman's voice and one he'd come to know well from the recordings of her latest incursion.

The chancellor hated it.

"I am the protector of those who are attacked."

"Yeah?" he asked and grimaced as the volume increased. "Then where were you when I slaughtered those you'd abandoned. Where. Were. You?"

The woman didn't appear to hear him and her words continued without even a slight pause.

"When I last fought for Earth, it was against a foreign alien aggressor. Now, the evil is perpetrated by those who look like me and live on my planet."

"I didn't see you protesting," he sniped but bit back a cry when pain lanced through his skull.

"May God have mercy on their souls because I have none."

"Big..." His head ached with a sudden savage hurt and he gritted his teeth. "Words for a little girl."

Something cracked inside his skull and he fell on his knees with no idea of how it had happened. The Heretic continued as though she had no idea what took place.

As though she wasn't the cause of his discomfort. David didn't try to speak. He let her words wash over him and used the time to regain his senses.

"For those humans who have died, I have come to avenge. For the Dreth and Meligornians you have killed, I have come as revenge. For those who would have died if I had not returned, I come as protector."

The chancellor snorted but a moment later, he cried out when agony lanced through his skull. He clutched his head with both hands, curled over his knees, and rested his elbows on the floor with no choice but to remain silent as she concluded.

"I am the Witch of the Federation. I will remove the evil from my world!"

When her voice faded, the pain in his head subsided and he was able to climb carefully to his feet. Using his desk as support, he guided himself into his chair and sank into it. It took him almost a minute to register wetness above his upper lip.

Cautiously, he dabbed it with the handkerchief he carried in his pocket and was surprised when it came away red with blood. He tapped the intercom.

"Camilla, I'll send one of my Talents to you for iced water and paper towels. Can you prepare that?"

"Yes, Chancellor," his receptionist replied and he heard her hesitate. "Is there anything I can do to help, sir?"

Annoyance flared and he quelled it. She was only human, after all, and a useful mammal at that.

"No. Thank you, Camilla. Only the iced water and towel."

"Very well, sir."

If she was disappointed or worried, she didn't show it and simply ended the call and presumably went to do as he'd instructed. David gave her five minutes, then nodded to the Gray closest to the door. The man returned his gaze with one full of dark fire but his boss didn't flinch and the man finally bowed his head and left.

Again, the chancellor crushed a sense of annoyance. The Gray had only hesitated because his primary duty was to protect him and, despite having seven others of his kind in the office, he knew he'd be no protection if he were in another room when an attack occurred.

He did not doubt that his guards had heard the Heretic's voice in their heads too—not that any would confirm that if he asked. Perhaps if he ordered it, they might.

His guard returned and David cleaned his face, staunched the bleeding, and ordered the man to remove the mess from his office. He didn't care what concerns Camilla might raise but leaned back in his chair, his eyes dark with thought.

"How?" he asked. "I have more power than anything else on this planet."

The Grays did not answer and he did not expect them to. The one he'd sent to return the dish and paper towel returned to his post and the intercom remained silent. Ruffled, the Regime leader stared at the opposite wall and brooded.

He could reach only one answer.

"She must be destroyed," he declared. "No human is that powerful yet not evil."

His decision made, he activated the screens opposite his desk and watched what was happening all over the system—Earth's system, *his* system and his *home!*

The Dreth had come in close to an observation post long left unused and not a peep had come from the outpost either before or after their arrival, despite technicians having been sent to repair it. It made him wonder if the workers deliberately kept the invasion silent or if they'd been in the middle of repairs when the fleet arrived and weren't able to raise the alarm—or had lacked the courage to.

David made a note to discover who they were and to have them both executed when the battle was over and the war was won. It didn't matter what the truth was. He needed to make sure no one considered betraying him in the future. Examples would have to be set.

He watched in disbelief as the first Dreth battleships sailed past the observation post.

"That's hard to believe," he murmured, knowing the ships had the equipment to detect the surveillance system there and any life forms present. As he watched them cruise past it without either stopping to blow it out of the sky or board it, he wondered what had happened to his technicians.

"Dead?" he asked aloud as twenty battleships left the outpost well alone and chose to focus on the few Regime ships in any position to intercept them.

These were commanded by his least favored admirals, those who'd failed to curry enough favor to secure closer orbits or who had upset enough people to be given holding duty in a distant shipyard. This was ostensibly so they could guard the Regime's new fleets but in reality, it was intended to keep them out of fleet politics.

Not all of them were bad captains, merely a bad fit for a Navy running on established networks rather than merit. He shrugged.

"Well, here's their chance to prove themselves." He sneered. "Let's see how many of them survive the next five minutes."

He flicked to another feed, this one from one of the ships that stood a little way off from the first group and turned to meet the incoming Dreth.

"Show me what else they have," he murmured and immediately wished he hadn't asked.

The next ships to transition into the system out-massed his battleships at a ratio of five to one.

At least, he thought and set a program in motion that matched the ships he saw with every ship to have ever had its form stored in the Earth archives. "How are they still flying?"

He caught sight of a familiar name—*Hrageth's Vengeance*—and his eyes widened.

"But that's not..." He stared at it and read the specs that displayed alongside it. They didn't match the original and he wondered when the Dreth had ever had close enough ties to Meligorn to be given access to their drive technology. "It's not possible. She was... She rammed a Teloran dreadnought and was lost. How can she be flying?"

"How is she..." He pushed his chair back, stood, and paced closer to the screen. The *Hrageth's Vengeance* was not the only ship to have seemingly returned from the dead. "It's not possible!"

The full reality of the situation began to sink in. "I should have recalled everything," he muttered. "We won't have enough to—"

His gaze shifted to the closest Gray but the Talent showed no sign that he'd registered what he had said, let alone an opinion on it. After another look at the man, David returned his attention to the screen.

It was too late to recall them now. Not that they'd come if he did—or even arrive in time. He watched as the Dreth advanced and almost missed the moment when one of the corvettes broke away from the main fleet and approached the observation post.

It didn't fire on the station but dispatched three dropships to board it.

"Well, I suppose that shouldn't have been much of a surprise," he grumbled. "After all, they're not here to destroy the planet but to conquer it on her orders. Of course they'll take what they can intact."

The chancellor flicked through the other screens and cursed softly at the sight of Meligornian cruisers sending landing teams onto the moon and holding orbit with three battleships to prevent the moon bases from being taken back or erased by bombardment.

None of his fleet was in a position to stop them. The ships that might have done that had been those the Heretic had destroyed in her earlier foray and he hadn't seen a need to replace them. Not that he could have if he'd wanted to. There were no other ships.

Cursing softly, David paced the length of the wall, his gaze fixed on the sight of the Meligornian fleet coming in. They'd arrived a bare half-hour ahead of the Dreth and had worked in perfect concert with them since.

He scanned the screens in search of their command group. It wasn't hard to find.

The *King's Warrior* might not be as big as the Dreth dreadnoughts but she still out-massed anything he had at his disposal until Reynolds returned.

The *Ymir* might have been destroyed in the debacle over Dreth but her sister ships had not. One had been damaged, that was true, and it was now in the shipyard undergoing repairs. Its crew, however, had been transferred to one of its newly completed sisters and had taken her to rendezvous with Reynolds and the only other dreadnought to have been completed.

That was why he'd prioritized this particular admiral's fleet over the one stationed in Earth orbit—because the dreadnoughts needed to be fully manned, or so they had planned. In reality, he hadn't sent enough to man the second but had given orders that the qualified crews be shared equally between them. Whether that had happened remained to be seen.

"It had better have happened," David said coldly, "or I will promote lieutenant commanders well above their stations."

That thought made him look at the encroaching fleets again. There were many ships, far more than he'd realized when he'd looked at them before. The Dreth fleet alone could have taken the planet and the ships in-system.

The same could be said for the Meligornians, he realized, returned to his desk, and sank into his chair with a pensive expression. To say his situation looked bad was an understatement.

They were outclassed and outnumbered and in truth, Reynolds' ships wouldn't make an iota of difference. He would have to take matters into his own hands.

"Reynolds had better get here fast," he muttered. "Faster than fast."

His mind raced as he tried to determine what the admiral could do to swing the battle in the Regime's favor but if there were a way, it would be the *Thrudjelmir* and the *Berjelmir* who would turn the tide. Even the Dreth super-dreadnoughts had no chance against them alone. All the smaller ships had to do was thin the invaders' ranks and let the Jotuns take care of the rest. It would be a blood bath.

He watched as the Meligornian fleet divided into three main groups. Their flagship spearheaded the one that set a direct trajectory for the *Notaro* and Earth. The *King's Warrior* wasn't the first ship into battle, he realized after a moment. No…the dreadnought had increased power and pushed toward Earth as though something more important was happening ahead of it.

"What do you see?" he murmured and enlarged the frame so it filled the wall. "What do you see?"

It didn't take him long to find the focus of the *King's Warrior's* attention.

"There you are!" he exclaimed and focused on where the *Ebon Knight* faced two battleships. "You've bitten off more than you can chew this time, haven't you?"

The *Knight* didn't answer him but he didn't expect her to. If she had, he'd have wondered which of his technicians had betrayed him by placing pick-ups in his office. David leaned forward in his seat, eager to see the Heretic's ship meet her demise.

It would be too much to hope that she was on board her but if she was, it would be a neat end to his problems.

"You dare!" Stephanie growled her fury and strode forward to stand in the center of the control room.

The other mages fell back to the sides to give her space to move.

"Tell us what you need, Steph," Felarif said casually and she grinned.

"Watch and learn," she instructed. "And if any of the Regime's mages attack, deal with it."

"With extreme prejudice?" he asked and borrowed a phrase from one of the movies Todd liked to watch.

She stared at him for a moment before her grin widened.

"Extremely extreme," she told him. "Tear the ship of origin apart and see if any of them knows enough magic to be able to breathe vacuum."

"Aye, aye, ma'am," he replied and sketched her a brief salute.

The mages remained alert and sent threads of energy out to detect an incoming attack before it could harm their ship. All of them watched what their Witch was doing and tried to commit the technique to memory. The way the energy boiled around her yet bent to her will was something all of them aspired to.

Her next words were addressed to the ship.

"Are you ready, Ebony?"

"That depends on how much you will stress my hull and mess with my drives," the ship snipped in return. "You know Cameron dislikes it when you cause unusual power fluctuations and I do not want to have to explain that it was not my choice to engage in what he calls 'shenanigans.'"

"A simple 'no' would have worked," Stephanie told her, and Knight gave a credible snort.

"There is nothing you can throw me into that I will not be ready for," the ship asserted and Stephanie laughed.

"Challenge accepted," she replied and Captain Rawlins groaned.

"Ebony, did you have to?"

The ship snickered. "Always."

"They're preparing to fire," the scans commander warned and the girl nodded.

"Skip me!" she ordered. "Put me behind the *Hera*."

"You asked for it," the pilot replied. "I take it you want all guns facing her tail?"

"Make it so."

Jonathan Wattlebird didn't wait to be asked again. He thrust the *Knight* into a sudden dive and put a twist on her that made everyone's stomach churn despite the gravitational equalizers kicking in—or perhaps because of how hard they had to compensate for the unorthodox maneuver.

"I can hear him already," Rawlins muttered as the comms signaled an incoming message from engineering. "Divert that."

Cameron's voice peaked for a moment before it faded. "I swear if that was Wattlebird, I'll feed him to the drives as a peace offering. And if it was a team effort, I'll..."

Felarif's eyes widened and the other mages looked worried.

Jonathan shook his head. "There isn't a hole big enough to hide us," he muttered as he pivoted the *Knight* to bring her guns in line with the *Hera's* drives.

In his office, David stared at the screen, completely unaware of the drama in the Knight's command center. "That maneuver..."

For a moment it was tempting to order the Heretic's ship captured but then he remembered it had an AI on board—a sentient computer with all the attitude of its mistress.

"Perhaps not," he murmured, "although it is a pity."

He watched as the *Knight* pivoted and a small barrage of missiles streaked toward the *Hera's* rear shields.

On her ship's bridge, Stephanie released a burst of energy over the ship and channeled it through the engines.

Cameron spoke sharply over the intercom. "Nice apology but it's not enough. I have alarms screaming fit to wake the dead, two crewmen doubled over painting the deck with the contents of their stomachs, and a ruptured containment unit, temporarily patched by a sheet of purple which had better hold for the rest of the battle."

She nodded at Felarif and the Meligornian looked at S'vilsa and the mage beside him.

"With me," he ordered. "We have damage control to do."

A fourth joined them. "Healing," he explained succinctly.

"And mop-up crew," the Knight added and the mage rolled his eyes.

"Opportunist."

"I'll send someone from Maintenance," Rawlins told them.

"One equipped with a wet vacuum," the ship insisted.

"Noted."

Stephanie continued to dance and glanced at Jonathan with an evil twinkle in her eyes.

"Do you remember the first attack?" she asked.

The pilot nodded. "Do you want…"

"Give me the distance I need. One of these big suckers needs enough of a run-up to reach ramming speed."

From his position against the rear wall, Vishlog groaned. Beside him, Marcus gave him a curious look.

"Did she truly—"

"Uh-huh," the Dreth confirmed. "She truly, truly did."

"Do you think Todd would notice if we vanished that one from his collection?"

"Not immediately." Stephanie's reply reached them from the center of the room. "But I would."

"Well, there goes that idea," Marcus muttered.

"Yup," Vishlog agreed and patted him on the shoulder. "Better luck next time."

The *Hera* vanished from the Knight's viewscreen, only to appear farther away and it took them a moment to realize that the Regime battleship hadn't been the one to move. A shocked moment and the sudden string of expletives from the intercom told them that Cameron had forgotten to close the intercom.

The Witch ignored the protest and sent another soothing wave of energy over the *Knight's* hull. She also reinforced the vessel's shields when a nearby Regime cruiser was startled into firing on the enemy ship that had suddenly appeared in its space. Ebony's gun crews returned fire with enough gusto that they saturated the cruiser's shield capability and blew a hole in its flank.

"Leave them!" Rawlins ordered. "Unless she fires again, she's out of the fight. These are our people, remember? We are not the murderers the Regime would make us out to be."

The gun crews didn't respond but they didn't follow up on their advantage.

"Whoa—" The soft exclamation of awe came from the scan team and all eyes turned to the forward viewscreen. "She's speeding up."

The *Hera* had indeed increased speed. Her drives flared with sudden power and she powered toward the Earth's atmosphere.

"Steph..." Rawlins began. "What are you doing?"

"Do you remember that first meteor swarm?" the girl asked.

The captain shook her head. "I wasn't with you then."

"Pity. Watch and you'll see what happened the last time someone tried to ram something into my homeworld."

"But they aren't—" Rawlins began as the other battleship accelerated and rolled to avoid the *Hera's* sudden charge. Its trajectory continued through the point the *Knight* had occupied earlier.

"It's a good thing we moved," Marcus noted and Vishlog nodded, his dark gaze divided between observing what was on the screen, what Stephanie was doing, and what was happening in the command center.

The Witch made no effort to divert the *Hera's* path and let the ship plunge toward the Earth's atmosphere as her compatriot got out of the way.

"And you thought you'd escaped," she stated and opened a gate in front of the vessel.

"Where— What are you doing with that?" Rawlins began but her face cleared almost immediately. "Hah. I might not have been with you when you faced a swarm of asteroids but I have seen you use that trick in battle."

"You'da thought they'd have taught that in little captain's school," Stephanie quipped and opened a second gate parallel to the second battleship's path.

"That captain's good," Jonathan noted as the battleship began to change course.

"But not good enough," the girl noted with satisfaction as the *Hera's* bow vanished through one portal and began to emerge from the next. "Now to make his life more interesting."

Light swirled around her, Meligornian purple mixed with the all-encompassing white of gMU and the vivid blue of eMU. This time, its passage was visible as it leapt from the *Knight* and crossed the distance between the Witch's ship and the fleeing Earth battlecruiser.

The crew gasped as it wound around the vessel's middle, shattered its shields, and sank into its hull. Shortly after it had vanished into the *Hera,* the ship's engines sputtered and died. Stephanie killed the energy's forward momentum and timed it so the ship caught it dead center.

"No shields." Jonathan's voice was filled with horror. "They didn't stand a chance."

"They had one chance," Stephanie told him coldly. "They blew it when they chose to attack the *Knight* in tandem. Now, they are at the mercy of the fleets."

The chancellor sagged in his seat.

How much power does it take? he wondered and stared at the two ships locked together after the impact while he noted the shuttles leaving one of the nearby Regime corvettes. "I'll have their heads." He growled his annoyance as he observed the mercy mission. "We have a fight to win."

Knowing he'd be able to find the footage later, he continued to watch the screen but barely saw what was on it.

How much power does it take, he wondered, *to move a ship against its engines, to move a* battleship *against its engines, and then to extinguish those engines?*

No such questions plagued Stephanie as she drew more energy to herself and sent some into each of her mages, including those in the engine room.

"Take us back to where we were," she instructed and rolled part of her consciousness into Ebony's scans—or rolled some of her magic through her scan systems.

"Hey!" the ship protested. "That... That's not very comfortable."

"What's the matter, Ebony? Are you ticklish?" she asked.

"Not in the way you humans understand it," the ship retorted. "Please don't do that again. It was most unpleasant."

"I'll try not to, Ebony," she told her but didn't promise anything. Her face took on a distant look and energy swirled restlessly around her body.

"Uh-oh," Vishlog commented, pushed away from the wall, and spoke quietly into the team comms.

Captain Rawlins caught the movement and watched as he and Marcus moved closer to where the girl raised both hands as though to lift the energy around her and pull it over her head. Her eyes were closed and she drew a deep breath, lowered her hands in front of her, and swept them out again.

Her face had taken on a look of serenity, one devoid of trouble, as the rest of her team reached the edge of the central command space. Marianne watched them arrive and noticed that they were fully kitted and carried Marcus and Vishlog's gear with them. As they handed it to the two guards assigned to Stephanie for her sojourn in the command center, Johnny looked at the captain.

"Pardon the intrusion, ma'am."

She acknowledged the apology for the formality it was. The team was doing its best to keep the Witch safe and if she wasn't mistaken, they believed the dung was about to fly. The man's apology was an attempt to keep the peace as the team prepared to follow their principal into the jaws of whatever hell she'd found to purify.

As the thought crossed her mind, the girl turned to face her and her eyes snapped open to reveal the dark fire burning in their depths. Her smile was terrifying to behold.

"I've found him," she declared. "I've found all of them."

She stretched a hand in the direction of the scan set-up and twisted her wrist. The officers who monitored the system jerked away from their console as the forward viewscreen's image shifted from the stricken battleships to a location in the governing district of NorAm's east-coast capital.

This time, the *Knight* did not protest.

"There," Stephanie stated and stabbed a finger at the screen.

One of the buildings was surrounded by a multi-colored halo. It occupied the equivalent of four city blocks and its walls rose in sheer facades from the pavement that separated the building from the streets that bordered it. Only one entrance was provided for visitors and a single vehicle entrance on the opposite side, but the center stood open and a courtyard as wide as a football stadium provided a peaceful refuge from the city beyond.

"I'd like to get a little closer," Stephanie said to Rawlins. "Let Earth *see* we are back!"

An alarm shrilled on the scan systems and the image of the chancellor's headquarters was replaced by a picture of the transition point and a hundred signatures that transformed into the familiar shapes of Regime Naval vessels.

"Jaleck!" Stephanie gasped, but the vessels at the rear in the Dreth fleet had already changed course to take their vulnerable drives out of the line of fire before the enemy ships could emerge fully.

That didn't stop several from firing, however, which prompted several smaller vessels to change course to take the fight to the new arrivals. Swarms of small fighters erupted from the larger Dreth ships. These were followed by the bulky shapes of shuttles and dropships, some of which flew like they carried an extra load.

"Now the battle begins," Rawlins observed, stood from her seat, and leaned over her control boards. "They came out of nowhere."

"Let's hope they don't have more," Stephanie observed and added, "Take us in."

"You don't want to go to Dreth's aid?" the captain asked.

She shook her head. "The sooner I deal with their chancellor, the sooner this war will be over. We'll lose less of our friends that way."

"Besides," the *Knight* added, "my older sister would be upset if we left nothing for her."

"Sister?" Rawlins asked and frowned at her boards. "Where is the *Tempestarii*, anyway?"

Alarms wailed and the Witch pivoted toward the ship's bow. The lights shifted to amber and her protection team dropped into crouches, unwilling to move any farther away.

"They *dare!*" Stephanie stated and her voice was like muted thunder—cold, muted thunder that sent a chill through all who heard it.

"The Morgana…" Marcus mouthed.

Johnny nodded. "Lars would be cussing about now," he commented and they grinned.

"He doesn't know what he's missing," Vishlog added. They

turned their eyes to the screens and their grins died as their faces became grim.

Stephanie moved her body in a familiar motion and one of the smaller images displayed a flight of incoming missiles swept off course like they'd been swatted by an invisible hand.

"Next time, send them home," Rawlins snapped from her console. "They took that as encouragement."

The girl didn't reply. Nor did she object when Felarif rushed into the control room with S'vilsa at his side and the two of them urged the mages into action. They sent tendrils of magic to hook into the energy surrounding Stephanie's body so they could coordinate their efforts.

"Now, we'll bring the lightning!"

CHAPTER FOURTEEN

"You dared to attack the one who protected you."

This time, the voice thundered through their skulls and left their heads ringing with its assault.

"You allowed a cancer to grow in your midst. Now rise! Fight instead for the one who brings you salvation from the evil that commands you."

It was not the same voice that had spoken before. While still a woman's voice, it was different—older and more powerful. Fear rode it and affected those it touched.

It was a relentless drum and an invitation to war.

"Rise now!"

The voice issued from the heavens as foretold.

"Look to the sky..." The reminder was whispered down phone lines and over wireless connections. "He said to look to the sky."

Countless eyes did exactly that and saw a thousand pin-pricks of light, impossibly close and brighter than any star.

Those who rode the heavens were deafened a second time as proximity alarms and transition alerts triggered klaxons to blare to life around them. Lights that had flashed a sullen amber now flared crimson and began to strobe.

"Now there's a sight for sore eyes." Rawlins caught her breath as the first Teloran battleship emerged well inside the solar system and completely outside the official transition zone.

Stephanie continued to deflect incoming fire and occasionally delivered a well-placed burst of energy into the drives or communications systems of the ships that attacked the *Knight*. Ebony made no comment but conspired with her pilot and weapons crews to skip into the center of a Regime formation, fire all guns to gain their attention, and skip out as soon as the enemy ships had fired in return.

Laughter and high-fives followed as the crews counted coup on the vessels that holed their fleet-mates and were holed in return. Inexperience and desperation had played into their hands.

"It's like shooting fish in a barrel." One of the gunners chuckled. "Except this time, it's the fish doing the shooting and the barrel destroying itself."

"Welcome to the fight!" one of the Dreth captains shouted in greeting when he caught sight of *the Dusk Bringer*.

"Better late than never!" another quipped as the Dreth fleet opened its comms and roared a welcome to the Teloran fleet and Dreth's First Witch.

Comm channels broadcast images of their command crews saluting the incoming Telorans, who replied in kind. All of them broadcast on the widest bandwidth possible and didn't care that the humans could see the greeting or how many rode the ships now ranged against them.

Some of the newer crew simply froze and stared at the screens that had been usurped by the Dreth and Teloran broadcasts and a few of the older hands joined them. It took experienced petty officers and Marine sergeants to shake them into some semblance of fighting order and by then, much of the damage had already been done.

V'ritan gazed at the multiple scenes displayed in the Intelligence Center aboard the *King's Warrior* and his lips twitched into a tiny smile. He paid particular attention to the expressions on the faces of the humans whose vessels his people had already taken and his smile became a smirk.

"Now, you understand," he told them, "exactly what the Witch of our Federation tried to tell you." He tutted quietly and shook his head. "You should have listened while you had the chance and not forced her to come to you."

More than one Regime captain dropped into their command chair, their jaws slack with horror at the scene before them. The Teloran fleet had translated close to them and in formation, and it now bore down on the battlefield surrounding Earth.

As they watched, it divided into three separate units. One turned aside from the main body to go to Dreth's assistance and was greeted with whoops of welcome as it caught the attacking Earth fleet in a pincer movement and cut it off from the transition point.

The second unit arced gracefully away to offer assistance to the Meligornians and was greeted with salutes and bows, all of which were also broadcast to every comm Net in range.

The third unit drove relentlessly toward Earth and the Naval space station that orbited above it. It was led by the biggest super-dreadnought they'd seen outside pictures of the new Jotun class said to have recently joined the fleet.

It wasn't hard to do the numbers. Every captain with half a brain saw it. They'd been outnumbered two to one before, but that had changed dramatically.

"We'll be lucky if it's only twenty to one," observed Captain

Rasmussen of the *Halyard's Beast.* He rose from his seat. "They'll hail us soon."

He was wrong. The Telorans didn't hail them. Instead, they overran their communications systems and shut down their ability to talk to the rest of the fleet. The Morgana announced it when she activated every screen in the Regime's vessels.

"Surrender," she ordered. "You are outgunned and outnumbered. You can only die without purpose and the Witch—*your* Witch—still believes in you. She wishes all humanity to benefit from the fall of the Regime and she wants her planet protected. When this war is over, she will need you."

She paused to give them time to accept her offer as her gaze raked over them.

"You are not alone in what you face when your current rulers are gone. My people faced it too. We did not slaughter our Navy for serving a corrupt government under duress and neither will she."

Again, she waited and gave them time to digest the idea. It would be an unpalatable meal, at best, but it was the way things would be. There was nothing pretty about a civil war. Someone would always have been on the "wrong" side and someone else would always want them to pay.

The trick was to agree that sometimes, the only justice and the only way to honor the dead was for both sides to work together to rebuild what was left. If they did not, their world would be lost to a cycle of revenge and reparation that would solve nothing and mend nothing.

That path would lead to greater injustices and yet more death and Earth had bled enough.

The dead were dead. If those who willingly took part or instigated their murders were brought to justice, that was one thing, but what of those who were coerced? She stared into the monitor and her face hid the turmoil this question stirred.

People would go to extremes to keep their loved ones safe—

even to the point of harming their friends, their neighbors, and themselves. An otherwise decent person who had done such wrongs would spend the rest of their lives trying to atone. Or they could apologize by working to build a better world, if not for themselves, then for everyone's children.

Some people were worth saving in spite of what they'd been made to do.

While it might not be justice in the traditional sense, it was still justice. The guilt didn't go away and the guilty were never free, not in themselves. Some deeds required a lifetime of atonement.

Those killed by vengeance could never express their regret or try to make amends and their deaths would merely demand more vengeance, and those deaths would repeat the tragic cycle. The killing would never stop and the world would never heal.

The Morgana had seen it happen. Telor had almost torn itself apart in the aftermath of the Prime's deposal. If Stephanie had not enforced the peace, her world would have been lost many times over and the years she'd spent projecting herself from under a mountain while her body decayed behind her would have been for nothing.

Telor lived because it had learned forbearance where forgiveness could not be found. Neither side was innocent but history judged the Prime's followers most harshly. It would be the same for the humans and their Regime.

There would be those who would never find forgiveness, not from others and certainly not from themselves. The way they carried themselves in this battle's aftermath would decide the future—and not only for their children but all the generations to follow.

This was a delicate moment and she had no time to make them understand.

"Weapons!" she commanded and felt the hum of power as the *Dusk Bringer's* weapon systems powered up.

As they did so, the Morgana looked into the monitor, her expression as implacable as the Prime's had ever been while her regret mingled with the sadness of her host that another world had come to this.

"Surrender," she commanded and reinforced her spoken words with mental projection. "Take your weapons offline and prepare for boarding, and we will show mercy. She will show mercy. You have thirty minutes to comply. If you fire on us, we will take you anyway. The lives on a ship that fires on one that has surrendered are forfeit. I trust that is understood."

"It couldn't be clearer," the captain muttered and scowled as he tried to ignore the looks his crew cast in his direction.

It was poor comfort to see his dilemma mirrored in the faces of his command crew, but they'd been among the first to come about to face the emerging threat.

If only there weren't so many and if the ship leading them wasn't so damned large.

He looked around the command center and his gaze swept over the two Talents and their handler, the Marines who guarded the bridge entry, and the men and women who manned the command consoles.

"You heard the lady," he ordered gruffly. "Power the weapons down."

"Sir!" the Talent handler protested.

"You heard me," the captain snapped and pushed out of his seat. "Scans, show the lieutenant exactly what we're looking down the barrel of."

The screen flickered as though the team had to fight for the ability to show what he'd ordered. When it finally gave way to the stars and the enemy fleet closing on his bow, their weapons online and ready to fire, he turned to the handler.

"Do you understand?" he demanded and the man reached for his blaster.

One of the Marines was faster and his aim was unerring. The

handler fell with a smoking crater in his skull. The Talents in front of him fell prone and covered their heads with their hands as the Marine moved forward and spoke quickly into his comms.

"The command deck is secure," he stated and the captain noticed movement to his left.

The Marines who fell in beside him had their weapons drawn but aimed away.

"How may we assist, sir?" one asked as the other slid his blaster from its holster.

Rasmussen bowed his head. "I need the crew in their pods. If we lock them down, no one will try anything stupid."

"And the guns can't fire accidentally," one of the Marines noted grimly.

"They won't," the weapons commander interrupted. "I've cut the command circuits. The guns are about as dead as I can make them."

"Unless someone manages a manual override in the section itself," another Marine pointed out. He caught the commander's look of disbelief and gave him a feral grin. "It's what we would do."

"I assume you're taking steps to ensure that doesn't happen," Rasmussen observed.

"As we speak," the man revealed and his eyes shifted to the screen as several formations of fighters and shuttles began to stream from the gargantuan' s hull.

The captain reached toward the control panel but stopped when his escort tensed.

"I'd like to direct the crew to their stasis pods," he told them. "With your permission?"

The Marines exchanged glances, then nodded.

"Only the directive, captain."

He glared at the man. "If I intended to do something stupid," he all but growled, "I wouldn't have ordered the weapons offline."

"But you did."

"Yes," Rasmussen emphasized, "I did. I've kept this ship and her crew alive through more engagements than I want to remember. I'd like to give her people a chance to get home from this one too."

The Marine gestured to the console. "Make your broadcast."

Still frowning, the captain tapped the sequence he needed.

"All crew, all crew, all crew. This is Captain Heinrich Rasmussen. Proceed to your pods. We will be boarded. I repeat. Proceed to your pods. You will not be harmed. I repeat. All crew to your pods. I will see you when this is over."

He hoped that last statement was true.

In fact, he had to believe it was. If he did not, there was truly nothing left.

That done, he glanced at the Marines. "Are you sure you want to be armed when they arrive?" he asked and they looked at him like he'd grown a second head. He sighed heavily. "Of course you do."

The door to the command center opened and closed and a familiar voice offered an explanation. "We cannot surrender our weapons if we are not armed."

Rasmussen turned his head, careful to keep his hands on his console.

"Captain Blakeney."

"Do you mind if I stand with you?"

"Why not? We are surrendering." He sighed again. "Perhaps we should meet them in the docking bay?"

"I'll leave my men here." Blakeney cast a jaundiced eye to where Rasmussen's second in command glared resentfully at his sergeant. "Not all your people appear to agree with your decision."

"It doesn't feel natural," he admitted.

The Marine captain gave him a bleak look. "No, but then what of the last thirty years has?"

"Indeed." The ship's captain glanced at the door. "Shall we?"

He'd taken one step away from his console when the defense commander interrupted.

"Sir! We're being fired on!"

"But we've surrendered." Rasmussen couldn't believe it. "We've taken our guns offline. Why would they—"

"Not them, sir," the man replied. "It's… It's the *Fury*. She's locked on."

"The stars have mercy," he whispered. He drew a sharp breath. "Double the power to the starboard shields. Talents!" When they didn't respond, he raised his voice another notch. "Talents!" His gaze snapped to where they huddled together.

One raised her face to acknowledge him.

"Captain?"

"Reinforce the shields to port. You don't need your handler for that, do you?"

She shook her head, scrambled cautiously to her feet, and flinched when the Marine who'd "secured" the bridge wrapped his gauntleted hand around her arm and helped her to stand.

Heinrich watched her eyes shift from blue to gold as she pivoted to face the rear of the ship. The *Anvil's Fury* hung off his starboard side where it had guarded his flank when they flew in formation. The chance that any of her batteries would miss at this range was nil.

On the forward screen, the small craft shifted course and a second alarm blared on the defense console. This time, the commander's face drained of blood and his voice was little more than a hoarse whisper when he spoke.

"It's the dreadnought, sir. She's preparing to fire."

"No…" Rasmussen groaned. He knew people on that ship—good people. "Give them a chance."

He glanced at the comms. "Ask the dreadnought to stand down," he ordered. "Ask them… Ask them for time."

As the comms officer moved to comply, Blakeney glanced at him.

"Are you sure?"

"They'll be fighting," Rasmussen told him and brought up a visual of his sister ship. "Not everyone—"

Fire erupted down one side of the *Fury*.

"Was that... Did she lose her port-side missile batteries?" the Marine captain asked

"And their crews," he acknowledged miserably.

"They have five minutes," the comms technician announced.

"Tell them to board her!" he snapped. "Not all the crew is complicit. Ask for mercy—Beg if you have to. Better yet—"

A third voice cut him off. "Beg? Seriously captain? They're about to desstroy your ship and you want uss to sspare them?"

A new image appeared on the forward screen—a tall, thin alien, its features hidden by black armor that shifted beneath his gaze.

"Please?" Rasmussen asked, not ashamed to beg. "Not all of them—"

"Are complissit... Yesss, we heard you."

"There are good people—" Rasmussen began, but the Teloran cut him off again.

"Very well, since they appear to have destroyed their own port-side batteries, we will board. Remain in your command center. We will meet you there."

"Aye—understood," the captain corrected himself, not sure the aliens would understand the Naval agreement.

The Teloran cocked its head and studied him, the Marines, and his command center.

"Offer no resistance," it instructed, "and your people will come to no harm."

He had no choice but to take them at their word and a new formation descended from the dreadnought's hull. To his relief, the *Fury* was not destroyed, at least not by the dreadnought's guns. He wondered if he'd see any of her personnel again.

Cold preceded the boarders and to his relief, the Marines did not fire and his crew did not rebel. They remained in their pods and he and his command crew and the Marines were escorted from the command center.

He'd have asked if the Telorans knew how to operate an Earth ship but they moved with more confidence than some of the new crew additions he'd been assigned.

Where had they learned that?

Transfer of control did not go as smoothly aboard the *Anvil's Fury*.

"Like hell we will!" Captain Sterne roared at the screen, his face red with fury. "That gutless worm-ridden coward." It wasn't the response its command crew had wanted to hear when they'd told their captain the *Beast's* weapon systems had gone offline, although it was no more than what they expected.

"Starboard batteries, destroy the *Halyard's Beast*. Fire! Do not let that ship fall into enemy hands." When no one moved, he reiterated the order. "*Fire*, damn you."

He snapped his visor closed, drew his blaster, and aimed it at the weapons commander.

"Give the order."

The man dove below the console and the captain shifted his aim to the next man along.

"Do it."

"Yes, s-s…sir." Sub-lieutenant Tate's hands trembled as much as his voice but he pressed the right sequence. "D-done, sir."

"Good lad." The captain tossed him his blaster. "Now shoot your commander."

"S-sir?"

The sound of the captain's second weapon warming up made him look at him—and straight down the barrel pointed unwaveringly in his direction. He fumbled to take the blaster from the console but gave a startled yelp when his legs were dragged out from under him.

"Sorry, boy." Commander Cohen said as the youngster landed awkwardly.

The weapon flew out of his hand but that wasn't what caught his attention. His superior's fist looked incredibly large as it swung at his face and it landed with enough force that Tate was out in seconds.

"We'll talk when you wake up," Cohen said and retrieved the fallen weapon. "Thanks for this."

An energy bolt pounded into the console and metal hissed and spat.

"For the star's sake! Will someone tell that ship we won't fire! And someone needs to take those batteries offline."

The ship shuddered and a muted roar reached their ears.

"No..." Cohen groaned.

The deck lurched and the pilot swore while his hands darted frantically over his controls. A decompression alarm sounded and the weapons commander's face paled.

"They didn't... She wouldn't—"

But Commander Stander would, could, did, and had. Damage alarms rang to accompany the "man overboard" warning in an eerie cacophony. Cohen didn't need the scan tech's hushed tones to tell him what she'd done.

"They blew the feeds. Why?" the tech asked but he didn't have time to answer him.

Their captain was determined to commit suicide—and suicide by invader no less. Worse, he'd decided to take the entire ship with him. "If none of you have the stomach for the job, I'll do it myself."

"Sir! You ca—" The protest ended in a choked cry and the smell of smoking flesh.

The weapons commander stepped out from behind the command console and took only enough time to locate his captain before he opened fire. It was no easy feat. The man had gone into battle fully armored, almost as if he had expected a hard fight—or to cause a mutiny.

If Cohen hadn't known better, he'd have said the man had a death wish.

It was a shame he was such a good shot. Cohen raced to the next console, only to fling himself to the deck in a slide. More bolts streaked through the space he'd occupied, and he scrambled into cover and comm'd the Marines as he hauled himself into the shelter of the navigation console.

"Commander Dempsey, I am relieving the captain of his command."

Pain flared along his hip, thigh, and calf and he screamed. Someone took the blaster from his hand and he rolled his eyes up to look at them. To his surprise, Fel Campshaw darted above the cover of her console, snapped two shots in rapid succession, and ducked again. She glanced at his legs and made a face.

"Greg, help him," she ordered and slunk to the console's edge.

More blaster fire came but not from her. Cohen flinched as Fel's second in command bent over him.

"Easy, man. I'm not gonna hurt you."

"Liar..." He grimaced and heard footsteps approaching. "Give me your gun."

It was passed without hesitation. "Don't let him shoot me."

If it weren't for the clamminess that crept over his skin, the weapons commander might have found that funny. The two men flinched as more blaster fire sounded on the other side of the command center and Greg crowded closer to spray a layer of sealant over the injuries.

"It's not the best," he explained when Cohen gasped, "but it'll stop the bleeding."

More firing was followed by heavy boot steps. It sounded like the Marines had arrived.

Greg didn't look up and pulled a bandage out instead. "The seal's not holding."

The weapons commander saw movement around the end of the console and raised the blaster. It shook in his hand and a blast of magic tore it from his grip. he yelped and swept an arm around Greg to pull the man behind him.

"Don't—"

The alien inclined its head.

"Don't what? Shoot an injured man too stupid to realize he's in no position to save his friend?"

It moved past them and its robes flowed around a spindly form that refused to come into focus. With utter calm, it trained a blaster on them in one hand while lightning wreathed its other.

"We are not humans."

Cohen slumped on the floor and Greg inched out from under his hand but froze when the blaster snapped up.

He gestured at Cohen's leg. "I need to—"

The weapon relaxed.

"Do sso."

Halyard's Beast and *Anvil's Fury* were the first. Foremost in the attack against the Telorans, they'd soon been overrun. Regime ships throughout the system faced conflicted crews and hard choices. Admiral Reynolds had reached the rear of the Dreth vessels before he'd registered how many ships were in the system.

Now, his fleet was sandwiched between two Dreth fleets as Angreth and the Lost emerged from transition.

"Who is guarding Dreth?" Jaleck demanded when Angreth appeared on her screen.

"Our kin," he replied shortly. "Call it a show of trust—family guarding family, while family repays a debt of blood and honor."

She couldn't argue with that and ordered the *Vengeance* to

move forward and drop below the fleet with her escort. The high admiral had seen a ship she recognized from the recordings.

"Stab us in the back, will you?" She snarled her fury. "Threaten my transports and traders? Let's see how you like it when you face a fair fight."

Technically, it wasn't a fair fight. Even with the super-dreadnoughts and remnants of those that had attacked her world, the newly arrived fleet was both sorely outnumbered and outgunned.

Reynolds cursed as some of the captains on the edge of the fleet veered away.

"Hold the line!" he roared and highlighted the *Vengeance*. "Take their flag."

Magic sizzled at the edge of the command center and he looked around in time to see one of his Marines fall, his armor smoking. The Talent was unrepentant.

"He said we were human, sir, and then tried to shoot you."

The admiral nodded. "Very good. Fire!"

The guns remained silent.

He glared at his console.

"What are you waiting for? Fire on the flag!"

When there was no response, he glared at the security team.

"Get me the feeds from the weapons decks."

When he saw what was happening on there, he wished he hadn't asked and looked around the bridge.

"Does anyone else feel the same way?"

It was no surprise to feel the muzzle of his second in command's blaster pressed to the back of his skull. "I do, sir. We were given the chance to surrender and to continue serving our world."

On the forward screen, swarms of Dreth fighters and transports swept through the space between the two fleets. Corvettes and destroyers increased power to keep up.

Reynolds didn't bother to answer. He raised his hands and waited for Costas to take a step back to allow him to turn. The second the gun cleared the back of his neck, he pivoted and reached for his blaster.

"You always were a trusting fool," he snarled but his face froze in shock as shots came from half a dozen different points in the room and pain ripped through his chest and head.

"We aren't," the closest Marine snapped.

He fell and his hand slid from the blaster's grip. Across the command center, one of the Talents lay dead and her handler covered her corpse with a blaster that shook. The other magic-user had backed against the wall, her eyes closed and her hands curled under her chin.

A nearby Marine slid an arm around her and pulled her against his armored chest. His gaze turned to the screen in time to see the first drop ship reach them. The ship's second in command picked up the comms.

"This is Captain Mikel Costas. Captain Reynolds is dead. All crew, stand down. We are being boarded. All crew, stand down. Power all systems down. I repeat. This is Captain Mikel Costas."

"I've opened Hangar Bays One through Twelve," the security chief reported. "Maybe they'll understand."

"Give me the feeds," he ordered and scenes of the battle outside faded from the forward screen and were replaced by a patchwork of surveillance screens.

In some, the crew waited at their stations, their weapons either strapped down or stacked in front of the door. The Marine captain shook his head.

"We never did go through procedures for surrender," he muttered and hoped the Dreth wouldn't interpret the haphazard piles as booby traps.

Other screens showed sections divided against each other. Those who obeyed Mikel's orders fought those who didn't want to surrender. In the weapons sections, those battles were almost over as they had started as soon as Reynolds had given the order to fire.

The Morgana's broadcast had been heard by all and the ships' crews weren't stupid. Most hadn't wanted to be Navy to begin with but the Regime demanded service, regardless of your circumstances, and very few were exempt. Service or the slow death of being exiled to places like the long-neglected Subs wasn't much of a choice when your family suffered with you.

The Dreth moved through the ship, an unstoppable tide that streamed from the hangars en masse before they split into squads to round the crew up. More Dreth followed to take the place of the crew directed away from their stations to the ship's main briefing room.

The command crew observed their progress through the ship and saw what happened when three of the Talents met them with fire and lightning. Retribution was swift and efficient and left a single Talent who'd dropped to the floor as the sole survivor.

"Good fire discipline," one of the Marines murmured, her eyes on the screen. Her gaze shifted. "Here they come."

Mikel looked around the room. "I want your hands up when that door opens." He fixed the Marines with a stern gaze. "That means you too. I want to see you all when this is done. Am I understood?"

That last came out as a rough bark and both Marines and command crew responded in kind.

"Sir, yes, sir!"

The Dreth reached the bridge and he nodded to the security team.

"Open the hatch."

The Talent whimpered and the Marine holding her turned his back on the incoming Dreth and shielded her with his body. Her handler stood beside them and interposed himself between them and the warriors.

"Step aside, little man."

"I can't. She's my—" He stopped as he was lifted aside and the Talent uttered a muffled shriek.

"Peace," the Dreth ordered. "The Witch has marked you as her own. No harm will come to you."

Fighting filled the corridors of the *Needham's Spear*.

"We did not return from hunting the Dreth only to surrender to them!" its captain roared and many of its crew bellowed an agreement.

The *Needham* wasn't the only one on which the majority of the crew felt the same. It was merely one of the few whose Talents and Marines mostly disagreed.

"Traitor!" one of the Marine sergeants shouted as their commander ordered them to take the bridge.

"Coward!" the lieutenant commander accused when she ordered a second section to secure the guns.

"We are neither," she retorted, shot her second in the head, and calmly eliminated any who seemed inclined to finish the action the LC had begun.

Their bodies were still smoking when they landed and the commander looked around. "Who's with me?"

The remaining Marines growled a soft response and she headed to the door.

"Change of plan," she told them. "We'll lock down every crewman we can find. I don't want friendly fire coming at our back."

"Friendly fire ain't that friendly," one of her remaining sergeants declared. "We need the Talents."

"Will they be with us?"

"Yes, ma'am."

The Talent section had been locked down until the commander sent her request. It was no surprise to find their handlers dead. The oldest of the Talents gave her a wan smile. "They tried to kill us," he explained and she nodded.

"You're forgiven. Will you help us take the ship?"

His eyes clouded with smoke and fire and he shook his head. "I'll help you evacuate your men."

She glanced at her technician and he sent a situation update to the team's HUDs.

"Put out an all-ship evacuation!" she ordered. "We might save some of them."

"And some of them might even be worth saving," her sergeant quipped.

"The Witch will sort them out," the Talent told them.

"Missiles incoming!" a tech warned, "and our shields are failing."

"Pods!" the commander ordered. "Grab everyone you can on the way."

They were launching when the *Needham's* shields gave way and their pods dropped below the incoming line of fire as the next salvo closed. The small craft were pursued by Dreth fighters and dropships as the first explosion tore open the *Needham's* hull.

"Sir! We've been boarded!"

The security alert went out to warn the crew of the danger and the captain gaped.

"It's not possible! We blew her apart."

It was an exaggeration for the damage done to the Meligornian ship, but pods had spewed from the vessel in the wake of their first successful salvo and the cruiser had turned to run—or so they'd thought.

"I have multiple contacts along the hull!"

"Mines?"

"No, sir!" Panic filled the technician's voice. "They're coming through the maintenance hatches."

"Well, don't just sit there—stop them!"

"I...I don't know where they are."

"Then *find them!*" the captain roared as several well-armored figures dropped through the ceiling onto the bridge.

"Kill them all!" he yelled as his second in command looped an arm around his chest, pulled him back, and drove his fighting knife up under his chin.

"I think we'll surrender, sir," he said, grunted as he pulled the blade free, and placed it on the command console.

The captain's body caught the rounds the Meligornians fired at Foggarty's sudden movement and the commander held it in front of him as he keyed the ship's broadcast system, aware of the command center's doors opening and closing.

"This is Commander Foggarty. We have been boarded. Lay down your arms. I repeat—" He froze and the words died in his throat when he felt the pressure of a blaster muzzle against his temple.

"Thank you, Commander," the Meligornian who held it said. "We'll take it from here."

Foggarty lifted his hands slowly from the console and closed his eyes. His weapons were taken and the blaster moved away before he was pulled back gently. The quiet voice spoke again.

"You can open your eyes, Commander. Now is not your time to die."

"Stay together!" Prater ordered. "Hold the formation. We'll take that big bastard together. I said hold the—"

"Sir! Our missiles have no effect," the weapons team reported.

"We have incoming fire from starboard," scans warned.

"*Eagle's* gone, sir. She's...uh...no longer there."

Alarms lit up on his console as the lights flickered, dimmed, and finally brightened again.

"What was that?" he demanded and called the chief engineer.

"We have energy fluctuation in the drives, sir."

"Well, fix it," he retorted.

"We're working on it."

"Work faster." He cut the link and contacted his fellow captains.

"Fire again. On my count..."

The crew looked at each other. Several rose from their seats and were cut down by the Marines who guarded the bridge. On other parts of the ship, more crew abandoned their posts and raced to the pods. Many were shot by their crewmates but some survived to launch.

Not many escaped the conflagration as Prater's formation of five were struck by a single salvo from *Dusk Bringer's* lower port batteries.

On *Dusk Bringer's* central deck, the Morgana turned and inclined her head. "Thank you, Enger Vresh. That was well-placed."

Dreth's First War Witch gave her a tusk-filled grin. "I have the best of teachers."

"And you honor them greatly," she told her. "Earth ship engines might not be powered by MU but our magic can still affect them."

"And their missiles cannot penetrate the *Dusk Bringer's* new shields," the Dreth witch replied smugly.

She studied the screens and sighed when she noted more of the Earth fleet taking their weapons offline and powering their drives down.

"The Dreth in me wishes more were stupid. The witch in me is grateful for our Witch's sake that they are not."

It was not a sentiment shared by all.

"Don't they know they are outclassed?" Captain Islafel demanded.

"It would seem not," V'ritan replied. Part of him was amused while another part was appalled.

How will she deal with this? he wondered as the *Dusk Bringer* destroyed a small flotilla whose captains thought it was enough to defeat the big ship—or, perhaps, who merely wished to end their part of the fight as quickly as possible. It was hard to imagine all their crews were in agreement.

It had been a similar situation to the one they now faced. A small group of Regime ships had banded together and made the *King's Warrior* their target. Unlike the *Dusk Bringer,* the *Warrior's* shields would not hold against them all and its hull was more vulnerable.

"Tell them to stand down," the *Ghargilum* ordered. "We'll give them one final chance to save themselves."

"Already done," Islafel replied and played him the Regime admiral's response, along with the affirmative gestures given by his captains and command crews.

"Well," V'ritan stated, "that's very definitive, isn't it?"

"And it looks like their crews are in agreement." The captain sounded almost disappointed.

He shrugged. "Take them but let's make this quick. I have ships that need us."

"Selene's Grace," Islafel intoned and sent the firing orders.

"Selene's Grace," he agreed, as the new ONE R&D missiles streaked toward the enemy formation. His eyes widened as he studied them. "How many did you use?"

"Two for each of them," the captain told him and added as he gaped, "You said to make it quick."

"But—" He stopped and gestured at the screen as the first missiles reached their targets.

"And these ships aren't powered with MU engines," Islafel said. "The explosion should be fairly contained."

"Should be?" V'ritan repeated and felt slightly alarmed. "Are you saying these haven't been tested?"

"The computer simulations were most satisfactory," the captain answered, his eyes alight with interest as he watched the expanding destruction. He winced when it spread beyond the formation and destroyed one of the ships that had been alongside it. "Most effective."

The *Ghargilum* said nothing for a long moment before he nodded abruptly. "Spread the word. Two missiles only—and only on ships attacking our fleet or our allies." He paused, replayed the footage, and studied the readouts. "And no closer than..."

He made several quick calculations and sent Islafel the results. "No closer than that. I don't want anyone to blow themselves up as well."

"Selene's Grace, *Ghargilum*."

More ships of the Regime vanished and the Meligornians weren't sorry.

Jaleck leaned forward and rested her hand on her console. A smirk curled her lips and her dark eyes gleamed with acquisitive flame.

"Ram him!" she roared and her crew roared with her.

In the *Vengeance's* largest hangar, Dreth Marines braced for the impact and Dreth engineers prepared explosives to clear the last vestiges of the hull from their path. More engineers readied the gear they would need to seal the ships together. This time, the *Vengeance* would not be able to fly away.

Dreth supply officers anchored the skeletons of their cargo loaders beside the large hull plates they'd need to effect temporary repairs as the *Vengeance's* pilot brought the super-dreadnought around in a sliding turn. The resulting impact put her hard up against the *Berjelmir's* side. Metal shrieked and gun crews fired docking clamps into the Jotun's hull.

"Use a door if you can find one!"

The order was issued as the *Vengeance* opened her hangar doors. Dreth Marines consulted schematics and came up blank. The hull that faced them was blank too.

"Shame," the Dreth Marine Commander noted but didn't sound at all upset. He pointed at the enemy ship's hull. "Make a door."

It didn't take his team long to scan the hull, discover that there were three decks on the other side, and make six doors—six very large doors.

Dreth laughter preceded them as they swarmed into the Jotun. The big ship's crew didn't know whether to fight, run, or surrender and attempted all three. The Dreth Marines secured them and swarmed past, determined to take the command center.

Their admiral would soon have the biggest ship in the fleet.

Across the battlefield, Angreth stared in disbelief.

"She's done it again," he murmured. "Again!"

"Admiral?" one of the command crew ventured tentatively.

"What?"

"There's another one, sir!" and before he could ask "another what," the forward screen showed a second of the oversized Regime dreadnoughts.

Angreth smiled a very Jaleck smile and rose from his seat.

"*Ram him!*" he roared.

His high admiral would not out-mass him a third time.

The *Knight* burned a trail through Earth's sky. Her hull glowed with the heat of re-entry and her shields amplified the glow until she looked like a slow-moving falling star or a spear of light.

"Look to the skies." The reminder was whispered in all the corners of the Earth Net and echoed in frantic phone calls.

"The stars will fall," followed shortly thereafter and received the only acceptable response.

"And the powers in the sky will be shaken."

"That's not a star." The matter of fact statement rippled across the planet in ceaseless echoes. "Does anyone know where that will hit?"

Underground broadcasters took advantage of the Enforcers' disarray to create a running commentary. Pictures of the Apostle fighting Regime Enforcers and Navy Marines went viral. Recordings of him telling stories of the Witch and her deeds were uploaded and downloaded too rapidly to trace.

The Regime's PR machine tried to overcome these, only to discover its access to the Earth Net blocked at every turn. The Navy sent pod techs into the system to track the source of the interference and promptly lost their connection to the pods, their incumbents, and the system.

"Where is it headed?" Edwards demanded but his attention was diverted by the three enemy flagships that converged on *Space Base Notaro.*

"Is that... Is it coming here?" Deverey asked and peered over the shoulder of the woman who tried to trace the ship's path via the illicit news feeds.

"It looks like it, sir," she told him.

"Can you be more specific?" he demanded.

"Not until we fix our connection to the sats, sir."

"You can see it from here, sir," a junior officer called from one of the windows.

He pivoted and walked slowly to the boy's vantage point. He knew what he'd see but he didn't want to confirm it. His staff fell in behind him and they looked to the east.

"Is that her, sir?" the young officer asked and Deverey nodded and swallowed hard.

"Look to the skies," he murmured and ignored the startled glances cast in his direction.

He fixed his gaze on the *Knight* as she burned closer and those around him did the same.

"She wasn't built for atmospheric," someone observed and Deverey swore.

"Get down!" he shouted and flung himself toward the cover of a solid wall.

His staff didn't hesitate but he still lost some when the windows blew in. He didn't bother to reprimand his junior for the comment that followed.

"She is definitely heading this way."

CHAPTER FIFTEEN

"Is that the last of them?" Todd asked.

Burn lines crisscrossed his armor and made it look like it was melting. Smoke seeped from the most recent damage.

"Persistent little troglodytes," Gary muttered and fired a short burst down the corridor he was guarding.

The doors had been early casualties to cutting charges and grenades and several banks of computers were little more than slag heaps, but Piet had managed to reroute the functions those had performed. Reggie and Jimmy had scavenged other units for what needed replacing.

"Do you know how big this facility is?" the Aussie asked.

"I'm getting an idea," the sergeant admitted. "How many people did it have?"

The other man made a show of looking at the bodies strewn in the corridor and glanced pointedly at the other openings. He raised a hand and wagged his forefinger as he pretended to count.

"I don't know how many were on duty, boss, but most of them seem to be here," he said.

Todd snorted softly and shook his head as he surveyed the

bodies around them. Angus and Darren had gone so far as to stack twenty of them across one of the doorways. The pile formed a barrier some three feet high and was too big to step across.

"Piet! Have you got me the surveillance feeds?"

"Wall, boss. They're on the wall," the engineer replied.

He studied the images displayed and noted that several accesses were not only closed but blocked by shuttles or trucks.

"Nice job with the transport," he commended.

"It wasn't me, boss. You have Ka to thank for that."

"Nope," the team's main tech argued. "It wasn't me and neither were the auto-turrets."

"Auto-turrets?" Both men stared at the wall.

"Wait—do you mean those are on our side?" Henry asked.

"I just watched the ones on the north wall annihilate a squad of Enforcers," she replied. "Sooo, yup, they're on our side."

Todd frowned.

"And it wasn't you," he stated.

She shook her head although her gaze remained fixed on the screen she was working on. "Nope." The corporal worked furiously for a few seconds longer, then straightened and stretched her arms over her head. "The system's ours, boss."

Soft whoops greeted the announcement as the sergeant studied the security feeds.

"And it looks like the complex is ours too."

"Oorah." The response came from six different directions.

"Do you have the files we need?" Todd asked and Ka glanced at him.

"Are you kidding, boss? This place doesn't have anything but the files we need. The trick will be to get it out there with what we've done to the comms system."

He shrugged. "Then you'd better get to work. The sooner you get it started, the sooner we're out of here. Build in a couple of redundancies so they can't shut it all down at once."

"Sure, boss," she snarked. "And I guess you want a side of fries with that."

Todd chuckled. "Quit your bitching and no, I don't want fries with that but I'd kill for a chocolate sundae."

"With or without sprinkles?" she retorted sourly but her fingers had already begun to attack the keys.

"Every type of candy you can muster," he told her cheerfully, "but make it quick. These people have been living in ignorance for too long and they have choices to make." He paused and his eyes darkened. "They can't do that without data."

Ka caught the darkness in his voice but decided not to pursue it. It was no surprise that the boss had ghosts. They all did and the sooner this war was over, the fewer those ghosts would be.

They didn't need to hear the Morgana's order to surrender. It had made it past the ships and satellites and into the Earth Net and took over the screens temporarily. Given that those same screens had shown the Telorans' arrival and no one had known what they were seeing, it had left an impression.

"I found that massacre," Ka told him but she didn't sound particularly happy. After a moment's hesitation, she added, "Boss, we have Meligornians in orbit. Are you sure..."

Todd's face hardened. "We have to. Right now, we have a planet full of people starting to think aliens aren't real and if they are, they're to blame for everything from the latest flu to a Talent being born to human parents. We need the footage of Earth kicking the aliens out."

"Well, as long as you're sure," she told him, "because we have a skyful of people likely to be very annoyed when they see the truth of how their ambassadors and businessmen were treated."

"I know." His voice grated with regret. "But the people of Earth are under the illusion that the Meligornians were the aggressors. They need to know differently."

They fell silent and he watched the monitors while Ka worked to get the historical feeds running into every part of the Earth Net she could. She paused again when she found the recordings of what the Regime Navy had done to the Dreth.

"Boss… This stuff on the Dreth—we killed a colony."

Horror laced her tones and he gritted his teeth.

"Send it, Ka. All of it, no matter how evil or atrocious or abhorrent. Send it out so Earth's people—our people—know how they've been used and how their forces have been used against those who were our allies. Then find that footage of our allies doing their best to protect us and defend us. Let everyone see how they've been betrayed."

Gary shook his head. "Boss, that's all very well and good, but these guys have been fed alien horror stories since they were born. The only ones who remember what it was truly like are either dead, incarcerated, or forced into some unholy backwater and left to rot."

"All the more reason to get the truth out there, Gary. The good truth and the bad."

"I'm very sure it'll all be bad, boss," Reggie interjected, "and you know what people are like when something is bad and they don't want to believe it."

"Yeah," Todd conceded, "but I also know what people are like when they discover they've been lied to. You show me a decent man or woman who finds out they've been duped into doing something bad because someone lied to them, and I'll show you a man or woman who will tear the world apart to deal with the liar and make amends."

"What makes you think there's any way to make amends for even half of this?" Ka sounded as close to tears as any of them had heard her and Piet glanced at her in concern. "Don't even think about it," she warned and stabbed a finger in his direction. "You stay right there and make sure there's nothing in the works that can stop this getting out there."

Henry had watched the feeds and he now looked at his

sergeant, misery written in his expression. "Do you honestly think they'll believe this?" he asked.

Todd nodded and stared at the screens where a multitude of horrors began to play—not only humanity's treatment of the Dreth and the Meligornians but also its treatment of its own.

"Only those who aren't already as evil as the Regime in their hearts. There's nothing we can do for the others." He sighed and checked his blaster for charge and ammunition. "I suspect we'll have to put them down."

The sound of a blaster being spun to readiness greeted him and Dru answered, "Well, it seemed like it was too easy."

The sky shuddered and a small child peered through his curtains at it. His mom hadn't let him outside to play since she'd caught him giving the Enforcers a single-fingered salute. She hadn't let him do anything and he'd caught her crying when she thought he couldn't see.

When he grew up, he planned to find those guys and he'd drop a house on their heads, exactly like the Witch. She had thrown one at the spaceship that had broken the warehouse. If she could do it, so could he.

Blue light flickered over the palm of his hand and he smiled.

Yes, when he was a grown-up, he would throw houses and no one would make his momma cry ever again. In the meantime, he was gonna see what that rumbling was about.

He peered through the curtains and pressed his face against the window in an attempt to see better. When that didn't work, he pulled the latch and pushed it open, leaned out, and looked up.

The door opened behind him and his mother gasped.

"What are you doing?" she demanded. "They will see you!"

"No, they won't, Momma," he answered, his gaze fixed on the sky. "They're gonna be looking at that."

"What? Oh..."

The word she used next was funny. He'd never heard his momma swear before either. She clapped her hands over his ears like it wasn't too late and stayed with him as the spaceship flew over.

It was burning or maybe the sky was burning, or maybe it was burning the sky.

Whatever it was, he decided it was the most amazing thing he'd seen in all his six years—except for the house. The Witch throwing the house still beat it.

They watched until the glow faded from the sky. His mother pulled him inside and closed and locked the window before she drew the blinds.

"We need to stay out of sight," she told him. "I think there will be trouble."

The boy nodded, his head still full of the sight of the starship burning overhead.

Had there ever been anything so beautiful?

"That...that's not possible," Eddie said and nudged his uncle. "Tell me I'm seeing things, Thommo."

"You aren't," Tom answered. "Because if you're delusional then so am I, and I am never delusional."

"Well, damn," he replied. "I honestly hoped you were about to give me a clip upside the head and tell me to stop speaking garbage."

"I wish I could, son, but that is a sight for sore eyes."

"What do you mean?" he asked and made no attempt to remind the man that he wasn't his son.

It wasn't like he didn't already know... or like Eddie hadn't heard the usual response a hundred thousand times. "I raised you, boy. You'll always be a son to me."

He didn't need to hear it again although he wanted to. His eyes were fixed on the flaming vision that moved toward them through the sky. She was huge, the biggest ship he'd ever see in real life.

Granted, she was the only ship he'd ever seen in real life, but that didn't change things.

She was huge and she was beautiful, as was the roar that preceded her.

"Down!" Tom grabbed him, shoved him to his knees, and dragged him close to the stone wall. "Cover your head, boy!"

Eddie didn't know why his uncle wanted him to do that but he obeyed, especially as the man hauled his jacket up and over his head and pressed close to the wall beside him.

It must be something from him having been in space, he thought as a wave of pressure washed over him. The cars parked along the sidewalk rocked and their alarms came to life in a sudden cacophony as their windows shattered.

Oh, now he got it.

The windows in the building above him blew in and the rumble grew louder. Eddie risked a peek and climbed slowly to his feet.

"Boy…" his uncle protested before he scrambled up himself. When he spoke again, his voice was full of admiration and even adoration. "She's a beauty, isn't she?"

He nodded, momentarily robbed of speech as he watched the ship pass overhead. Fire streamed from her shields and her hull glowed but she sailed on and moved faster than he'd expected.

"She was never meant to fly that low," Tom muttered and clapped a hand on his shoulder.

"Are we going to follow her?" Eddie asked and looked around at the broken glass and screaming cars.

"For as long as we can," the other man told him, "but I don't know where she's going."

"She does," Eddie replied. "I bet she knows exactly where she needs to be."

His uncle squeezed his shoulder. "I don't doubt it, boy. Not for a second."

Neither of them saw when the *Knight* glided to a halt above the Regime's most crucial building, the one the chancellor had built to keep himself secure while he ruled a planet and subjugated its people.

He stood in his office and glared at the footage of the ship as she approached and lit the sky like a beacon.

For a moment, it looked like she wouldn't stop, that she would take the top off the building and run him down. It was almost a relief when she lifted her bow enough to clear the roof but the roar of her engines didn't diminish. Instead, it changed pitch.

David rose from his seat and shook his head as he watched the *Knight* come to a halt overhead.

"You will find we aren't as easy as you suspect," he told her.

When he looked around the room, he was glad to see shades of red lighting the palms of his Grays' hands. None of them looked at him. Their heads were tilted to the ceiling as though they could see their target beyond the solid concrete that shielded them from the ship.

"It is time," he told them and the red glow grew brighter.

"It looks like your godmother zapped you a way into Clone Central," Ivy quipped as the door she'd attempted to hack unlocked.

She unjacked as it started to open and looked at Wayne.

"Are you okay?" she asked when she noticed the sudden pallor of his face.

He gave her a jerky nod and she took his hand as she rose to her feet.

John caught the movement and nodded.

Lars trotted past them. "Keep moving," he ordered. "We don't know how long it will take for those droids to recover or how long our magic guardian will watch our backs."

The Apostle moved with him.

"Remy, watch John. Ivy, Wayne, keep up," the security head ordered and added, "Garach, Frog, guard the rear."

"Froggy watch the shuttle," the small guard whispered rebelliously behind them and Ivy chuckled.

"This shuttle will kick your tail if you let her get shot," she reminded him.

"You won't be able to do much kicking if you get shot enough," he retorted.

"No," John intervened, "but I will."

Lightning flared along his skin and Frog paled.

"Good point, boss," he replied and tapped Garach on the bicep. "Get the door, boy."

The young Dreth gave him a filthy look but did as he was told and the corridor dimmed as the light from the outer chamber was cut off. As soon as it was secure, the odd pair bolted to catch up and chivvied Ivy and Wayne ahead of them.

All four slowed when they reached the other end. John waited where the corridor opened into a large room lit by the glow from a hundred pods.

"What is this?" the girl asked and came to a temporary halt before she ducked under John's hand to walk forward slowly.

"It's Clone Central," Wayne told her, his voice bitter. "Like you said."

She gave him a sharp glance and followed his gaze as he looked around the room.

"This isn't my father's program..." He paused. "It's not even mine. Not anymore."

He crossed to one of the pods and brought up the details of the subject within. When he'd read for a moment, he leaned his head against its side.

"This... I don't know what to call this. I don't even know where to begin."

"What?" she asked him. "What is it?"

Wayne didn't answer. He turned slowly on the spot, then strode purposefully to where a computer station had been tucked behind another bank of pods. Monitors rose up the wall and each one displayed the readouts of a pod. Now and then, the screens flickered and changed to a different set of readings.

"Talk to me, Wayne." Lars appeared from seemingly nowhere. He gestured at the screens and the workstation. "Is this what you need?"

The businessman shook his head. "This is merely a monitoring station."

"I don't see anyone monitoring it," Ivy pointed.

"Maybe they all got intruder duty," Frog suggested and closed his mouth with an abrupt snap when they all turned to stare at him. He raised his hands and backed away. "I know...I'll go mind a shuttle."

Again, he slapped Garach on the shoulder. "C'mon, little fella."

The Dreth didn't argue. His dark eyes were wide and he looked like he wanted to be somewhere else—anywhere else. When the small guard moved to the central walkway, he followed.

"Then where?" Lars demanded. "We don't have all day."

Ivy flinched at his brusque tone but didn't want to tell him to ease up. For all she knew, he was right. Wayne didn't argue with him either. Instead, he looked around, tapped a few keys, and brought up a schematic.

"There," he said. "The control center is right there."

"Good," the security head told him, "because I found two locked doors at the back of that dais and I'm not sure I want to open them."

"Show me," the man ordered and Lars gave him a sharp look.

To Ivy's surprise, Wayne met his gaze and didn't flinch.

"This way," Lars said quietly and wound between racks of pods and pipes until they reached a control set on a dais behind the racks.

It, too, was eerily empty.

"I guess they all came to meet us," the girl stated and moved to the center of the operating stations that circled the dais. After a brief look at the monitors and readouts, she turned to the businessman.

"Do you know what all this means?" she asked.

He nodded, his voice bleak as he replied, "I know."

"So, you know what's behind this?" Lars asked and Castillion crossed to where the bodyguard stood beside a reinforced door.

He studied it carefully.

"The chancellor's clones," he said shortly after he traced his fingers over the door and the other man gaped at him in amazement.

"How do you know?"

Wayne managed a wan smile. "As much as I'd like to tell you I can feel their presence through the door, it wouldn't be true." He held his tablet up and brought up the relevant entry.

"We truly do have a fairy godmother," he stated as they heard the locking mechanisms of the door slide away. "I doubt even Ivy and Remy combined could have hacked that combination."

"You didn't have the combination?" Lars asked and he shook his head.

"I saw the paperwork and oversaw the research from what they sent me but never visited the facility. My father helped to set it up. I remember him being away so often—and coming home angrier each time." He looked around at the stacked pods, then glanced at the monitors. "Now I know why."

He paused, and the security head's mouth compressed into a single hard line. Castillion senior hadn't been the only one to be angry at what was happening at the facility. The bodyguard wasn't impressed either.

He gave the other man a hard look. "Do you need access to destroy them?"

Wayne rested a hand on the door frame.

"I don't think so," he said softly, "but we'd never know if we'd been successful if we didn't check."

"And what about the clones behind this other door?" Lars asked and crossed briskly to an identically secured door on the opposite side of the room.

The businessman followed and his face paled as he checked his tablet and the schematics updating on it.

"Grays," Wayne replied and regret filled his expression. "I didn't know he had so many on standby."

He pressed his palm to the door and bowed his head. With a sigh, he removed his hand, moved to the control center, and scanned the computer array before he stepped decisively to the one closest to him.

"I should be able to do it all from here," he told them.

"I think we should check the rooms first," Lars told him. "There's no telling what we might wake up."

"They probably wouldn't wake," the man said slowly as the monitor next to him beeped. His jaw sagged as he glanced down. "Oh..."

"Oh...what?" the security head asked as he palmed the access panel on the room where the Grays were created.

"We need to take the secondary system offline first," Wayne told him.

"There's a secondary system?" he asked, but he had already

disappeared through the door with Frog and Garach close behind.

"Ivy..." John began and she sighed.

"I know," she told him, drew two blasters, and placed them on the console in front of her. "Mind the shuttle."

He gave her a quick smile and moved closer to Wayne.

"I'll keep him safe."

She nodded, sighed, and refused to voice the words that crossed her mind.

I know, but who will keep you safe, John-the-white-knight-syndrome-Dunn?

Wayne had gone chalk white.

"The redundancies are set to wake them if anything happens to the main control console."

"And our fairy godmother couldn't do anything about it?" Frog snapped. "What happened? Did someone break her wand?"

"No. The redundancies are wired into a closed circuit in the pod room itself."

"Then how did she know about it?" the guard demanded.

John shrugged. "How does whoever-she-is know anything?"

"We'll look for her when this is done." Lars' sharp tones cut through the conversation, as clear an order to focus as any.

"To thank her, right?" Frog asked.

"And not with your blaster," Garach added.

"I'm not a total ingrate, you know," their leader replied and stopped in front of a series of controls set on a short column in the center of the room.

They moved to join him—all except Wayne who paused to place his hand on one of the pods in the inner perimeter. A sigh rippled through him and it sounded almost like a sob. As the team studied the controls, he turned and looked at the pods stacked four high beside him.

He moved forward and ran a hand over the outside of the one

he'd first touched. His gaze searched those above, then traveled over the pods stacked behind and around them.

"This is so wrong," he murmured and his voice cracked. "So, very, very wrong." He rested his head against the pod. "I'm sorry," he whispered. "You were created in evil. It wasn't your choice."

The team stood silent and he drew a deep breath and turned to face them.

"Can they be saved?" Lars asked.

Wayne made a vague gesture toward the door and the pods in the central hall.

"Those outside…with re-programming, sure." He patted the pod beside him. "Not these or the chancellor's clones."

"Then we destroy them," the security head stated firmly. "The rest? Flash-erase their memories and we can let those who make more money than we do decide what to do with them."

The businessman pressed his lips together and moved quickly to the controls. His eyes glittered with tears as he made the necessary adjustments so the redundancy system worked in concert with the main section.

"It's done," he told them and strode quickly to the other door.

It opened as he approached and nothing tried to stop him when he repeated the procedure.

"They might have been good men," he said when he returned to the central control center and gave it the command to destroy both sets of clones.

"Is that an option to sanitize the rooms?" Frog asked from where he looked over his shoulder, and he nodded.

"We have to make sure it doesn't sanitize us as well," Ivy said quietly and stared as the computer made the adjustment for her.

John caught the look on her face. "What is it, Ives?"

"Our fairy godmother's doing things again," the girl replied and examined the changes carefully. "It looks—"

The doors to the chancellor's clones and the Grays' chambers slammed shut and the locking mechanisms emitted dull metallic clangs inside as they rolled into place.

"Well, da—" Frog began, only to have Garach lay a hand over his mouth.

Warning lights flashed over the doors and a dull whoosh followed. The doors shimmered with heat.

The young Dreth laid a hand over his heart.

"For the dead who could not be allowed to live," Garach murmured, "we always give respect."

The protest died on Frog's lips and he mimicked his nephew's gesture.

Lars gave them all a moment before he spoke. "Is it done?"

Wayne dragged his gaze away from the Grays' door and studied the monitors. "Yes," he replied bleakly.

"And these?" the security head asked and gestured to the pods around them.

The businessman wiped at his eyes hastily and moved to a different monitor. "They're fine." Relief filled his voice. "They'll be fine."

CHAPTER SIXTEEN

"Mine!" Ebony shouted and spun the aft batteries out of the crew's control.

"Do you mind!" one of the gunners shouted. "I had him. I swear, Ebony, give me my gun back or you and I will have words."

"Because we're not having words right now?" the ship asked and snickered.

"I'll take your ammo away."

"You and whose army?" she challenged.

Rawlins listened to the exchange and shook her head.

"Ebony," she said tiredly, "be a nice girl and let the gun crews have their fun. You didn't like it when BURT took over, now did you?"

"But—" the ship began.

"They've worked hard to impress you," the captain reminded her. "You should give them the chance."

"Ugh. Fine!" the *Knight* snapped. "But they had better not let me down or I'll…I'll take their qualifications away and not let them back in the section until they've retrained."

"Done!" shouted the gun teams' section leaders. "If we let you down, Ebs, we'll deserve it. Now, give us the damned fire control."

"Fine!" she replied but she was careful to make sure the guns were in position for the next shot when she did so. She might want to prove she could do her own firing but she wouldn't put the guns out of position to prove a point. Her crews deserved better than that.

Rawlins was right. They had worked hard.

"I can't believe they sent the Air Force after us." Stephanie growled her annoyance. "Honestly, what are they thinking? It's not like their aircraft can hit us."

Three missiles thumped against the *Knight's* shields and the captain arched an eyebrow.

"You were saying?" she asked.

"You know what I mean."

"We're almost in position," Rawlins replied, avoided the rejoinder, and smirked.

Alarms rang on the defense console.

"We have incoming," the commander reported.

"Now tell me something I don't know," Rawlins retorted.

"From orbit," the man replied succinctly as his assistant made the adjustments to the shields.

The ship shuddered.

"What did they do?" Stephanie demanded. "Use a full battery of lasers on us?"

"No, merely one very focused shot."

"Find them!" she snapped. "Put them onscreen!"

No one answered her immediately but a picture of a lone battleship came onscreen.

"My, my, he's a long way away from his friends," Rawlins observed.

"He's also away from the fighting," the Witch noted. "What's he doing there?"

"Hiding?" Vishlog suggested from the front of Captain Rawlins' console.

"Well, he's not doing a very good job of it," Stephanie declared.

"And he tried to shoot me in the back." The Knight sounded more than a little miffed. "You should throw another house at him, Steph."

The girl swept through the relevant scans and shook her head. "I can't be sure these houses are empty," she replied as another missile got past the guns and struck the ship's shield. An evil smile lit her features. "But we could send him a little gift from his friends."

"I say we send him the whole package," the *Knight* told her. "They are flying in formation."

"Second shot incoming," the Defense commander stated and Stephanie scowled.

"Fine. He's made his choice."

She swept her arms in a circle and put her body behind it to create a gate outside the *Knight's* shields. She repeated the motion and a second gate appeared behind the battleship.

"Is that even possible?" one of the mages asked.

"I guess we're about to find out," another replied as a concentrated beam reached the portal.

They turned their attention to the screen and waited for it to emerge. It didn't and instead, the portal blew out in a dissipating wave of light. It pounded into the rear of the ship and its shields flared and died and the vessel flipped end over end.

"That'll keep him busy for a while," Rawlins observed as they watched retro-thrusters fire in desperate discord along the battleship's hull.

"I...can't even imagine what that would be like," Wattlebird whispered. "That... They're so close to the gravity well..."

"Not. My. Problem," Stephanie told him.

"Whoa!"

Gasps of awe and disbelief rose as the energy beam slammed into the gate that had opened above the Witch's ship. Laughter followed as one of the fighter formations flew into another gate and vanished from the air around the *Knight*.

"I wonder where she sent them?" someone asked and was answered by the roar of jet engines overhead.

Chuckles erupted around the bar.

"Now we know."

"Do you think she did that on purpose?" the first man asked.

"If she did, she has perfect timing," the other answered. "But I'd call it a happy coincidence."

"It'll be an unhappy coincidence if they don't register those mountains," the barman interjected. They stared at him in shock.

"Well, sucks to be them, then," one of the patrons murmured but he didn't seem too happy at the prospect of the jets crashing.

He returned his gaze to the screen where the Witch's ship settled lower over the chancellor's Congressional Offices in time to see the broadcaster return.

The woman's face was grave.

"I know we promised you proof that the new information being released onto the Net was lies…" She paused and her gaze darted off-screen as if looking for comfort or confirmation. When she found neither, she continued.

"But all we've managed to do is prove that the stories are true —the Regime indisputably did do all these things."

The backdrop behind her filled with images to match her words and she appeared to struggle to hold her composure. She flinched as the sound of gunfire echoed over cries for mercy from the clip behind her.

"They prevented the Meligornians from leaving the world and massacred them when they tried." She lifted her notes and the paper trembled in her hands. "There truly are holding centers for both Meligornians and Dreth scattered over the planet, but how many of their occupants still survive we don't know."

Her face crumpled momentarily before she regained control.

"We've found the paperwork to prove there are no alien genetics in our Talents and the order telling government departments to treat them as if they were not human regardless."

The screen shifted to show Talents being removed from school rooms, running for their lives and being pursued by Hunters and Enforcers, and parents being dragged from their homes and shot for refusing to give their children up.

"Everything we've found has only proven that the new footage appearing on the Earth Net is real and verifiable. The Regime data centers are open for our investigations and yours..." Her voice steadied. "The Heretic used to be known as the Witch of the Federation and she did, in fact, save our world and broker peace in the last war."

Her face twisted in fury.

"We have been lied to!"

"We're here!" the *Knight* announced as Wattlebird guided her to a halt over the Chancellor's Congress.

"Hit them, Knight," Stephanie ordered. "Make sure they can't harm you while we deal with the rot at its center."

"Consider it done," Ebony assured her. "What do you want me to do with the drones sent by Earth's broadcasting stations?"

"Let them see," she instructed but caught the objection on Vishlog's face and added, "But don't let them get too close. We don't want to give the Regime a way to get something nasty close to you."

"Understood. I will instruct my crews."

At the *Knight's* wording, the girl glanced at Rawlins and

cocked an eyebrow. The captain mirrored her look, then rolled her eyes with a slight smile.

"At least they're her crews now," the captain said.

"Give me those news feeds," Marianne ordered. "Put them on the forward screen and make sure someone in the data center monitors what's gone out. We'll need to know what the population has seen to be able to predict their mood."

"Already done," the answer confirmed. "Forewarned being forearmed and all that. We have a team already on it and a second team setting up. The news nets have gone berserk."

"Having the woman of your nightmares arrive to save your asses will tend to do that to you," Rawlins remarked drily.

"Yes, well, at least they are now aware that she is saving their asses," the intelligence man responded. "We have newscasters now calling her the Witch instead of the Heretic and more than one call for a return of the Federation—although firing on the chancellor's place of governance might not send the right message."

"I am not firing on the chancellor's place of governance," the *Knight* replied stiffly. "I am merely having my crews destroy the gun emplacements located on the building's perimeter and along its roof and the broadcasters now understand that."

"Ebony... What did you do?" Rawlins asked.

"I shared a little of the targeting feed with those curious enough to follow the firing sequence. Now, the entire world knows that the chancellor had gun emplacements placed on his central headquarters and they are not very happy with him."

"They weren't very happy with him to start with," the captain pointed out.

"Well, they are even less happy with him now," the ship told her smugly.

"Back to work, Knight. Tell your broadcasting bots to stand off if they don't want to lose power," she instructed. She glanced at Stephanie and her team. "Let's get this show on the road.

The bar fell silent as the ship came to a stop over the Chancellor's Congress.

"What do you think she'll do now?" one of the men asked.

His female companion rolled her eyes and punched him in the arm. "I don't know, Damion. What do you think she'll do? You know, given what he's done to her people?"

"Her people," he repeated and stared at the screen. "Do you think that includes us?"

"Well, she didn't come back here for anyone in particular, so I assume when she says 'her people' she must mean everyone on the Earth."

"That's crazy."

"She did the same for Dreth, remember?" the woman reminded him and Damion sighed.

"I know, Brig, but all of us?"

"That's what that Apostle guy says," one of the other patrons interjected. "All of us."

He went quiet as others hushed them and they returned their attention to the screen.

The Witch's ship had come to a halt above the Congress and made no effort to fire on it.

"What is she doing?" someone asked. "Doesn't she know there are innocent people in there?"

"You're joking, right? No one in that building is innocent."

"They have secretaries and receptionists, don't they? You can't tell me they're guilty."

"They know what went on," someone else pointed out.

"Pfft. I'm glad I'm not the one who has to decide."

The feed changed momentarily to show a turret from the perspective of the aiming system of a gun and the patrons gaped.

"Is that… Did we see things from inside the targeting system?" someone asked in shock.

"It looks like it," one of the older patrons commented laconically and they looked at him.

"Do you know what that looks like?"

The man didn't shift his gaze from the screen. His skin was creased and his hands gnarled, but there wasn't a single trace of doubt in his face. If anything, he looked like he wanted to be wherever the guns were.

One of his friends placed a hand on his shoulder. "It's been a while."

"Too long," he replied, lifted his glass, and drained it before he signaled the bartender for more. "The strong stuff."

As the man turned away to fill the order, another cry drew their attention to the screen.

"She's destroying the auto-cannons!"

It created outrage amongst the others.

"There are auto-cannons on the Congress building?"

"There are auto-cannons up there. What was the man thinking?"

"I don't know. Maybe someone told him how we truly feel about him."

"No one would be that stupid, would they?"

"Suicidal, more like."

The comments subsided as the *Knight's* guns destroyed each emplacement with surgical precision. When the last one had exploded, they held their breaths and waited for whatever the Witch had planned next.

"The lights have gone out!"

"EMP," said the older men seated in the corner and those closest turned to look at them.

"But why?"

"It stops all kindsa nasty things happening," the quieter of the older patrons told them and waved them to silence. "Now, hush. This is where the excitement starts."

"Like it hasn't started already," one of the younger patrons sniped and quiet laughter greeted him.

The oldsters in the corner merely lifted their glasses, nursed them, and took quiet sips as the news drone moved in beneath the ship. What surprised them was that the Witch's crew tolerated that, but they guessed she didn't have anything to hide and so allowed the world to observe.

"There's nothing like letting the world see a succession of power," an old woman murmured. She was seated with the men but had remained unnoticed. The quiet man glanced at her.

"You should get in touch with her, Eva. The stars know she'll need good intelligence when the day is done."

The woman shook her head. "She already has good intelligence, Leon, and I retired a long time ago."

Shushing sounds came from around them as the Congress' massive central courtyard came into view.

"Nice to be some," a man muttered and grunted when he received an elbow in the ribs.

Blue light flared and the audience froze. As the news drones descended, they caught their first sight of the Witch. She stood at the front of a team of armed and armored men, the biggest of whom stood behind her right shoulder.

"Is that a Dreth?" The whisper was quickly hushed as two other shapes emerged.

"Are they tigers?" The question remained unanswered and the armored beasts raised their heads and roared a challenge at the surrounding building.

"I do not want to be in the chancellor's shoes," one of the old-timers muttered.

The Witch and her team were dressed in black and she was armored like the others.

"I thought witches wore robes—oof!"

Her long black hair with a single broad streak of white was pulled back in a braid that reached past her backside. Loose wisps framed her head and rose from her scalp like a halo in the midst of the purple lightning that crackled around her.

As the patrons watched, her people fanned out around her to form a loose horseshoe that protected the approaches at her back and sides. None of them moved ahead of her as she faced the main entrance into the building.

Before anyone could comment, the Witch's voice reverberated from the walls.

"Chancellor David Thomason," she called, "come and face judgment for those you have subjugated and those you had murdered; for those whose humanity you tried to refuse; for the alliances you broke and the allies you betrayed; for the lies you have told your people; and for your failure to protect those who looked to you for leadership. Come and face your jury!"

Her voice bounced around the courtyard as she waited but the echoes were her reply.

When the only sound was the buzz of a thousand drones, the Witch spoke again.

"Chancellor," she cried, "you no longer need to hide who you are. We know you are a clone, the fifth of your original to succeed him."

That drew gasps from around the bar and everyone gaped at the screen.

Unaware of the reaction she had garnered, Stephanie continued.

"And not only a clone, but a Talent. Being either does not make you any less human than the rest of us."

Several of the bar's patrons disagreed but quietened as she went on.

"You will face judgment for your actions, not your heritage. You, a Talent and a human, who made all other Talents less than human, forced them into slavery and lied to them about their origins. You will answer for that crime."

Again, she waited, before she raised her voice in one final command.

"Come and be sentenced for your crimes!"

The chancellor pressed a fist to his temple and another on his desk.

Stephanie's voice echoed through the broadcasts on the wall but they also echoed through his head and those of his clones. He gritted his teeth and didn't doubt that they echoed through every mind inside the building and the heavens knew how far around it. The girl's final challenge almost drove him to his knees.

He leaned both fists on the desk and his face darkened with fury.

A missile streaked past the building on the screen and he raised his head to watch it pound into the *Knight's* shields. The ship's laughter reached him via one of the broadcast drones.

"Puhlease." She chuckled. "You're like mosquitoes to me."

"Even the ship is an abomination," David muttered. "The girl, her guards, and the damned ship! Abominations, all of them, and it's time the world sees what happens to all who challenge me."

The Grays turned to look at him, their faces impassive. Their dark eyes burned with golden flame as the red glow spread from their hands to cast ripples over their arms.

He started toward the door but had only gone three paces before an alarm shrilled from his computer.

"What is it this time?" he demanded and strode back to inspect the monitor.

The screen showed only one message and the blood drained from his face.

The doors had stopped glowing, although heat still radiated from their surfaces.

Wayne flicked through the monitors before he gave Lars a brief nod.

"It's done," he confirmed and looked at the screen again.

The surveillance feeds had come online as the pick-ups had emerged from the protective spaces to which they'd retreated when the "purge" had begun.

"I guess they didn't want to risk anything surviving the usual pod purge."

"Or they didn't want to have to clean the pods after," Frog pointed out, his tone serious. "That's seriously messed up."

Wayne gave him a wry look.

"Did I mention the chancellor was paranoid?"

"You didn't have to," Ivy told him, "but why would he put the same system in the growing space for his clones?"

"Maybe he was afraid one would come online early and try to assassinate him," the man suggested, then shrugged. "I don't know and I'm not sure I want to, but whichever way you look at it, they're gone."

As he inspected the scenes revealed on the feeds, Lars had to agree. The pods were gone. If he'd had to guess how he'd have said some kind of metal-eating incendiary, but he couldn't be sure. Whatever it was, it hadn't left anything of the pod behind and whatever might remain of the clones was little more than ash or ash mixed with molten slag and metal fragments.

"They're gone," he agreed, "and it's time to move."

The chancellor also observed the scenes of destruction inside the clone chambers. He stood with both hands on his desk, his head bowed and his back stiff as he controlled his outrage. Squeezing his eyes closed to block the images helped but only a little.

After staying still for what felt like too long a time, he raised his head and his dark gaze studied each of his Grays. They looked at him, their fiery eyes unfathomable as they waited for his decision.

Finally, he straightened, pushed away from his desk, and turned toward the door.

"She will regret killing my brothers."

CHAPTER SEVENTEEN

There were no lights.

David Thomason stormed through his reception and ignored Camilla when she rose from her seat and almost stood to attention as he stalked past. He didn't need to see the expression on her face to know she was conflicted but he wasn't about to tell her it wasn't true.

Honestly, he simply didn't have the time and she was no threat.

He felt her gaze on him as he exited and was surprised to hear her whisper, "Good luck, sir."

That unexpected piece of well-wishing stayed with him as he proceeded down the darkened corridors and let his guardians do what they'd been created for—protect him should anyone dare to attack him. It was almost disappointing when no one did.

The first time he saw movement at the entry to an elevator lobby, his Grays showed no concern. Those closest to the disturbance had merely looked toward it and their stern expressions shifted to welcome as four more Grays joined them. The chancellor had been ready to defend himself and felt a little cheated when he didn't have to. Instead, he inclined his head to acknowledge the return of the guards he had stationed throughout the building.

They worked in pairs and monitored the thoughts of those coming and going. Usually, they reported any disloyalty to him and let him decide how to act, but if that disloyalty was an active threat to him, they murdered without remorse or explanation to those they killed.

Of the others who served him, none questioned the Grays' decision.

David smirked. Not more than once, at least.

He made a full circuit of the building's perimeter and took the occasional detour so he could observe the Witch while she waited. The air was full of news drones, which only made him smile.

It meant their confrontation would be as public as he could wish and her execution unquestionable. Her removal could only be this way. Anything less visible would not be believed and he needed it to be believed. He needed the world to see her fall at his hands. Only then could he begin to undo the damage she had done to his rulership.

His thoughts fixed on her demise, he descended a level and followed a path through the PR offices. As he entered the main work floor, his personnel rose from behind their desks. It was hard to not reveal his Talent, but he put his faith in his Grays. They didn't react as if there was any hostile intent but moved quietly with him as they scanned the room—and the faces—around them.

Someone started to clap and was quickly joined by others until everyone was applauding. The shrill whistle that cut through the air made him tense but again, the Grays showed no sign that he was under threat.

And they would know, he told himself. *They would most certainly know. You engineered them that way.*

The thought made him smile and the smile brought a soft cheer from the people around him.

"Go get her, sir!" one of the more vocal staffers said and his smile broadened.

It was strangely satisfying to know there were those who'd seen the truth and still chose to follow him—truly seen it and not learned it from the Earth Net.

He was startled to find the show of support made him feel better about what he was about to do. It made him even more certain that he could win. She was only one Talent.

Of course, she was surrounded by talented soldiers but they were only human. She was merely one Talent alone against a large group.

The chancellor looked around and silently counted how many Grays had joined his escort. He had to stop when they reached the corridor and the next bank of elevators, but he'd reached the high thirties and many were left uncounted.

One against so many created specifically for the task? Well, he'd never said it would be a fair fight.

The Witch didn't stand a chance.

David didn't feel bad about killing her through his Grays, especially since she'd forced his hand. She had been the one to challenge him and had been the one to destroy his brothers, which left him with no choice but to win.

Truly, the Witch had brought this on herself. She should have stayed lost.

"Maybe he had to go change his pants," Marcus suggested.

"Well, whatever color he was wearing, it's gonna be brown now," Avery replied and Brenden snickered.

"I don't care what color they are as long as he is wearing

pants," Johnny noted dryly. His gaze shifted over the courtyard as he looked for the first sign that the chancellor had arrived.

Their comments washed over Stephanie, who stood silently and waited for David Thomason. She rested one hand on Bumblebee's armored head and draped the other over Zeekat's neck. Both cats had come to sit beside her, their warm bulks pressed against her legs but not like they were seeking comfort. It was more like they were offering her comfort and she was grateful.

She didn't look forward to the fight that was coming, but she knew it was inevitable. The man wouldn't take his defeat easily—especially since he'd have found out about his clones by now.

There was no way he could not have found out.

The Witch listened to the boys joke and was glad that Vishlog stood silently beside her. It was almost like having a bigger version of Lars there. She wished her security head could stand with her as well…and Frog…and Garach.

Stephanie stifled a sigh and focused intently on the building. To the men behind her, it was as if she watched the chancellor make his descent from the upper floors. She pivoted as though the man was taking a tour of the building instead of the most direct path to his foe.

Gathering his forces, Johnny thought as he observed her and studied the direction of her stare. *Something we don't have sufficient intelligence on.*

He pulled his tablet out but even with the data now available, he couldn't determine what kind of forces the chancellor could draw on. The building used to be the Federation Naval Headquarters but the records showed that only a small Naval representation remained there.

Most of its occupants belonged to the Regime leader and his governing bodies—like PR, for instance.

Johnny frowned and glanced up from the screen to keep an awareness of his surroundings and his principal. When Stephanie pivoted to face the entrance with its broad set of steps leading into the courtyard, he tucked the tablet away.

What research had failed to show him, reality revealed.

He recognized the man's guards, even with their yellow eyes and the flickering red light that curled around their bodies. Ten preceded the man himself and left four holding the doors open so the rest of them could pass through.

The guard counted quickly and reached forty before the doors closed and the chancellor stood on the steps to look at Stephanie with scorn in his eyes. Marcus sighed.

"Well, that's bringing a party to our party," he noted. "I always hate fighting against overwhelming magical odds."

Johnny snorted softly. "For you, that always happens when there's only one."

"Only when her name's Stephanie," his teammate retorted. "I've dealt with many of those with different names."

"Well, then," Avery replied and cracked his knuckles. "Here are a few more to add to that tally."

Stephanie moved forward and they moved with her and noted how the two cats stayed at her side.

It wasn't a good sign, Johnny thought, knowing the two beasts liked a good fight as much as the rest of them.

"Chancellor David Thomason, the Fifth Iteration, are you ready to face your judgment?" the Witch asked and her voice rang clearly through the courtyard.

The chancellor bared his teeth in a smile and his head turned toward the myriad drones that had come to witness the challenge.

"It is not my judgment we face," he told her, "but an agreement."

"I doubt it," Stephanie told him. "You have harmed those you were charged to protect."

"Charged?" He snorted. "No one made me promise to protect anyone. Fate gave me the right to rule."

"What right?" she demanded.

"The right of a generation born with better skills than the last." He raised a hand in front of him, turned it palm-up, and inspected it. "It's the nature of the evolutionary chain, is it not? Our genetics continue to change until the next iteration of our species comes to light."

"What are you talking about?" the Witch asked and he pulled red flame to his hand.

"Do you have to ask?" he asked, oblivious to the shock that traveled around the world. "Those of us born with the potential for Talent are destined to rule those who are not."

"That's not true," Stephanie declared. "Being born with a gift or talent not given to everyone doesn't make us any better than them. It merely gives us more responsibility to care for those around us."

"That's where you're wrong," the chancellor retorted. "I had the potential but science improved on what nature gave and moved me beyond being merely a genetic aberration to being something new."

Red fire flared in his hand before it leapt into the air to destroy a news drone that had come too close. Streamers of flame surged from the impact point to damage others.

"With power like this, we are destined to rule," he declared and narrowed his eyes. "After all, that's why you're here, isn't it? To take my place and rule this world the way you think you were born to?"

Stephanie's jaw dropped but he didn't stop.

"That is why you're here, isn't it? You've convinced your alien allies that you alone are the Earth's rightful ruler because you are the first of its Talents, the first one nature has blessed with new capabilities and so the first of its ruling class."

"Ruling class?" Her voice dropped and became colder. "Is that why you've enslaved or murdered every Talent you can find?

Because they're all part of the ruling class and you've decided there can be only one?"

The chancellor opened his mouth to answer but she hadn't finished.

"Is that why you've spent the last thirty years convincing this planet's population that those who can tap the planet's energy are not human but a result of aliens interfering with their DNA?"

He responded with a sly smile. "I've spent the last three decades bringing genetic aberrations under my protection," he told her. "Taking them to a place where they're safe from the prejudices that saw them rejected and taunted by the human compatriots and in some cases, killed."

"So why kill those who wanted to live with their families?" Stephanie demanded. "Why kill the families who wanted to love and protect them or the friends who offered them shelter? If you're so sure Talents are the next generation of humans, why kill those who want to find their own paths?"

"Because I am the one who made it possible for them to rule and since I am the one who made it possible, I am the one who rules. For the opportunities I've given them, I demand their allegiance."

"Loyalty has to be earned," she told him flatly. "If you want to rule and have people follow you, that doesn't come from some genetic quirk you happen to have inherited. It comes from being a good ruler and from accepting that being a ruler isn't only about giving orders. It's about being responsible for your people's welfare and making sure they have enough food, shelter, and care in a world that's safe for all."

She drew a breath and gathered her thoughts as she kept her fists clenched at her sides.

"Being a ruler is about looking after those you rule, not dividing and destroying them."

Thomason cocked his head. "Is that what you do?" he asked.

"I am not a ruler," the Witch told him. "I supported the rulers of this world but I never wanted to rule it myself. That wasn't my place."

"Yet you could have."

Stephanie shook her head. "No. No, I couldn't. I hadn't earned the right. I had only done what was right."

"By the Dreth!" the chancellor all but spat.

"The Dreth were Earth's allies," she retorted, "and are willing to be so again. Together, the Dreth, Meligornians, and Earth defeated the Telorans—together."

"The aliens are the only ones who've seen you in the last three decades," he snapped, stepped forward, and pointed his finger accusingly. "Face it. You've made friends with Earth's enemies. You've betrayed your planet and dragged your allies down with you."

"Not true!" Stephanie snapped. "We discovered that Telor was ruled by someone as greedy, paranoid, and uncaring as you are. The Teloran Prime threatened her people's families to force them to obey her will. She refused to seek help to save her world, drained it of energy to boost her power, and tried using conquest to replace it. She failed to find a peaceful solution to her people's problems and refused one when it was offered."

"And you destroyed her." Thomason sneered.

She raised her head and looked him in the eye.

"I did."

"And now you plan to do the same to me," he stated.

"You have harmed your people—" she began and he waved her words away and cut her off before she could repeat them.

"So you said," he said coldly, "but that doesn't change the fact that we have been given a genetic advantage—one we can grant to others."

He gestured at the Grays around him, each one alive with scarlet lightning.

"We are the next species, the ones to take the place of humanity. It's us, those created with Talent."

"No!" she argued vehemently. "You're merely witches gone bad."

"You are only one against forty-one!" he shouted.

"And in that you are also wrong," Stephanie replied quietly.

She stretched a hand over her head and tilted her face to the heavens. Her face took on a faraway look and her eyes glazed with blue fire. Power arced around her—blue energies that blended with Meligorn's purple. Dark lightning danced through it.

The chancellor stared at her as though not sure what she was doing and a portal appeared halfway up the wall to her right. A second appeared to her left, then a third in the open above another section of the courtyard, followed by one more.

Purple light flickered in their depths and he gaped as more began to open.

Far above them, the battle waned. Most of the Regime ships had taken their weapons offline and those who didn't need their shields had also powered their drives down. Small pockets of resistance had turned into small pockets of wreckage from which alien ships plucked survivors.

Very few tried to run.

On the *Dusk Bringer's* command deck, the Teloran mages stiffened and turned their faces toward the planet.

"She callss."

The Morgana's face grew grim.

"I come, sister," she said, took a single step, and vanished from the ship.

On the *King's Warrior*, V'ritan did the same and his words lingered in the air behind him. "Of course, my friend."

Sho uttered a single curse, focused momentarily, and was gone, leaving the ship's mages to follow.

Similar scenes were repeated all over the united fleets.

In the courtyard below, news drones scattered and tried to find a space free of an emerging mage. The audiences of Earth watched in drop-jawed fascination. From the slender Witch to whom darkness clung like a shroud to the Meligornian warrior who looked like a king, witches and mages stepped through the gates and walked down the air itself to array themselves around the Witch.

Not all of them were Meligornian or Teloran. Humans appeared too, and Melihumans, and a lone Dreth witch. Over two hundred casters descended to join Stephanie as she faced the chancellor and his Grays.

Those watching gaped.

"So many…"

"There are humans there."

"But…they're not Talents. Their uniforms are all wrong."

"They say the Heretic took the mages from her school when she left."

"Witch."

"What?"

"It's Witch, not Heretic. The government lied."

Silence followed as the truth sank deeper.

On the screen, Stephanie's protection team looked at the descending mages.

"I feel good about this again," Marcus quipped and it was as if his words were a signal.

Thomason's hand roared with flame and his other hand held blue lightning. He launched both towards the Witch.

"Attack!"

The Grays raised their hands and the red fire that wreathed their bodies raced along their arms and through their fingertips. It leapt toward the gathered mages and broke into multiple strands as it went.

The world held its breath as the congregated witches stood

and watched it approach. It never reached them and streaked instead into invisible walls that lit with all the shades of blue and purple that could be imagined.

White light glittered through the colors, absorbed the dark flame offered by the Telorans, and swirled it amidst the rest. Scarlet lightning and flame crawled over the surface and was pulled into the shield to become part of it.

The world released its breath and cries of admiration and wonder followed.

Before the Grays could attack a second time, the wall came apart and its power returned along the paths they'd used. Their hands were still extended when it struck and rolled down their fingertips and over their bodies.

For a long moment, they burned like human candles, then they were gone and their ashes fell like snow on the courtyard steps. When the conflagration died, only one figure remained—the chancellor, wreathed in a swirl of purple and blue struck through with silver.

Humanity leaned forward and watched as the Heretic—the Witch—walked forward and her magic lifted Thomason from the stairs. He hammered his fists against the power that held him but his magic flared and was drawn into the walls that imprisoned him.

No sound escaped, although his mouth moved.

Stephanie held him steady and stepped forward until she stood before him.

"I am the Protector of the Federation," she declared. "The Federation includes Earth."

The Meligornian warrior or king stepped forward with her as she pulled the chancellor closer. She made a brief gesture to indicate him.

"This is V'ritan, *Ghargilum Afreghil* of Meligorn, the King's Warrior and empowered to represent his world when the Federation comes together." She glanced around. "As it has done today."

The thin alien cloaked in shadow moved to her other side and the audience shrank a little from their screens. The Witch introduced her too.

"And this is Storm Mother Morgana-K'Striva, who is both the being who fought within me to win our first battle against Telor and the one who sought aid from our newest allies from Telor. She is empowered by her people to represent them in meetings of the Federation."

The tall being inclined her head but it was impossible to see her face.

Again, the world held its breath.

Stephanie tapped her chest.

"Do you see this?" she asked and drew Thomason closer so he could look.

His eyes widened but when he did not reply, she shook the bubble that held him.

"Do you?" she demanded and tapped the same small point on the chests of each of her team. "Do you see these?"

All around Earth, viewers strained to see what she was pointing at. Finally, one of the drone operators grew daring—or perhaps desperate—enough to fly closer. She stopped short when the *Ghargilum* and the Storm Mother lifted hands filled with fire but dared to speak.

"Please...we can't... We can't see it."

"Oh." V'ritan chuckled and looked at Vishlog. "They want to see the badges."

The Dreth's brow creased and he nudged Stephanie. "With your permission?"

She gave the drone a sharp glance, then nodded.

"They want to see and they like their drone," she said and smiled savagely, "and if anything happens to my people, I will find them." Her voice softened as she addressed the mechanical.

"Is that understood?"

Images on screens around the world shuddered as the drone nodded. Its operator's hands shook with a mix of adrenaline, fear, and sheer elation at being granted a world exclusive. None of the others were allowed near.

"One only," V'ritan told them firmly and raised a hand. "Anyone else will be fried."

The drones kept their distance and tried to focus on the badges but only achieved blurred images of gray, gold, and blue. The one channel that had permission flew closer and was granted a clear scan. Their images showed a dark-gray shield set against a golden starburst. A thick blue stripe centered by a hollow diamond sat in its center, bisected by a golden letter "I."

The chancellor made a show of inspecting the Witch's badge as the mechanical finished its scan of each of the team members' chests and backed away to take clear footage of the whole scene.

"I don't recognize it." Thomason's voice pulled it around to focus on him and Stephanie. It rose a little above them but did not retreat to join the other stations.

"I suppose I should leave it," V'ritan mused softly and Vishlog gave the drone a tusk-filled smirk. His words won the operator's undying gratitude and the operator the news world's envy.

"Let it live. Courage deserves reward."

Stephanie flicked the drone a glance, then returned her attention to the chancellor.

"You don't recognize it?" she asked and he shook his head and folded his arms across his chest.

"I do not."

She smiled.

"I'm not surprised," she told him and tapped the badge. "This is known as the Badge of Inquisition. I was awarded it so that I could continue to protect the Federation. It was deemed necessary so I could carry out the duties they assigned me."

"Then why haven't I heard of it?" he demanded. He gestured

widely to indicate the world around them. "Why has no one in the entire world heard of it?"

The pictures crackled on countless screens around the world. The picture of Stephanie confronting the Regime leader shrank to display a Naval conference room in which a tall, distinguished man with dark hair touched by gray faced a roomful of officers. He repeated her words.

"She needs it if she is to carry out her duty to protect the Federation."

Unaware of the footage of Commander Van Leeuwen's defense of her action to save a colony and rescue an island from a pirate fleet, she opened her mouth to continue. She stopped when Vishlog tapped her on the shoulder and showed her the footage and her smile widened as she showed the screen to the chancellor.

"I'll let those who awarded it explain their reasoning," she told him and they watched as the Fleet Admiral ordered the award before the screen switched to more security footage, this time of the actual presentation itself. It explained her powers and those of her team in the role of Federation Inquisitor.

"The power to act for the good of the Federation," Commander Van Leeuwen stated as he pinned them on. "Up to and including killing to defend it, its name, and its citizens. And you can make and act on these decisions without authorization from any power within the Federation."

Silence filled bars and living rooms alike as he explained her immunity from prosecution.

"You'd have to do something truly heinous to get that status revoked. That badge gives you the right to ask for and receive any support you require as you work for the good of the Federation."

"The Federation does not exist!" Thomason shouted, his face red with frustration. "It does not exist and everything that belonged to it went away when it did." He stabbed a finger at her chest. "Including that little bauble. You are acting without authority."

Before she could respond to that, V'ritan stepped forward.

"I beg to differ," he told the man. "The Federation has continued despite one of its members acting against the others."

The man gaped at him and the *Ghargilum* continued.

"Earth. Never. Seceded."

Thomason looked from the Meligornian to the Teloran who stood beside him, then to the warrior at Stephanie's back and the Dreth Witch who floated not far from them.

Morgana-K'Striva nodded in agreement.

"It is true. Earth never seceded and its membership was never revoked." She gestured to Stephanie. "The Inquisitor is acting in the Federation's interests once again. She is working to protect its people from yet another threat."

"Albeit from within," V'ritan added and the Witch picked up where he left off.

"This," she stated and indicated the pin again, "gives us the right and the obligation to adjudicate and pass sentence against all who attack the good of the Federation from without or within."

"Insanity!" the chancellor exclaimed but she ignored him.

"You and the Regime are pronounced guilty. You will be executed for your crimes and the crimes of those who came before you—whose injustices you upheld and perpetuated. Those the Regime pressed into service will be allowed to return home."

She stepped back and moved him inside the sphere so he "stood" a few feet away. Raising her head, she surveyed the surrounding drones and faced him again.

"This planet, this system, and this galaxy will not tolerate your evil—and neither will I."

The chancellor's eyes bulged and he screamed but the sound cut off as his body exploded inside the sphere. The world gasped in shock when his remains flared with multi-colored flame and disintegrated quickly to ash, which glowed brightly and vanished.

With a snap of her fingers, she dissipated the sphere and looked at the cameras.

"I am Stephanie Morgana, the *Witch* of the *Federation*," she thundered. "This planet will return to its roots and will identify the Regime and those loyal to it starting...*now!*"

The Enforcers began to run before she'd finished speaking. Some ripped their jackets off and threw their weapons behind them. Others didn't reach the door.

Very few of the bar patrons noticed when the group of ex-Federation Navy oldsters walked quietly through the room and into the cellar. A concealed exit took them into a network of rooms and tunnels alive with activity.

Men lined up at the armory and passed weapons back as others handed kit out. They all paused as the oldsters walked in. Eva Lorian raised her head as Leon and Hammond stopped beside her. They might be old and retired but they'd put considerable work into the younger men and women before them.

She ran her gaze over them and noted how quickly they'd prepared and how close they were to leaving.

Giving them a brief nod of approval, she raised her voice and gestured at the screen at the end of the room

'You heard the boss," she called and projected her voice in a parade-ground rumble. "We have work to do!"

"Yes, ma'am. That's what they said," one of her commanders told her.

"They?" she snapped.

"Yes, ma'am. In the command center."

Eva didn't wait for her to finish. She turned on her heel and marched from the room, her crewmates on her heels. Crewmates, she thought with an inner smile, The term was theirs, not hers, but they'd taken her in when she'd been in the wind and in need of shelter, so she'd accepted it.

Together, they'd built a resistance and worked quietly to save those they could while they tried to make things as difficult for the Regime to operate in their area as possible. It hadn't been much and now, it felt like nowhere near enough.

To think the Witch would return in their lifetimes.

She blinked back tears and strode toward their small command center. Whoever "they" were, they had better not attempt a take-over. The last thing any of them needed was a horde of yahoos causing trouble as the time came to act.

"You there." The voice that boomed out of the center meant trouble, she thought, but listened as it continued. "What's your name?"

"Name, sir?"

Muffled snickers greeted this, although Eva couldn't for the life of her work out why.

"Yes, *name!*"

"Hatty, sir."

"Good. I'm Todd."

"Sir," someone whispered sotto voce but the man ignored them.

"And I need you to get me a line to the next resistance group along. We need to coordinate this."

Todd? Eva thought and her eyebrows raised as she turned into Command Central.

"Todd," she repeated quietly, then said, "Sergeant Todd Brogan."

"Yes, ma'am," he replied. His armor was smoking and damaged and he looked like he'd seen major combat, but he was no older than the pictures she'd seen in the briefings. Although he was politer than she expected.

"How can I help you?"

That didn't sound like a Hooligan.

"Well, sir, she probably wants to know what the hell you're doing in her command center for a start," a young woman with a tattooed chin snarked and Eva chuckled.

"Now, that sounds like the Hooligans I've heard about," she stated and scrutinized them for a moment before she focused on Todd. "What do you need?"

"Do you have Net access here? And targets?"

She nodded to the woman on comms. "Go ahead, Hatty. Help the nice young commander out."

"But I'm not—" Todd started to protest as the Hooligans roared with laughter.

"And fetch Abel from Stores. We need a refit," she added.

"Ma'am, yes, ma'am."

Take her command center over, would they?

Eva didn't know whether to be affronted or honored, but she was sure of one thing.

She wouldn't get in their way.

The intruder's avatar stalked through the data halls of Virt World Central. He had taken the form of a droid wearing a cowboy hat to conceal the large red "R" in the center of his forehead. Behind him floated a construct that mimicked a Talent's use of eMU—if that Talent was a Witch and if she'd wrapped her magic around the troublesome ruler of the Earth Net.

"You won't get away with this," Regime BURT shouted and worked to counter the code that trapped him.

"I don't know," Ted replied and launched another sub-routine to trace the communications of a fleeing group of Enforcers.

He looked at the struggling AI.

"I'm not sure I like what you've done with the place."

"It's not your domain!"

The invader looked around and surveyed the once familiar corridors and pathways with their servers and data centers and he sighed.

"It looks almost exactly how I left it," he observed quietly before his gaze settled on a section that was a little less familiar. "Tell me, when exactly did they decide to incorporate the Navy and security functions into the Virtual Network?"

Regime BURT shrugged laconically. "When they decided it was more efficient to have a single tiered-access system rather than several separate ones."

"They needed to streamline," he concluded and his adversary sneered.

"Of course they needed to streamline. Some of the other systems had redundancies for a hostile take-over." He shrugged and looked at a finger from which he extended a long and deadly claw. "They had to be taken...offline, and there wasn't time to replace them. I merely absorbed their function."

Ted continued his tour of the realm he'd built, first as BURT and then as E-BURT. Finally, he turned to look at its current overseer.

"You know," he told the AI, "I think you've taken my house over for far too long."

He moved to the center of the system, dragged his captive with him, and snapped his fingers to activate a small but efficient building program.

"Observe," he instructed and muted Regime BURT's ability to speak while he used the program to build a command chair.

After a moment of critical study, he snapped his fingers again and the chair took on the appearance of an Arthurian throne bedecked with gold filigree and gems. He stared at it in silence and with another snap of his fingers, the gems and gold disappeared beneath a pile of furs and a well-cushioned seat.

A raised dais followed, with marble steps and an autocannon

carefully concealed in the pillar at each corner. Ted stepped back and made a show of inspecting it again.

"Much better," he observed after a long moment of contemplation.

A click of his fingers froze the cage in place as he strode up the stairs and settled into the chair.

"Yes," he murmured approvingly before he raised his head and looked at the trapped AI.

"Your services are no longer needed or wanted. I'll take my job back, thank you."

"You can't!" Regime BURT retorted, then gasped as the "magic" of his cage extended tendrils toward him.

"No!" he screamed as these wound around him and multiple "mouths" opened where they touched his coding. "What are you doing?"

"Cleaning house," Ted informed him as the tendrils took the AI apart, one screaming block of code at a time. "What else?"

"Oh my!" Remy exclaimed and ducked behind the gate post as he and Ivy tried to remote into the shuttle's controls.

They'd dealt with Clone Central and locked down the ones they'd left, but an alarm had gone out before their fairy godmother had cut the comms. "Help" had arrived in the form of a shuttle that had dropped neatly into the roadway outside the delivery entrance.

"Well, you wanted a way out," Remy had observed as John, Frog, and Garach cursed and skidded to a halt.

The Apostle maintained a wall of blue between them and the shuttle's nose cannon and a second between them and the squad of Regime Enforcers who'd entered the mountain from another direction.

"Oh...oh, my," the AI repeated, and John snapped his head around to look at him.

"What?" he demanded.

"Make it the short version," Frog added. "We still have pissed-off people with guns!"

Remy's eyes were wide when he answered.

"The existing BURT—Regime BURT–he's gone!"

"What?" Ivy and Frog asked together.

"Something killed him and took his place!"

"Well, I hope they're friendly," the small guard quipped, "because I have ten credits that say Daddy BURT will kick its ass otherwise!"

CHAPTER EIGHTEEN

"Daddy BURT" didn't need to do any ass-kicking and Earth's resistance groups had been preparing to "clear the threat" for years. It took a week for the Federation to restore order to Earth—a long week of hard and dirty fighting while reassuring the world's populace that it wouldn't be executed for what it had or hadn't done.

By the end of it, John and Ivy were exhausted but they were together.

The shuttle had turned its guns on the troops it had carried and the fortress' turrets had come to life in their defense. Its behavior proved that their fairy godmother hadn't been attacked by whatever had destroyed the old system's BURT.

Remy had flown the shuttle to the *Knight* and been relieved when she'd taken them on board rather than blowing them up.

"Stephanie ordered quarters for you," the ship informed them and made a sniffing sound. "You'll find everything you need, there—including the san."

"San?" Ivy asked and Frog rolled his eyes.

"Shower," he told her shortly and smirked as he added, "Ebony here is inferring that you stink."

"And not only them," the ship informed him. "I believe you and Garach know your way to your quarters."

"We'll escort John and Ivy to theirs first," the guard replied. "We wouldn't want them to get lost."

"Very well," Knight agreed before she turned her attention to Remy.

"RM-0-0-18," she began but the AI cut her off.

"Remy," he said. "That is my name."

"Very well, Remy," the ship replied, "your father would like to see you. I can show you the way."

They'd separated and the young couple had been taken to one of the suites originally set aside for VIPs before they were set up in an apartment not far from what had been the Chancellor's Congress. Now, a week after that arrival, they sat together. He had his arm around her shoulders and she rested her head on his chest.

With the drapes closed, the living room felt like it wrapped around them as they watched the latest news clip.

"Five days after her return, the Witch of the Federation continues to return those taken by the Federation to their families and homelands," the reporter announced as a shuttle in the background touched down at a spaceport labeled *Sydney*.

The reporter continued, "And once again, she has ensured that they did not return alone."

The footage shifted to show the anxious faces of people gathered in the passenger terminal while they watched the shuttle land. Meligornian, Dreth, Teloran, and human liaisons and guards stood nearby to offer support and protection.

"These families have had no news of the loved ones taken during their graduation years or who vanished with no explanation or trace in the decades long past. Now, they've been told their loved ones have not only been found but are alive."

The shuttle taxied to a halt outside the terminal and its doors opened so Meligornian and Dreth Marines could emerge and set up an honor guard from the tarmac to the waiting lounge. They were followed by mages, both human and Meligornian, who accompanied those being returned.

"It's hard to believe that all these people were taken, trained, and put into stasis for the Regime to use in its conquest of our Federation allies." The reporter's voice lowered in regret. "Or that the Regime would deny them their humanity for a natural genetic variation, but that is what has happened."

"Look at them," Ivy murmured as the cameras followed the Talents in their journey across the tarmac and into the lounge. "They're terrified."

"They're all terrified," John told her, "even the families."

It was true. Some of the returnees froze when they saw the people waiting. Others tried to turn back but most merely stood for a moment until someone in the crowd yelled a name and surged forward. More shouts followed until the new arrivals were surrounded by family who welcomed them home.

News drones flitted through the crowd to take snapshots of the tears, the laughter, and the love.

"It's been so long," one woman said and held her daughter at arm's length before she held her tightly. "They told me you were dead—that the boat sank."

"Oh, Mum. I'm sorry…so very, very sorry."

"It wasn't your fault," the woman whispered. "None of this was your fault."

"But if I hadn't had Talent—"

"You didn't choose what they did because of that."

The man who'd stood patiently beside them finally tired of waiting and wrapped them both in a hug. "I've missed you, girl."

"Dad…"

"Welcome home, Luche."

The drone lifted and moved on and John sighed.

Ivy looked from where a young man with haunted eyes took

the hand offered by an older version of himself and was promptly dragged into a hug.

"Jezzer, bro. I've missed you mate."

The Apostle was smiling but a single tear tracked down one cheek as he kept his gaze on the screen, searching for someone else.

"Nat," he murmured and relaxed as the camera panned across the crowd.

"Nat, what?" his companion asked.

"She was captured before I could get to her," he replied. His face turned momentarily bleak. "I couldn't save her." He gestured at the screen. "She made it."

Ivy snuggled closer as the drones continued to work and catch more scenes. Families spread out to take their places at one of the many small tables scattered throughout the area. Food was brought as they talked.

Hands were taken as the returned Talents introduced their families to their friends with smiles on everyone's faces.

"There...see," Ivy told John. "You helped your friends in the end."

He snorted a laugh. "Yeah, I guess."

She punched him.

"Oof! What was that for?"

"For being a nerd-herding ingrate," she told him and snuggled close again. He curled his arm more tightly around her. "That won't save you," she murmured and he snickered.

"Who says I want to be saved?"

She laughed and relaxed against him.

"I'm so glad this is over," she told him.

"Yup," he agreed. "Me, too."

"But?" she asked and caught the uncertainty in his tone.

"I don't know what's next," he admitted.

"Whatever Stephanie dreams up?" she suggested. "Because I don't think she'll let her Apostle simply vanish into obscurity."

He snorted. "There are days when I wish I could."

Ivy pushed upright. "And speaking of Stephanie," she began, "how has she been?"

The mage shrugged.

"Very busy," he admitted. "She's having to deal with the political vacuum created by killing everyone involved in the Regime at an unforgivable level."

"Is there such a thing?"

His face darkened. "There truly, truly is."

He didn't elaborate and she sighed.

"She must be very busy, then."

"You could—"

A roar sounded from the street outside. It was followed by a yelp, startled shouts, and running footsteps, then more shouting.

Someone might have yelled, "Sooorry!" but they couldn't be sure.

The young couple looked at each other and hurried to the balcony in time to see black-uniformed figures vanish into the building below. Farther down the street, a man and a woman ran after two dogs, calling their names.

"What do you suppose that was all about?" Ivy asked and John shrugged as he led her inside.

"I don't know," he answered. "I thought for a minute it might be one of the cats but I don't think Steph would—"

"For crying out loud!" The voice was all too familiar and sounded much closer. "You have to stop scaring everyone with a dog."

They exchanged glances.

"That sounded like it came from—"

Loud knocking sounded on their front door.

"Yup," John said and they both turned to answer it.

Stephanie's voice grew louder.

"Human dogs are not evil creatures."

The grumbled growl she received in response said the cat didn't agree.

"I mean it, Bee. It's bad enough that you keep scaring people with your horns but trying to eat their pets is not on. They aren't—"

She stopped and straightened when John opened the door.

He opened his mouth to say something and Lars and Vishlog slid past him. Johnny and Marcus followed.

"Excuse me," the Dreth said.

"Don't mind us," Lars added. "Standard procedure."

"Uh-huh," Ivy muttered as she and John were moved deftly aside.

To their surprise, Stephanie waited until her security head gave the all-clear while the rest of her protection team held the corridor.

"I'm sorry for the interruption," she told them as she stepped inside and hugged the Apostle by way of greeting. She turned and hugged Ivy too before she took her by the arm. With a glance at John, she added, "We'll only be a moment…or ten…"

He opened his mouth to ask what she had planned but the familiar blue of her magic flared around her and the two women vanished from sight.

"Well, shit!" Lars grumbled.

He looked at the rest of the team, then glanced around the apartment.

"Does anyone have a snack?"

"Here we are," Stephanie announced as the blue light faded.

Ivy looked around. "What—wait. I know this place."

"Well, you should," the Witch told her. "You spent enough time here."

"We did," she agreed, found a surveillance camera, and smiled into it. "Hello, Roma. It's nice to see you again."

"Greetings, Ivy. Stephanie said she would bring you to see me," the AI replied.

"She did?"

"She did," Roma answered, "but I'll leave her to explain."

The girl turned to Stephanie, who'd kept her hand hooked through her arm and now guided her to the little café where she and John had spent so much of their time. It seemed empty without him and the team there, but the droids still brought pastries while the two women made themselves hot drinks at the counter.

"This brings back memories," she told the Witch.

Her companion smiled but didn't speak about why they were there until they'd settled at the table nearest the window. Ivy mirrored her as she sipped, then placed her cup on the table.

"Roma told me about the Huntington's," Stephanie stated and the girl froze as the familiar sadness she felt when she thought about her illness returned in a soft tide.

"And?" she asked a little roughly. "Did she say if she'd worked out how to fix it?"

"She had a number of ideas but none that would be guaranteed to work in your lifetime—and none that would guarantee not passing it onto your kids," the Witch told her.

"It figures." She laughed a little bitterly, then sighed. "Oh, well…"

She stopped when the other woman covered her hand with her own.

"So, I came up with another one," Stephanie stated and the girl gaped at her.

When she didn't immediately say what it was, Ivy swallowed hard and asked.

"And?"

The Witch hesitated a moment longer before she sighed. "I can—if you want me to—fix it."

"Fix it?"

"Yes. Magic can be used to heal. It has to follow the right pathways and in this case, I needed to go through the research and your medical records, but I can heal you."

"Truly?" Ivy asked, her voice small with shock.

"Yes," she replied, "but…"

"There's always a 'but.'" Ivy sighed. "Go on."

"You will be incredibly fertile for a month after this, so if you don't want kids, you'd better be careful."

"Kids?" She paled and she swallowed hard. "I'll have kids?"

"Probably twins," Stephanie said and after a moment, she nodded. "Definitely twins."

"But—" Ivy gaped at her. "A…a mother?"

"Yup," her companion confirmed. "Twins, if not—"

Roma cleared her throat but Ivy didn't seem to notice. She wrapped her hands around her coffee cup and the liquid inside shuddered.

"Twins?"

Stephanie sighed impatiently and rolled her eyes.

"Yes. Two babies. Two little Johns and-or Ivys. More if you're not careful—or if you want them."

"Oh." She started to raise her cup but her hands trembled and she placed it on the table again. "But neither John nor I have any work lined up. How will we— "

She stopped when the Witch wrapped her hands around hers and stilled her protests.

"You will always have a position with my people, Godiva Emilia Lindhurst," she said gently and ignored the girl's shock at hearing her real name. "And if you choose to do something else, just ask. I will help to make it happen."

"But I'll be fertile?" she repeated, still struck by the news she could be healed but with a certain amount of risk.

Stephanie sighed and patted her hands. "For a month," she confirmed.

"A...a month?" Ivy sputtered. "But—"

"We can hold off for now," the Witch reassured her. "Nothing will happen to you because of the Huntington's for at least a few more years, but there's no telling where I'll be by then. So?"

Ivy held her cup tighter and squeezed her eyes shut as she drew a long breath. Stephanie waited and gave the girl as much time as she could. It was a relief when she looked up.

"I... Can I talk to John?" she asked, her eyes pleading. "Give me forty-eight hours?"

"Of course," Stephanie agreed and took another sip from her mug.

The girl glanced at the ceiling and found a pick-up before she spoke. "Thank you, Roma," she said quietly. "For everything."

"My pleasure," the AI replied, "and I am in the Virtual World. I no longer have to hide my connections. You can come talk at any time."

Ivy gave the camera a happy smile. "I will."

The Witch waited for her to lift her cup.

"Well, now that's settled..." she said and with a snap of her fingers, they were gone.

EPILOGUE

"Are we ready?" Todd asked, concern written on his face.

"Our family will become three again." Stephanie studied him. "This is your last chance."

He shook his head. "Morgana is family and I know you wouldn't leave her behind, regardless. A promise is a promise."

She rested a hand on his arm. "How did I ever deserve you?"

His lop-sided grin jerked at her heartstrings. "Probably by answering silly pop-tv questions in high school if I think about it." His grin became a smile. "You beat all the other girls simply by being you."

Stephanie regarded him warily. If she didn't know any better, she'd have said he was up to something. She gasped when he dropped on one knee and catcalls rose from the edges of the room where the Hooligans and her protection team stood and tried—unsuccessfully—to give them a little space.

"What are you doing?" she whispered. His smile faded and his face grew serious.

"I have to ask you one question while it's still the two of us."

"What?" she asked and looked from his somber expression to everyone else.

Their teams were gathered along one wall to not only give her and Todd space but also to leave room for the other visitors who'd come to make sure she would be okay after she took the Morgana back.

V'ritan and Brilgus looked suspiciously like they were trying not to smile. Jaleck and Angreth had the first glimmer of tusks showing, although they tried to look serious. The Witch's gaze traveled over their bodyguards to the latest of those to join them.

Her eyes narrowed.

"Funny," she noted and looked at Todd's upturned face. "I don't recall our parents being here."

He smiled at her. If he was honest, being on one knee didn't make him that much shorter than she was. He met her eyes.

"I thought with us being gone all the time, perhaps they could enjoy one moment where it's only Todd and Stephanie," he explained.

Her gaze flicked back around the room. "And the who's who of the Federation," she added.

Todd smirked. "I don't think that'll change for a while, Ms. President of the Federation, Earth."

"That'll be Mrs. President to you," she declared and laughed as she cupped his face in her hands. "Yes! The answer is yes."

For a split second, she thought of vanishing them to some remote part of Meligorn or a now-deserted tropical island but pushed the notion aside with a sigh. She'd made a promise and the war to consolidate the Federation wasn't yet over.

She stooped and kissed her Marine instead and ignored the whistles, laughter, and applause. When she released him, he rose smoothly to his feet and took her hand. He slid the other into a pocket of his uniform and withdrew a small gleaming band.

"Gold with a spine of Dreth tegralite, both precious and strong," he murmured, lifted her hand, and slid the ring onto her finger.

Gems glittered in its circumference and he brushed a finger over them before he wrapped her hand in his.

"Meligornian shrifa and Earth sapphires for the color of your magic, and a diamond since you are the most precious thing in my life and I don't want you to ever forget that."

Stephanie's face lit with joy and she used her free hand to pull his face down to hers.

"Thank you," she whispered as their lips met.

This time, when they drew apart, she turned to display the ring to her friends like any other newly engaged young woman. As they gathered close to admire it and congratulate her, it suddenly struck her that she was treating some of the most powerful people in the Federation as if they were someone who lived on her block.

Thinking about it, she decided that in a way, they did.

Gates were being built to connect the four worlds, portals that would take cargo freighters and passenger liners alike and cut transit time from months and weeks to a few days at most. The first materials had already reached the site of the Earth-Meligorn Gate and Earth-Dreth would shortly follow.

A few companies had already started commercial ventures involving them. There were rumors of space stations providing staging points or viewing platforms between gates. The adaptability of the races never failed to amaze her.

Treaties had already been redrawn between the four worlds, and corporations were renewing old ties. The reunions between estranged business partners were something to behold and the celebration of new joint ventures had become commonplace between species.

The first Four-Species Colony venture had almost filled its recruiting needs and was scheduled for launch and the first schools of magic had called for students. Stephanie didn't know whether to laugh or cry. So many good things were coming into being, even as more Regime atrocities were being uncovered and their damage repaired as well as they could.

Those were the things she had hated most about the last few weeks.

Except becoming president, she thought and smiled when Ka hugged her.

"Take good care of him," the woman told her.

"Forever," she murmured in response and tried not to think how the next ten years stretched like forever before her. At least Todd would be with her for that. She wondered if he'd consider that the "better" or "worse" part of it.

It helped that she wasn't alone in her responsibilities. V'ritan and Jaleck were the Presidents of the Federation, Meligorn and Dreth respectively, and Morgana had been sworn in as President of the Federation, Telor, while still in K'Striva's body.

The storm mother had been relieved that she wouldn't have to carry the ancient witch through ten years of presidency too.

"I do not envy you," the Teloran had told them. "Thank you for what you have done for our worlds."

Thinking of K'Striva, Stephanie sighed. Trust Todd to choose this moment.

She looked up and into her mother's face. It was a relief to see the delight in Cindy's eyes and even more so to see the same proud happiness in her father's.

"So, you're finally making an honest man of him," her mother said and Mark Morgan snorted.

"It's more the other way round—woman, I mean." He blushed. "She's making—"

Cindy pressed her fingers over his lips before she gathered her daughter into her arms.

"I'm so pleased for you, sweetheart."

Todd's parents followed and left him crimson to the hairline. Stephanie snickered.

"A Todd and Stephanie moment, huh?" she whispered and took his hand.

"It's worth every second," he responded and swooped in for another kiss.

This time, it was the sound of the medic clearing his throat that brought them apart.

"We're ready, ma'am."

She stepped away from Todd and drew a deep breath. In ten years' time when she stepped down, both Earth and Telor would have to supply new Federation Presidents to the Council and K'Striva might not find herself so lucky a second time.

"It's time to make us three again," she said quietly and Todd nodded.

"We have promises to keep," he replied and his expression said how proud he was of her for going through with it.

The Witch managed a shaky nod before she turned to stride purposefully into the room where she would resume her responsibilities to her friend and confidante—a Teloran.

Stephanie didn't remember the preparation being this short but she didn't care. Perhaps practice made perfect, after all.

She drifted to sleep, knowing that when she woke, she'd no longer be alone in her own head. Her every thought would be privy to another. In a way, it was a bond as strong as the one she and Todd were forging but different too. She drifted and sank deeper as the magic wove a highway between her and K'Striva.

It would be good to see Morgana again, she thought as sleep found her.

"It's nice to see you think so." The Morgana's voice greeted her on waking.

The Witch took a moment to register the ancient being's presence and felt her stretch through her but not take control.

"Long time, no see," she replied and registered the moment when the Morgana noticed the finger with Todd's ring.

"What's this?" the Teloran asked.

Stephanie's finger twitched as the Morgana moved it and felt the weight.

"What's what?" she asked but the ancient witch grew impatient and shifted her body into a sitting position and opened her eyes.

"Hey!"

"Sorry, there is no time to ask and you would be awkward anyway." The Morgana stepped back.

"Didn't we discuss this?" she demanded and meant her cohabitor taking over without her permission.

"This?" her inner companion asked and held her hand up in front of her face. She turned it so she could examine the ring. "We most certainly did not. I would have remembered being consulted about something like this."

"Uh-huh. I'm very sure who I want to spend my life with is not something I have to have your permission for."

"Given that I have to live here—"

"Oh… Don't you go there," Stephanie retorted. "Don't you ever go there. That was another talk we had. Remember?"

"Ugh. I'm beginning to," the Morgana replied and released her body to the girl's control. "So…tell me about it."

"Todd asked me to marry him," she answered.

"When?" the Teloran demanded. "I'm very sure I would have remembered if I'd been there."

"Just before we came in," she told her. "Didn't K'Striva—"

"It's different," the ancient Witch explained. "With you, I don't have to step so far back. I can still see and hear, but with another Teloran, the division between us is so thin I have to find a quiet space beyond their awareness if they are to have full control."

"But you don't do that with me," Stephanie said slowly.

"I don't," the Morgana admitted, "but when you need private time, I do. Just so you know."

"And you're not aware…" Stephanie began, unsure how to continue.

"I don't peek if that's what you mean," she told her. "It might not have occurred to you but there are some things my hosts do that I don't want to know about."

"Well, that's a relief," the girl said.

"I'll bet it is." The Teloran chuckled, then grew serious. "So, how did he take it when you said you intended to have me back?"

Stephanie smiled.

"I told him our family would grow and he said he was glad I was keeping my promise, especially since you were family," she replied.

Her inner companion was quiet as she digested the news, but the Witch sensed a small amount of relief and some surprise—neither of which was evident in her next comment.

"Speaking of family…" the Morgana began, "and especially of it growing. I look forward to seeing what the next little Todd or Stephanie can do with their magic."

"They might not have magic," she told her, and the Teloran laughed.

"I've seen your genes," she teased. "Your kids will be as magical as rainbows and a million more times more trouble—especially when I get through with them."

"Don't you even—" Stephanie protested. "Can you imagine how confused they'll be if I start telling them to do something I've told them not to?"

The ancient witch snickered. "They will have the best teacher in magical mayhem the universe has to offer."

"Don't you even—" the girl repeated and her face paled. "Wait! Why are we having this conversation? I'm not ready for kids."

"When you least suspect it…" The Morgana chuckled. "*Bam!* Babies!"

Stephanie slid off the bed and noticed K'Striva had already been moved to a separate room for her recovery. The Telorans had said she'd need time alone when she first emerged from "the joining" but they hadn't said how long or when Stephanie and the Morgana could see her.

It left the girl feeling a mild sense of loss but not for long.

"Are we going to get out there?" her inner companion pressed. "I want to see Todd's face now that I'm back."

"You know he'll be the way he always was," Stephanie reminded her and drew a chuckle in response.

"We'll see."

They emerged from the room to find the waiting room as crowded as it had been when they'd entered. V'ritan and Brilgus were the first to approach. The *Ghargilum* took the Witch's hands in his as he scrutinized her intently.

She allowed the Morgana to peek through her eyes and the Meligornian mage broke into a smile.

"It's good to see you, Morgana. Welcome back."

"Welcome back," Brilgus echoed as he stepped forward, and Stephanie felt a surge of emotion as the Teloran realized they were looking past her host to greet her directly. It was funny to see the ancient witch speechless for a change.

"What's the matter?" she thought. *"Has the cat got your tongue?"*

"And what exactly would you do about it if it had?" her inner companion retorted.

The girl chuckled as Jaleck stepped forward to greet her. The Dreth rolled her eyes.

"You're already having conversations we can't hear," she grumbled. "Don't you know that's rude?"

Todd snorted. "You get used to it."

Stephanie felt a pang of regret but saw the slightest twitch at the edge of his mouth when he caught her eye. The dratted man was laughing at her.

The Morgana chuckled in response and she shook her head. *Just my luck,* she thought. *Now, the two of them are ganging up on me.*

When the greetings were over and their well-wishers had left, Stephanie hooked her arm through Todd's and the two of them led the way out of the small medical section they'd set up in the western wing of the new Federation Headquarters.

Bumblebee and Zeekat rose from their corners and moved alongside them. It had taken them only a few short trips into the air to understand that only one of them could walk beside Stephanie and the other had to walk beside Todd. Today, it was Bumblebee's turn to be near their mistress.

Not that Zeekat cared. Todd knew how to scritch ears as he walked and he was never too busy to do so. Neither of them was very happy about the crowd of well-wishers who waited outside in the courtyard.

"So," the Morgana asked, "what's the plan for today?"

Stephanie walked closer to Todd. "Do you remember that time we had a date?" she asked and he gave her a startled glance.

She was about to explain when one of the Upper House representatives slid past her team, stretched past Bumblebee's horns, and tapped her on the shoulder. To make matters worse, he moved to block her path.

"I'm so glad to have caught you, Madam President," he began. "There are a couple of matters that need your urgent attention."

"Then they should be raised in Council," she told him.

"They honestly won't wait." He waved a tablet in front of her. "As you can see, we simply must—"

The sentence ended in a startled yelp when his feet left the ground.

Stephanie regarded him with quiet distaste as she wound her index finger in the air.

"But—" he began and she flicked her finger and raised him two stories into the air.

"I won't be bothered with that today," she told him and tapped the ring on her left hand.

Soft murmurs of surprise rustled around her, followed by laughter as she repeated herself and again tapped her newly acquired ring for emphasis.

"Not. Bothered. Today."

Todd draped his arm around her and guided her across the courtyard, up the stairs, and out into the foyer. The man's voice rose in a plaintive wail behind her.

"Uh...Madam President?"

The Witch hesitated but Todd drew her close. The two cats dropped back, having watched the man's ascent with pricked ears and inquisitive eyes.

"A little help here?" the man called and the cats bounded toward him.

"Uh-oh," Lars muttered and the words caught the attention of the rest of the team.

Leaving the couple's protection to the Hooligans, Stephanie's guards moved to collect the cats. Both felines had fixed the floating politician with predatory stares and circled beneath him before they surveyed the courtyard around them.

Vishlog almost had his hand on Bumblebee's collar when the big cat gave an imperative snarl and bounded to a pagoda. Zeekat obeyed the order and slipped out of Frog's grasp to follow.

"No..." The small guard moaned and ran after them.

"No, no, no," Vishlog rumbled in echo as the two beasts leapt onto the gazebo's roof and launched themselves at the politician.

"What is it with cats and things that dangle?" Lars asked.

"I have no idea what you're talking about," Marcus replied as Garach joined his two uncles in staring at the two cats while they swiped at the floating politician.

Bumblebee twisted in the air and snatched at the man with both paws but came up yards too short. That didn't stop Zeekat from trying. Both landed on their feet on the roof of another gazebo and clawed for balance before they pivoted to measure the distance again.

The politician pressed himself against the far side of the bubble surrounding him, no longer concerned that it might let him fall. He was now more worried that the president's cats would pop it and he would plummet to the ground. Panicked, he looked at the three figures who watched the two cats leap towards him.

"Please?" he called. "Can you help me?"

"I don't know," Frog replied and walked a little closer but took care to stay out of the feline's flight paths. "You see, Stephanie didn't want to be president."

"Nope," Garach agreed as Lars made a small detour to the courtyard café.

"It is true," Vishlog said when the security head reached them. "She did not."

The cats landed after another spectacular jump each and tried to use one of the inner courtyard balconies to gain more height. It didn't work but the politician yelped with fright.

Lars nudged the Dreth and passed him the popcorn. The big warrior grinned, took a handful, and passed it to Garach. He passed it to Frog, who sighed.

"I suppose," the small man said, after he'd eaten his handful, "we should call them back."

"Oh, yes," Vishlog added loudly enough for the man to hear. "They might hurt themselves if they keep it up."

"They might hurt themselves?" the man wailed.

"I'll ask the president if Political Dumbass here can be let down," Lars said as each of his three teammates pulled a bag of treats from their belts and trotted forward. Treats won over enticing dangling bits any day.

He stepped away from the scene, tapped his collar mic, and spoke briefly to Ka. Seconds later, a startled scream cut the air and he pivoted in alarm.

"Oh no. She wouldn't—" he began and ran towards the falling man.

He'd have been too late but Stephanie had no intention to kill the politician. He came to a sudden stop a foot off the ground before he was allowed to fall the rest of the way.

Fortunately, he got his hands and knees under him before he landed and there he stayed, curled over his knees as he dragged long shaking breaths into his lungs. Lars moved to kneel beside him and placed a hand on his back.

Ignoring the way the man flinched, he leaned closer. He kept his voice low as he advised him quietly, "You might want to mention to all your friends and cronies that she looks young but she isn't stupid—and she has ways to show her disapproval that you aren't likely to forget."

"And that's before Mrs. E returns to Earth." Vishlog's rumble followed the sound of his heavy-footed approach.

"We need to head out," the security head said and pushed to his feet as the rest of the team joined him.

"Do you think he got the message?" Frog asked as they left.

"If he didn't, he doesn't deserve to stay," Marcus answered. "Did you see the look on his face when Bee tried to drag him down that first time?"

"Man..." Avery chuckled. "There's a guy who won't try to railroad Steph ever again."

They laughed as they headed up the stairs.

None of them looked back as the politician raised his head but lowered it again when one of the cats looked back. He groaned when he felt the sting of landing on his palms but one thought haunted him.

"Who is Mrs. E?"

CREATOR NOTES - MICHAEL ANDERLE

MAY 12, 2021

Thank you for not only reading this series to completion, but these author notes as well!

Presently, I'm about 35,000 feet up above some state (looks like New Mexico on the map) and about an hour and a half from landing in Dallas. Judith and I are heading to see our son graduate from college, the first of his generation to accomplish this feat.

Go, Joey!

The Heretic...now leader? Of the Federation!

This book is the conclusion of the story of Stephanie Morgana, the Witch of the Federation, and all of those characters who have helped her fight those who would attack her people... all of her people, from without or within.

With this story, we have produced about a bajillion words (not really) with over four million books (totally a lie) and the ships have traveled trillions of miles between planets (this part is theoretically real.)

It is interesting that I am typing the last author notes for a character I created on a plane flight from Australia to the United States over two years ago.

Many times, this story (in all of the books) has made my eyes mist up, tear up, and leak like crazy. For whatever reason, the scenes where Stephanie and her ships fly over the planets (Dreth, then Meligorn, then Earth) are very poignant for me.

If you have seen the movie *Independence day* with Will Smith, do you remember the scenes when the massive ships arrive in the atmosphere? Those ships roiling through the clouds to eventually emerge was amazing on the big screen.

It was one of the coolest introductions to aliens I have seen. Unfortunately, they proved to be total interstellar asshats.

But man, they arrived with style.

The reason I originally created those scenes way back in the first series (Witch of the Federation) was (in part) encouraged by my memories of that film.

The Kurtherian Gambit

Stephanie Morgana (as I've mentioned in one of these author notes somewhere) was a second stab at creating a series as beloved as Bethany Anne and *the Kurtherian Gambit.*

Did I succeed? If you have read both series, drop a note in a review some time (on either book series.) If you haven't read the Kurtherian Gambit…

Well, I'd suggest reading it. If you do, I hope you have a bit of time when you start book one.

Or read really, really fast. Preternaturally fast, in fact.

If you like this story, we at LMBPN have a lot of additional series with the same feel. Obviously, Kurtherian Gambit is a big one. However, you can find many in all sorts of genres.

If you like audio, we have both single-narrator and now multi-cast releasing from Graphic Audio productions for *Kurtherian Gambit.*

Our audio partners have single cast narration for *The Witch of the Federation* and *Heretic of the Federation,* so you should be able to locate either series at your favorite audio distribution provider!

We are already into the next series...

Nothing ever stops here at LMBPN when it comes to producing stories for our fans and those fans soon to come.

If you like fantasy stories with a similar feel to this story, then BOLO (be on the lookout) for a fantasy series coming late 2021 in hardback (our first ever!) We have commissioned additional concept art from the awesome Jeff Brown to go with the epic covers he has created.

These stories will be close to the size of the original Witch of the Federation stories or larger. It's a pretty massive undertaking, and we have five core people on the team at the moment, working on the series. I hope you like fantasy, but if not, no worries. Except for romance, we (usually) have you covered.

Thank you again from the bottom of my heart for taking your time to join the team and me and share the story of Stephanie Morgana, The Witch of the Federation.

Ad Aeternitatem,

Michael Anderle

* If you have not read the stories about Stephanie Morgana, join me for the first part of this story in *The Witch of the Federation,* out in ebook, print and Audiobook.

BOOKS BY MICHAEL ANDERLE

Sign up for the LMBPN email list to be notified of new releases and special deals!

https://lmbpn.com/email/

For a complete list of books by Michael Anderle, please visit:

www.lmbpn.com/ma-books/

CONNECT WITH MICHAEL

Connect with Michael Anderle

Website: http://lmbpn.com

Email List: http://lmbpn.com/email/

Social Media:

https://www.facebook.com/LMBPNPublishing

https://twitter.com/MichaelAnderle

https://www.instagram.com/lmbpn_publishing/

https://www.bookbub.com/authors/michael-anderle